Fatal Flowers

WITHDRAWN
FROM THE
TORONTO PUBLIC
LIBRARY

D0826455

ST. MARTIN'S PAPERBACKS TITLES
BY JESS DYLAN

DEATH IN BLOOM
PETALS AND POISON
FATAL FLOWERS

Fatal Flowers

JESS DYLAN

St. Martin's Paperbacks

NOTE: If you purchased this book without a cover you should be aware that this book is stolen property. It was reported as "unsold and destroyed" to the publisher, and neither the author nor the publisher has received any payment for this "stripped book."

This is a work of fiction. All of the characters, organizations, and events portrayed in this novel are either products of the author's imagination or are used fictitiously.

First published in the United States by St. Martin's Paperbacks, an imprint of St. Martin's Publishing Group.

FATAL FLOWERS

Copyright © 2022 by Jennifer David Hesse.

All rights reserved.

For information, address St. Martin's Publishing Group, 120 Broadway, New York, NY 10271.

www.stmartins.com

ISBN: 978-1-250-76952-7

Our books may be purchased in bulk for promotional, educational, or business use. Please contact your local bookseller or the Macmillan Corporate and Premium Sales Department at 1-800-221-7945, ext. 5442, or by email at MacmillanSpecialMarkets@macmillan.com.

Printed in the United States of America

St. Martin's Paperbacks edition / June 2022

10 9 8 7 6 5 4 3 2 1

For Alan and Cindy, the best in-laws
anyone could ask for

Look before you leap, for snakes among sweet flowers creep.

—*English proverb*

Chapter 1

The camera stared at me like a one-eyed robot, cold and unblinking. I stared back. The modern bullet-shaped contraption was out of place, anachronistic even, under the painted eaves of the century-old Victorian. Flower House was welcoming and cheerful, the front porch overflowing with barrels and boxes of many-hued flowers. The security camera was the opposite.

I wrinkled my nose at the thing and stuck out my tongue. Feeling sassy, I also wiggled my hips in a childish dance of defiance.

A feminine voice crackled from an invisible speaker. "It works. No need to put on a show."

I froze, then giggled. I'd almost forgotten there were people on the other side of the camera. My friend Deena was inside at the computer in our small office—along with the security company tech who had installed the front camera and its twin above the back door, as well as burglar alarms on all the windows.

"Good," I replied. "Now we can finally check this item off our to-do list."

This task had been hanging over my head for far too long. Most business owners would have invested in a security system after the first break-in—which followed the first murder on the premises last spring. I cringed at the recollection, as well as the word "first." There had been a second murder a few short months later. Intruders, vandals, killers—we'd had them all in the short span of time since I'd taken charge of the shop. Not that it was my fault. It was purely coincidental. The incidents at Flower House very well could have happened when my old boss, Felix, was still in charge.

And how different would things be then? If Felix hadn't decided to retire and leave his shop to me, all so he could go gallivanting off on a fanciful treasure hunt out West, I might be the one traveling the country, chasing my own dreams. I'd wanted to be a singer-songwriter, carrying the spirit of my Appalachian roots in my heart as I sang my way to the big time. Instead, my heart and my voice remained firmly planted in my hometown, where my roots only sank deeper.

Deena emerged from the front door with the security technician, a freckle-faced young man in a company jacket. As he handed me a pen and a clipboard, he tried, unsuccessfully, to hide an amused smirk.

I signed the contract and returned the pen with a bat of my eyelashes. "Thank you, sir," I said brightly.

He handed me a business card. "Call if you have any questions, day or night."

"Oh, I will," I assured him.

Deena chuckled as the guy walked away, toward his car on the street. "Is there anyone left in this town that you haven't charmed to pieces?"

I ignored her comment and pointed at the camera. "It's like an evil eye, isn't it? If Granny's protection charms don't keep the bad guys away, this camera ought to."

"That's the idea," she agreed. "It's also like insurance. We may never need it, but it's worth it for the peace of mind."

"Especially for Calvin," I said. "Not that he ever complained." Calvin was a former botany professor, who had shown up here out of the blue last spring at Felix's invitation—except Felix, the scatterbrain, had forgotten and skipped town. Calvin stayed anyway and turned out to be a godsend. He'd rented the upstairs apartment and accepted a job taking care of the greenhouse out back, not to mention helping out with anything and everything else that needed doing in the shop.

"True," said Deena. "I still don't know how he could sleep at night. It never seemed to faze him that so much mayhem happened in the shop below his apartment." She gave me a sidelong glance. "Speaking of Calvin, have you heard from him lately?"

"Yeah, I got a text a couple days ago. He still says he's coming back. Sometime soon."

"Good," said Deena. She opened her mouth as if to say more, then scrapped the thought. "I better go get the café ready. The garden club will be here for their monthly meeting in less than an hour."

"That's today? I'll come help in a minute. I want to freshen the blooms out here." I moved absently toward the porch display and picked up a watering can. Lately, the mention of Calvin had been throwing me into a pensive mood. He'd been gone for a little more than a month, and the idea that he might not return bothered me more than I cared to admit.

Calvin Foxheart. I felt a grin tug at my lips in spite of myself. His name suited him. He was cute and kind of nerdy, yet brave and strong too.

Biting my lip, I pinched off a dried orange marigold blossom and crumbled the seeds onto the soil. There was a time when I wasn't sure if I could trust Calvin. Eventually, though, he'd proven to be a true friend—and then some. Our growing attraction to each other was undeniable.

I gazed into space as the memories replayed themselves in my mind. We'd begun spending more time with each other, both at the shop and outside of work. It was fun to get to know him better. I enjoyed his company and loved the way I felt when he was near. In fact, we would have become even closer if not for a series of thwarted opportunities. It was almost comical, all the times we'd been interrupted or distracted at the exact moment we might have shared our first kiss. Whether it was an ill-timed thunderstorm, an important phone call, or a murderer in our midst, there was always something coming between us. Most recently, it was Calvin's family, who needed his help on their farm in Iowa, while his father recovered from hip surgery.

I kept telling myself we'd surely laugh about all the interruptions someday. I tried to ignore the irrational voice in my head—the one that wondered if the universe was conspiring to keep us apart.

"Ridiculous," I muttered. It was just life being life—unpredictable, messy, and inconvenient at times—in between all the magic and beauty.

A car door slammed shut, pulling me from my daydreams. I hadn't even heard a car drive up, but that might have been because the motor was so quiet. If I wasn't mistaken, the snappy red vehicle along the curb was a Mercedes-Benz. The young woman walking toward me was dressed in a matching beige skirt and sweater set—an outfit that suited someone with such an expensive car. So did her perfectly styled straight golden hair and model-worthy makeup. She gave me a friendly smile when she spotted me on the porch. But as she got closer, I saw that the smile didn't quite reach her eyes. The telltale lines spoke, instead, of worry and sadness.

"Howdy," I said. "Welcome to Flower House. Are you here for the garden club meeting?"

Her eyes flickered in confusion. "No. I was hoping to speak with someone about wedding flowers."

I set down the watering can and wiped my hands on my corduroys. "Absolutely. Come on in, Miss . . ." I trailed off, in a questioning tone.

"Marissa," she supplied.

"Nice to meet you, Marissa. I'm Sierra Ravenswood, the owner and manager here." It still felt funny to identify myself in that way, but I figured the more I said it, the sooner it might feel natural.

I directed Marissa across the foyer that opened to the shop floor, then to the left, through the arched entryway that led to the café room. Decorated in a charming French provincial style, with polished antique furniture, a crystal chandelier, a plush velvet sofa, and painted vases bursting with sensual bouquets in every corner, the café had become an attractive destination for individuals and groups alike. The monthly garden club was one of the regular meetings that took place here.

Deena had already pushed together three small tables in the seating area next to the front window, so I chose a table near the bakery case.

"Would you like coffee or tea?" I offered.

"No, thank you." She spoke quietly, which had the effect of requiring her listener's full attention. Or maybe she was used to being discreet.

"You sure?" I asked. "We have some nice specialty teas: calming lavender-chamomile, soothing ginger-lemon." I didn't know why, but I had a feeling she could use a touch of comfort. Perhaps it was the way she kept twisting her engagement ring (which, incidentally, featured the biggest diamond I'd ever seen this up close and personal).

"Actually, that does sound nice," she said. "I'll have lavender-chamomile."

Deena had overheard and appeared beside us with teacups and a miniature kettle of hot water. As she handed me a jar of honey, I noticed her eyebrows quirk expressively above her shining brown eyes. Was she trying to tell me something?

I returned my attention to Marissa, who was pouring water over the tea in her cup. I started to push back from the table. "I'll go grab our wedding portfolio and bouquet catalogues. Be back in a jiffy."

It might have been a stretch to call our slim binder of photos a "portfolio," but Deena and I were optimistic—and I believed in the Law of Attraction. *If you want to attract more wedding jobs, act as a wedding florist would act.* At the moment, our collection included more prom corsages and anniversary bouquets than bridal photos, but it was a start.

Marissa held out a hand to stop me. "You don't need to do that."

I paused. "Oh, okay. You already know what you want?"

Deena returned to the table with a plate of daisy-shaped sugar cookies sprinkled with bits of edible flower petals. Again, she appeared uncommonly excited about something. Probably it was the prospect of landing a wedding client.

"Deena," I said, "would you do me a favor and grab our price sheet?"

Marissa shook her head dismissively. "I don't care about the cost."

Now Deena and I exchanged a glance. It dawned on me that she must recognize Marissa. This wasn't a surprise. Aerieville was a small town, and Deena had always been more social than I was—back in high school and even now, a decade later.

"I'll get you a notebook," Deena offered.

"Thanks." As Deena left the café, I stirred my tea and asked the obvious question. "So, Marissa, when is your wedding?"

"September twenty-seventh."

I nodded. "Lovely. Fall weddings are so beautiful. And since it will be around this time next year, you can see what's in season now and take inspiration from what's currently blooming."

"It's not next year," she corrected.

"Oh. It's two years out?"

"No. Two weeks. September twenty-seventh this year."

I dropped my spoon and stared. I almost asked if she was joking, but it was clear she wasn't.

"I know it's short notice, but I'm prepared to pay a premium and any extra charges. Or, I should say, my parents will." She touched the edge of a cookie. "Pretty," she murmured.

"Um." I wasn't sure what to say. I wanted to ask why she was in such a rush to get married, but I knew that would be rude. Maybe her fiancé was in the military and would be leaving for a tour of duty. Or maybe she was expecting. In fact, this wouldn't be the first last-minute wedding job I'd handled. I knew it could be done. It was unusual and challenging, but it wasn't impossible.

She took a sip of tea, then resumed fidgeting with her ring. "The wedding and reception will be at my parents' house, and we'll need decorations for both. The colors are cranberry and gold. The last florist designed my bouquet with calla lilies and roses, but you don't have to stick with that."

"The last florist?"

"We had another florist, but she backed out." Marissa's eyes slid toward the window. "I'm not sure why."

I heard the front door jingle, followed by the drift of

voices from the foyer. It sounded like Deena was greeting the garden club members. Marissa pushed back her chair. Was she leaving already?

"How large is the wedding party?" I asked. "And how many guests are you expecting?"

She reached into her purse, then handed me a business card and stood up. "Taz will give you all the details. He's the wedding planner."

I glanced at the card and the bold-lettered name, Taz Banyan, Nashville, TN, before returning my confused gaze to Marissa. "I don't—" I began, but she interrupted.

"You'll do it, won't you? I was hoping to use a local florist at least, since all the other vendors are from out of town. Like I said, money is no object."

As I looked into her pleading eyes, I felt a strange sense of inevitability wash over me. As odd as this encounter was, and as stressful as the job might be, I knew I couldn't say no. Of course, I didn't want to turn down any business, but it was more than that. This was a woman in need, and where there was need, I had the urge to help.

"Yes," I said, with a brief nod. "We'll do it."

We were so busy the rest of the morning, I had to put Marissa out of my mind. Between serving the garden club ladies in the café and helping a couple of walk-in customers, we had online flower orders to fill. Mondays weren't always this busy. Then again, birthdays, anniversaries, and get-well wishes could happen anytime—and every day was a good day for flowers.

When Felix was in charge, he didn't bother much with advertising or promotions. He was content to run a slow business, since it gave him more time for his hobbies. When I took over, I soon realized such a lax business model wasn't sustainable. With help from Deena and Calvin, I decided to open the flower-themed café, in the hopes that it would draw in more customers. It worked, and we became busier than ever. I was already thinking of hiring more staff when Calvin announced he had to go away for a while.

As luck would have it, around the same time, my grandmother told me about a family she knew who had come upon hard times. The single mother had been laid off, and her older kids were looking for work. That's how I came to meet Toby and Allie Johnson. All summer, Toby, nineteen, made deliveries for us and took care of yardwork. Allie, aged seventeen, worked the cash register and kept the shop floor tidy. They were good kids, if a little too timid.

I wrapped up a delivery for Toby, and told him to take a lunch break before coming back. Then I walked up front, where Allie was wiping down the check-out counter. Her dishwater blonde hair was pulled back in a headband, making her look even younger than she was.

"It's lunchtime, Allie. I can mind the register, while you go eat."

"That's okay, Miss Ravenswood. I'm not hungry. Thank you, though."

"Well, take a break anyway. Why not go outside and get some fresh air?"

Deena poked her head out of the café. "Anyone want a watercress and chive blossom sandwich? We have a few left over, and they're best eaten fresh."

"If Gus were here, he'd be happy to help you out," I joked. My young corgi loved to eat, and he wasn't picky. He was usually a fixture at Flower House, charming customers or hanging out in the office. He also liked to be at the center of all activity—which meant he was often underfoot. That was why I'd dropped him off with my brother, Rocky, before meeting the security tech at the shop this morning.

Allie was biting her lip as she eyed the sandwich tray. I gave her a nudge.

"Help yourself, Allie. You need to eat."

"Well, okay. That sounds good. Maybe I'll take it to the park down the street?"

"Good idea."

Deena wrapped up some sandwiches, while I poured iced tea into a thermos. Allie gratefully accepted both, with a promise to be back soon.

After she left the shop, I glanced out the window. "She's such a shrinking violet, isn't she?" Deena wrinkled her nose at my pun, making me grin. My thoughts of Calvin must have put his goofy sense of humor into my consciousness. "How can we boost her confidence?"

"We could give her more responsibilities," said Deena. "Which we'll have to do if we get the Lakely wedding."

"Lakely? As in Mayor Lakely?"

Deena shook her head. "I *knew* you didn't recognize her. That was Marissa Lakely you were talking with this morning."

"Ohh. . . . That makes sense. She mentioned her wedding is taking place at her parents' house. The mayor lives in a mansion, doesn't he?"

"Yes, but that's because of who his wife is. Marissa's mother is Annaliese Bellman. Of the Bellman family?" She gave me a questioning look.

"Right. They're in . . . real estate, aren't they?" I probably should have known these things, but I'd been away from town since high school and only moved back at the beginning of the year. And I'd been a bit preoccupied ever since.

"Real estate, land development, and a few other enterprises. They're only the wealthiest family in Aerieville. It would really up our profile if we got to provide the flowers for that wedding. But they'll probably go with a larger florist."

"Actually, we did get the job. But there's a catch." I told Deena about the two-week turnaround.

Her shock quickly turned to skepticism. "You probably misunderstood."

"I don't think so." Part of me was hoping I had. The enormity of the commitment I'd made was finally starting to sink in. Of course, I hadn't signed a contract, but I had given my word.

I found the wedding planner's business card and showed it to Deena. "I guess I'd better call him now."

"Please do." She handed me a pen and a pad of paper.

The front door jingled as a customer came in, so I headed to our small office down the hall. Formerly a den, the cozy room still felt more like a gentleman's study than a business office. I sat in the armchair next to the redbrick fireplace and punched in the planner's number. After four rings, I expected the call would go to voicemail. I was startled when a brusque voice came on the line.

"Taz here."

"Hello! This is Sierra Ravenswood from Flower House. Marissa Lakely asked me to give you a call. I understand you need a wedding florist."

"Oh, yes. Thanks to Tammy, the diva. She made a *big* mistake, walking out on me like that. She just lost herself a *lot* of future clients. I'll never work with her again. And, with my influence, neither will any other wedding planner in the state."

"Um." I was so taken aback by this unexpected outburst, I was at a loss for words. Taz didn't seem to notice.

"I told Marissa I'd find another florist, but she said she wanted to go local this time. I hope you can take direction. You won't be too precious about your designs, will you? As

I *tried* to tell Tammy, the bride is the star of the show. The flowers are the backdrop."

"I understand."

"Good. Be here at six, then. I'll show you what we need."

"I'm sorry—be where?"

He sighed impatiently. "Bellman Manor. For the vendor rehearsal. We're meeting at six thirty, but if you get here at six that should be enough time for me to catch you up."

"Uh, okay. I think I can make that."

There was silence on the other end of the line. I looked at my phone and saw that the call had ended. He'd hung up on me.

Dropping my hand into my lap, I shook my head. What had I gotten myself into?

Chapter 2

Deena and I arrived at Bellman Manor at six on the nose. Nestled in the hills on the outskirts of town, the private estate felt like another world. A long tree-lined driveway led us to the expansive Tudor-style home: a three-story brick mansion, striking with its sharp peaks and multiple chimneys. On instinct, I drove around to the back. The driveway ended at a structure that might have been another house, except for the four closed garage doors. To the side was a concrete pad. I parked there, in a row of other cars that clearly belonged to visitors or staff. A painted panel van featured the image of a fierce-looking rattlesnake, above the words "DJ Sidewinder ~ Rattler Entertainment."

As we got out of the car, another van pulled up next to us. The woman who emerged wore a pale pink smock and crisp black trousers. Her brown hair was coiled in tight braids at the back of her head. When she opened the rear doors of the van and pulled out a tower of food containers, I rushed to her side.

"Need some help?"

She glanced at me and nodded. "Sure, that would be great."

She handed me an insulated food delivery bag, which I passed over to Deena before accepting a covered tray. As I did so, I introduced myself and Deena.

"We're from Flower House. I'm guessing you're the caterer."

"You got it. I'm Regina Ervin." With her arms full, she nodded her chin in greeting.

"Are these refreshments for the meeting?" asked Deena.

"Not exactly," said Regina. "They're for Taz's final approval." She pursed her lips as if she was holding back further comment.

We were met at the back door by an older woman in a light blue housekeeping uniform. She took us through a short vestibule, past a sunny breakfast nook and a spacious modern kitchen, then around a corner into the great room. And great it was. I felt like I had entered a museum. Polished antique furniture gleamed along the walls, leaving open the center of the room where a massive Persian rug softened our footsteps. Far to our right was the home's entry way, a recessed area framing tall, arched double doors. To our left, a sweeping marble staircase flowed like a waterfall from a spindle-railed balcony above.

My mind immediately shifted into decorating mode. The bannisters begged to be draped with tulle and white roses. As we made our way across the room, I saw that the far wall showcased a carved limestone fireplace, standing regally beneath a mounted family crest. It would be the perfect backdrop for the marriage ceremony.

Regina set her containers on a round table in the corner. As Deena and I took in the surroundings, I wondered where everyone else was. Although Taz had said he wanted me to arrive early, the line of cars near the back door must belong to someone.

As if on cue, a side door opened and a slender man breezed

our way. Ignoring me and Deena, he addressed Regina with surprised delight—though, from his syrupy tone, I couldn't tell if he was being genuine or sarcastic.

"You came! I'm honored. I thought sure you'd send one of your minions."

Leaning forward, Regina returned his air kiss with a tight smile. "I don't think of my assistants as 'minions,' Taz. But of course I came. You asked me to be here, didn't you?"

Taz laughed loudly. "I could always count on you, Reggie. You're a doll and a sport."

I watched the exchange with fascination. Was Taz always this patronizing, or was there a special history between him and Regina?

From his appearance alone, I gathered the wedding planner was something of a character. His glossy black hair was gelled into a gravity-defying faux hawk, and his goatee was unapologetically patchy. I admired his burgundy suit—I had a penchant for bright colors myself—though even I had to admit it was a tad over the top for everyday wear. On closer inspection, I noticed the polka dots on his skinny tie were actually tiny skulls. Deena and I exchanged an amused glance.

Taz eyed the food containers. "I can't wait to taste your goodies, Reggie. Be a dear and take them to the dining room. That's where I've set up my command center."

"Of course," Regina echoed. She gathered up the containers and stalked out of the room. Deena took the tray I'd been holding and indicated with a nod that she'd follow Regina.

I cleared my throat and took a step toward Taz. "Hello. I'm Sierra." At his blank look, I elaborated. "From Flower House? You asked me to meet you at six o'clock."

His eyes flitted over me, from the fringe of my short hair, down my Kelly green sweater set and brown cords, to my two-tone sneakers. His lips curled. "I hope you can style floral arrangements better than you style yourself. You look like a tree."

My face flooded with heat. Before I could formulate a response, he glanced at his watch, a chunky gold wrist band, and frowned. "And you're late."

"I'm sorry," I began.

"Never mind. I can talk fast." He strode across the room, obviously expecting me to follow him. Obviously, I did.

With sweeping gestures, Taz pointed to various areas of the great room, as if he were a director on a stage. As he went over the ceremony logistics and described his vision for the proceedings (fairy-tale romance meets sophisticated Gatsbyesque black-tie affair), I recovered from the sting of his insult. He was probably joking anyway. *Right? Nobody is that mean.* I peeled off my cardigan and draped it over my arm, ready to get busy.

Pausing in the center of the room, Taz spread his arms wide. "We'll have eight rows of ten chairs, beginning here. Five seats on each side of the center aisle for a total of eighty chairs." I nodded, repeating the numbers in my mind. *Should I be writing this down?* Surely he'd give me a checklist later.

Taz moved on to the fireplace and continued talking, even more quickly. "The four groomsmen will stand here, the bridesmaids here. Marky will stand there, in the center. We'll have LED candles on the hearth and flowers on the mantel. I want every inch of the mantel covered with flowering vines dripping elegantly, three feet over the edge and spread at six-inch intervals."

"Excuse me." I held up a hand like a pupil in a classroom. "Did you say the *marquis*?"

"I said *Marky*, as in Marky Farrell, the officiant."

"Oh. He's not a reverend, then?"

Taz gave me an impatient look. "He's a family friend.

The Lakely-Bellmans and the Princelys, not to mention their assorted relatives, all come from mixed religious backgrounds. Hence, the secular ceremony."

"Princely?" I assumed this must be the groom's name, but so far I hadn't heard a word about him. "I haven't met Marissa's fiancé yet. Is he from around here?"

"No," said Taz shortly. "Michael-William Princely is not from 'around here.' And he won't be here until next weekend. He's a political aide in Washington—not that it should matter to you."

Aye-aye, Captain. I shut my mouth to keep from asking any more questions Taz would deem trivial. *Why is he being so mean to me?*

He returned his attention to the center of the room. "A white carpet, thirty feet in length, will extend through the hall. The flower girl is eight years old, so she can take direction. The rose petals must be dark red. Think *crimson*. And whatever amount you imagine will be enough, triple it. Got that? Our mantra is *Abundance*. That little girl will *not* run out of petals."

Okay, I'd better take notes. I reached into my purse and rifled for some paper and a pen. Finally, I found both and hastily tried to jot down Taz's instructions. To my dismay, the ink was dry. Meanwhile, Taz was still walking and talking.

"The string quartet will be here. The musical director is Gordon Winslow. You may have heard of him." I hadn't. I shook my pen in vain.

Taz opened a heavy wooden door, giving me a glimpse of an elegant, formal sitting room. "The wedding party will assemble and wait in here. This is where you should bring the wearable flowers and bouquets—by nine a.m. sharp." He cast me a warning look. "Don't be late."

I could only stare at him in return. I didn't even know what time the wedding was scheduled to start! *This guy has some nerve, talking to me this way. Does he want a second florist to walk out?*

He turned to the staircase. "The bride will descend these steps, eighteen in all, preceded by the maid of honor. I want flowing greenery along the rail and two jumbo vases here on the floor."

Deena walked up to us then, as Taz gave me a pert look. "Any questions?"

I held up my useless writing utensil. "Do you happen to have a pen?"

The look he gave me could have withered a silk flower. I felt myself blushing again, though I was more irked than embarrassed. It was no wonder the last florist quit! This guy really was *not* very pleasant. You'd think he'd be more gracious, considering I was stepping in so last minute. I was essentially doing everyone involved a huge favor!

Before I could utter a more relevant question, a musical ringtone captured Taz's attention. He pulled a phone from his pocket and answered it. Of course, he didn't excuse himself or even step away.

"Kendall, darling, where are you? Don't tell me you're going to be late for the vendor meeting. I need to go over the photo ops with you."

Deena nudged me and held out a pen.

"Thanks," I whispered.

Taz rubbed his forehead. "Certainly, there will be a photo booth. Why do you sound so surprised? I'm sure you can handle managing the booth *and* capturing candids of the guests." He rolled his eyes, evidently listening to complaints on the other end of the line. "Settle down, honey. I have everything timed out. We'll talk at the meeting."

He ended the call with a sigh, then checked the messages on his phone. For a moment, he seemed to have forgotten me. I was about to speak up, when he cursed under his breath.

"Everything okay?" I asked.

He glanced up distractedly. "Take five, Sarah. I need to deal with something."

"Sierra," I corrected.

"Whatever. Listen, go take a look at the ballroom upstairs. We'll need centerpieces for every table and bouquets near the guest book and party favors, et cetera. After that, meet me in the dining room, and I'll look at your portfolio." With that, he slipped into the sitting room and shut the door behind him.

I turned to Deena and grimaced.

"That bad?" she asked.

"Worse. I forgot our portfolio."

"In the car?" she said hopefully.

I shook my head. "At the shop." I was beginning to feel this job slip through my fingers. Taz was already unimpressed with me. If he told Marissa I wasn't working out, she'd have no choice but to let him find a replacement.

"I'll go get it," Deena offered.

"I'm not sure there's enough time," I said.

"Taz seems plenty busy with other issues," she pointed out. "I'm sure it won't matter if he meets with you at the end of the meeting."

I smiled gratefully. "You're right. We might as well try."

While Deena hurried off, I jotted down a few notes, then made my way up the marble staircase. The first landing was a large balcony-like space, beyond which was a hallway with a number of closed doors. I continued up to the third floor, where a pair of French doors opened into the ballroom. It was an enormous space, with shining parquet flooring, gilded panel walls, and a vaulted ceiling. The room was largely empty, with the exception of a grand piano in the corner near the entrance and a scattering of bare round tables. A large crystal chandelier hung majestically from the center of the ceiling.

I whistled under my breath and dropped my sweater on a table. Walking slowly across the room, it began to sink in what a special break I'd been handed. Marissa's wedding was bound to be the fanciest, most high-profile event Aerieville had seen in a long while. Having this family on our client list, and their wedding photos in our portfolio, would raise Flower House's reputation like nothing else could. I'd better not squander the opportunity.

As I crossed the broad floor, I realized I should have looked for a light switch. The only source of illumination was the fading sunlight streaming through four tall arched windows along the exterior wall. The effect was peaceful and slightly melancholic. Something about the long, unfamiliar shadows, combined with the old-fashioned architecture and the pervasive, empty silence, gave the space a lonely, almost haunted feeling.

I looked out the window and felt my breath catch at the panoramic view. Beyond the wooded acreage surrounding the estate rose the Smoky Mountains, sparkling in the distance. In the highest altitudes, many of the trees already showcased brilliant leaves in shades of red, orange, and yellow.

Every autumn, I found myself more and more thankful to call the Appalachians my home. I felt privileged to live in such a beautiful area. But alongside the exhilaration of fall, with all its change and newness, I also felt a little wistful this time of year. It probably had as much to do with the waning summer as with an awareness of the passage of time: my birthday was coming up at the end of September. This year,

I would be turning twenty-nine, which seemed particularly momentous—and slightly alarming. Shouldn't I be further along life's path at this point?

As the sun began its descent behind the mountains, I had a sudden realization: the loneliness I'd felt from the ballroom was really coming from me. I was missing Calvin again.

What if he doesn't come back? Or what if he returns only to get his things and move away for good? After all, he wasn't from Aerieville. He had no family here. And there weren't any nearby universities, if he should decide he wanted to take up teaching and research again. Why should he stay?

A tinkling of piano keys intruded on my thoughts. I turned abruptly and squinted across the darkening room.

"Hello?" I called.

No one answered.

I paced to the front of the room and located a plate of light switches. Flicking them all, I brought to life the chandelier, a hanging lamp above the piano, and several sconces along the walls. I was still alone in the room. Perhaps it had been a vibration from the floor below that tripped the piano's strings. Or maybe it was a mouse.

Over the next few minutes, I used my phone to snap some pictures of the room. Then, reluctantly, I turned off the lights and headed back to the staircase. On the landing between the second and third floors, I paused to take a few more pictures of the balcony area.

From the adjacent hallway, one of the closed doors opened with a soft click. I looked over to see a young man slip out of the room. His back was to me, and his shoulders hunched, as he slowly pulled the door shut behind him. For a moment, he bowed his head as if lost in thought, before turning to skulk up the hallway. When he caught sight of me, he straightened in surprise.

"Oh! Hey." In a flash, the guy's somber expression brightened. He was a short man, close in height to my own five-foot-four frame, with sharp features and long sideburns. He stuck out his hand. "I'm Nick Siden, aka DJ Sidewinder. I don't think we've met."

Sidewinder? Ha! Clever name. He probably meant it to sound fierce, but it sounded cute to me. I returned the handshake with a polite smile. "I'm Sierra Ravenswood, the florist."

"So, Tammy really quit, huh?"

"I guess so. I haven't heard the full story yet. Creative differences, I think?"

Nick snorted. "There were differences, but not of the creative sort."

"Ah." When Nick didn't elaborate, I decided to prompt a little. I was desperate for any information that might help me get along better with the wedding planner. "I gather Taz has a strong personality. It must make it difficult for some people to work with him."

"Yeah, that's one way of putting it. He knows what he wants, and he's not shy about doing whatever it takes to get it. He's good at his job. Smart too."

"Have you worked with him a lot?"

"A few times. I've learned it's best to go with the flow with Taz Banyan. Just give him what he wants, put up with his demands, and you'll be better off in the end."

I wondered if that included putting up with his insults and condescending manner. It didn't seem right, no matter how well the job paid.

Nick looked thoughtful. "Actually, I could probably learn a thing or two from Taz. He's got ambition like nobody I've ever met. Less than three years ago he was mopping floors. Now he's the hottest wedding planner in the state. Been featured in national bridal magazines and everything."

"Oh, wow. I had no idea." If I wasn't nervous about this job before, I was now. "We'd better not keep him waiting, then. I think it's time for the meeting."

Nick checked his watch, then gestured toward the staircase. "Right. After you."

We crossed the great room at a fast clip and reached a set of partially closed pocket doors. Through the opening, I saw Regina, the caterer, sitting at a long, formal dining table, chatting with two individuals I hadn't yet met, a man and a woman. On the table in front of the woman was a professional-looking camera attached to a wide, leather strap. I didn't have a chance to make any other observations before the door slid open and Taz loomed on the threshold. I cringed, half expecting him to berate us for being late. In fact, he did start yelling, but not at us.

"Where is Anton?" he demanded, looking past us. "He was just here! He knows I need to talk to him."

"I haven't seen him," Nick said mildly. To me, he said, "Anton Cooley is the hair and makeup guy."

Taz bit the inside of his cheek, as if he was trying to decide what to do. "I need a drink," he muttered.

Nick chuckled. "Should we break into the bar?"

Ignoring the suggestion (presumably a joke), Taz seemed to collect himself. He glanced at the cell phone he was holding, then stuffed it into his pocket and focused on Nick. "Do you have the reception playlist?"

"Right here," said Nick, patting his breast pocket.

"There's been a change in plans for the first dance," Taz said briskly. "Michael-William wants to surprise Marissa with a special song from their first date. You'll start out with the expected song and segue into the surprise song after they take the floor. Kendall will be ready to capture Marissa's expression."

For a split second, Nick's eyes twitched in an expression

of annoyance. I wondered if it was because this change was one more in a long string of demands from Taz. Regardless, true to the DJ's earlier advice, his face quickly became passive again, and he nodded. "Sure. No problem."

I'd been curiously watching the two men, as if I were merely a bystander. It startled me when Taz jabbed his finger my way.

"You. Come with me."

While Nick went into the dining room, I scurried after Taz. He stalked into the large kitchen and gestured toward a gleaming cappuccino machine. "Make yourself useful and brew up some coffee. God knows I'd prefer—"

He broke off abruptly as a woman entered the kitchen, her high heels clicking loudly on the tile floor. In an instant, Taz transformed like a chameleon, morphing from a gruff and uptight autocrat into a warm and friendly chum. He smiled broadly. "Well, look at you, Miss America! Dressed for the runway and radiant as the sun."

The woman smiled back. With her delicate features and expertly applied makeup, she resembled an older version of Marissa, only with shoulder-length auburn hair instead of Marissa's long blonde tresses. She wore a simple, yet elegant, royal blue satin wrap dress. As she approached us, she snapped closed a matching blue handbag and rolled her eyes good-naturedly.

"I'm meeting Frank and Marissa for dinner in the village. It's a nice excuse to dress up." She swished her skirt with a laugh, then turned from Taz to me. "Hello, there. I'm Annaliese."

I stuck out my hand. "I'm Sierra Ravenswood, the florist."

Her skin was smooth and cool, but her smile was warm. "Ravenswood," she echoed. "Your family owns the little health club on the square."

"That's right. Dumbbells." I cringed involuntarily. The silly name had been a source of embarrassment for me ever since I was a kid. I'd grown used to it, but I should've anticipated Taz's derisive smirk. If not for Annaliese's presence, he surely would've had something insulting to say.

She pulled open a drawer and removed a set of keys. "Taz, before I go, I have two updates for you. First, we received four more late RSVPs. I hope that won't be a problem."

"Of course not. I always count on late replies."

"Perfect. The second thing is a small favor, I hope. Do you think Anton will have time to do my mother's hair and makeup? She's feeling a bit left out."

"He'll make time," Taz assured her. "We want Grandma to be happy. No worries."

"You're the best." She turned to me. "He really is. I can't tell you how many crises he's averted already."

I raised my eyebrows, wondering what qualified as a crisis in the context of wedding planning. Alas, I wasn't to find out. The housekeeper entered the kitchen, carrying two jackets and a bulky purse. She handed one of the jackets to Annaliese.

"Do you need anything else, Mrs. Lakely?"

Annaliese accepted the jacket and slipped it on. "No, Gretchen. Go on home and have a nice evening." To Taz, she said, "I'm not sure how late we'll be tonight. Don't feel like you need to wait up." She gave me a pleasant nod and headed for the back door.

I smiled, thinking what a nice woman she was—and what a contrast to Taz. It was too bad she was leaving. Then her last words sank in. *Did she say "Don't wait up"? Is Taz staying here?* Who knew wedding planning was a 24/7 job? Then again, if he was from Nashville, I supposed it made sense. Aerieville was a three-and-a-half-hour drive from

Nashville—as I knew well, since I'd lived in Music City myself for a time, before lack of money and prospects had forced me back to Aerieville.

As soon as Annaliese and Gretchen left, Taz's face hardened and he whipped out his phone. I busied myself with the cappuccino machine, hoping its operation would be intuitive. Why couldn't they have a plain old basic coffee maker? After a moment, I opened the nearby drawers and cupboards, searching for coffee and, if I was lucky, an instruction manual.

Shuffling footsteps sounded behind me, as someone else entered the room. Almost immediately, Taz erupted in a frustrated tirade. "Finally! Where have you been? If you want to get ahead, you have to take these jobs seriously."

I glanced over my shoulder to take a peek at the newcomer, presumably the missing Anton. He was about Taz's size, with a similarly colorful outfit. However, instead of a groomsman-like costume, he appeared to be dressed for an aerobics workout video, with paisley leggings, a long shoulder-baring sweatshirt, and a scrunchie-tied man bun.

He sauntered over to the refrigerator, a luxury stainless steel model, and perused the contents. In a soft, amusement-tinged voice, he said, "Relax, love. Just because I'm not neurotic like you doesn't mean I don't take the job seriously." He helped himself to an apple and crunched into it with relish.

Taz visibly seethed. "I wouldn't be so *neurotic*, if you—" He broke off suddenly, with a glance at me. Whatever he'd been about to say was left unsaid. Apparently reconsidering his words, he said, "Timing is everything. You're styling the bride's grandmother now. We need to go over your schedule."

"That's why I'm here," said Anton, around a mouthful of apple flesh. He looked my way and winked.

Regina rounded the corner into the kitchen and regarded

the three of us with barely concealed irritation. "Are we still meeting? My samples won't stay fresh forever."

Taz turned on me and barked, "Where's the coffee?"

"Um," I stammered.

Fortunately, Regina came to my rescue. Nudging me aside, she said, "Find some cups, will you?"

I gladly obliged. I could have pointed out that serving coffee wasn't exactly a florist's responsibility. But at this point I was inclined to follow the DJ's advice to go with the flow. If nothing else, this was proving to be a unique experience. It might even make for a good story someday.

Chapter 3

Seated at the dining room table, coffee cup in hand, I tried my best to blend in with the other vendors. Like them, I listened attentively and took notes as Taz ran through his master schedule, referring often to a thick, leather-bound organizer. He had everything meticulously planned, from the hours leading up to the wedding and every minute of the ceremony to every moment of the reception and beyond. Based on his gravitas and hyperattention to detail, you would have thought we were prepping for a rocket launch.

In truth, I was awed by the whole process—and more than humbled to be a part of it. In the midst of my notetaking, I observed my peers around the table. *What a high-level bunch of professionals!* Regina, owner of her own catering company, was the picture of cool competence in her crisp pink smock and chic braids. Sitting back in her chair, she eyed Taz with a laser-like focus that showed she was all business.

To the right of Regina was the photographer, Kendall. I guessed her to be in her mid-thirties, though she sported a youthful appearance. She had an urban, artsy style with asymmetrical pink hair, a silver nose ring, and a black turtle-neck. I recalled Taz's phone conversation with her earlier. It had seemed she was annoyed by his pile-on of her photography duties. But if she was still upset, she didn't show it. She listened passively, now and then exchanging enigmatic glances with some of the other vendors.

Of course, Taz hadn't bothered with introductions. When I'd followed Regina into the dining room carrying a tray of coffee cups, I'd felt the curious stares of both Kendall and the other vendor I hadn't met yet. It didn't take me long to figure out he must be Gordon Winslow, the musical director. He rested one beringed hand on a violin case and nodded in assent when Taz mentioned the "Wedding March." Gordon appeared to be the oldest of everyone in the room and not only because of his thinning white hair and lined face. From his buttoned-up shirt and rigid posture, he had an air of dignity and refinement that made me feel I was in the presence of a British nobleman. I couldn't help wondering if he resented taking direction from a young upstart like Taz.

Without warning, Gordon suddenly directed an icy glare toward me. Blushing, I looked away. *Had I been staring?*

I doodled in my notebook for a moment as Taz discussed the parts of the day that wouldn't concern me, before resuming my study of the other vendors. If Gordon was the oldest, Nick must be the youngest. In contrast to the musical director, DJ Nick appeared mellow and relaxed—well, except for a nervous twitch that sometimes pulled at the corner of his mouth or furrowed his brow. Other than the mild twitchiness, he seemed perfectly at ease, with his hands folded calmly on the table in front of him. He met my eye and, thankfully, gave me an encouraging smile instead of daggers.

Speaking of relaxed, the cosmetologist, Anton, continued to display the blasé attitude he'd shown in the kitchen. The way he slouched in his chair, I half expected him to swing one leg over the arm. Like a teenager at the dinner table, he seemed to be splitting his attention between Taz and his phone.

I took Anton's example as permission to sneak a peek at my own phone. *What's keeping Deena?* She should have been back by now. It wasn't like her to leave me hanging. Yet, I had zero messages and no missed calls.

Taz was describing the transition between the ceremony and the reception, when Anton spoke up. "How many guests will there be?"

For a moment, Taz glowered at the stylist, apparently miffed at the distraction. "As I already said, we're planning for eighty. Not that it affects your job. Now then, the ushers—"

"Does that include the wedding party?" Anton interrupted.

"Why?" asked Taz suspiciously.

"I want to make sure I bring enough product samples for everyone. I'm thinking small vials of body oil and hand cream, tied up in cute little organza drawstring bags. They make perfect parting gifts."

To my surprise, Anton's statement provoked an intense reaction from nearly everyone at the table. Several people spoke at once.

"That's not fair!"

"If he gets to include advertising, how about the rest of us?"

"At least business cards! They're small."

Taz clapped his hands sharply. "Everyone, quiet! Don't be ridiculous. No one is hawking their products or services to the wedding guests. That would be *beyond* tacky."

He shot Anton a warning look, then resumed his presentation. Anton shrugged, and Kendall muttered something under her breath. I continued to sit quietly like a wallflower. (*Ha. Wallflower. Calvin would like that one.*)

Before long, it was clear Taz was nearing the end of his checklist. And still no word from Deena. I tapped my foot under the table in a bout of nervous energy. Any minute I expected the wedding planner to turn on me. I just knew he was going to put me on the spot and make me feel foolish and incompetent.

The second I had that thought, I checked myself. I knew better than to allow anyone to *make me* feel anything. I was a big believer in the power of my own attitude. If I wanted to be viewed as a professional, I should act like one. If I wanted to be treated with respect, I needed to respect myself.

I sat up a little straighter and took a long, slow breath. Affirmation style, I tried on a few different statements in my mind: *I am a competent person. I am a talented professional florist. I am worthy of respect.*

My phone buzzed, jolting me from my internal pep talk. I grabbed it from the table and quickly read the incoming text, which was from Deena. Then I read it again.

So sorry! I tried to print our latest photos & the printer ran out of ink. Then Rocky showed up with Gus and, long story short, Gus destroyed the portfolio. BUT I'm transferring the photos to my email, so you can still show the pictures. The files are huge so it's taking forever. I'll send them soon. I hope.

It was all I could do not to slap my forehead and groan. *Gus! How could you?* Actually, I couldn't be too mad at the pup. He'd been acting out ever since Calvin left. If anything, he probably missed the guy more than I did. Still, what was I supposed to do now? Somehow I didn't think Taz would have the patience to look at our photos, one by one, on my tiny phone. It was too bad we didn't have an updated gallery on our website. That was another task that fell by the wayside in Calvin's absence.

Suppressing a sigh, I started to type a reply to Deena, when my ears tuned in to what Taz was saying. It was the word "flowers" that caught my attention. I looked up sharply and tried to follow his rapid-fire directions.

"After the one-on-ones, we'll reconvene here for a final check-in." He stood up and pointed at me, before turning to the others. "Okay, florist first. Gordon, wait for me in the great room, so we can test the acoustics. Kendall, you'll be up after that. Then we'll meet Nick in the ballroom. Nick, go ahead and get your area set up. Got it?"

"You bet," said Nick.

"What about—" Regina began.

Taz cut her off. "Anton, you can tag along with me."

"Oh, can I?" said Anton, more than a little sardonically.

I needed to speak up, and now. *Confidence. Competence.* I sat up straight and raised my hand. "Um, could you start with someone else maybe?" Hearing myself speak, I cringed. *Don't be such a pipsqueak!* I cleared my throat. "That is, I'm waiting for my colleague to send me our updated portfolio. I should have it soon."

Taz glared at me for a beat, then shrugged. "Fine." He beckoned Gordon with one finger. "Let's go hear that violin."

I breathed a sigh of relief. Emboldened now, I spoke up again. "Does anyone have a laptop I can borrow?"

Everyone was getting up from the table, and no one seemed to hear me. Taz and Gordon exited through the pocket doors into the great room, while Anton slipped out the door leading to the kitchen. Kendall left too, muttering something about needing to make a phone call.

Regina stood rigidly, staring at the doorway. Speaking to no one in particular, she said in a low voice, "He's doing this on purpose. It's like he wants my cake to be dry when he tastes it."

I tried to give her a reassuring smile. "I'm sure it will still be delicious."

She ignored me and left the room.

Nick chuckled lightly. "You're right. It *will* be delicious." Leaning across the table, he pried off the plastic lid from one of the food containers, revealing an array of frosted mini-cupcakes. He popped one into his mouth, then pushed the container toward me.

It was tempting, but I shook my head. "I don't suppose you have a laptop?" I asked.

"Not on me. What do you need one for?"

I explained my predicament. "I'm not sure what Taz has in mind, but I'd like to show him my work and share some ideas I have for the wedding decorations."

"Oh, you can use Frank's computer for that."

"Frank's computer?" *As in Mayor Frank?*

"It's in his office. I'm pretty sure Taz has borrowed it before. He has the run of this place, so I'm sure it's fine. Come on, I'll show you where it is."

Nick replaced the lid on the cake container and led the way through the side door. Instead of turning right, toward the kitchen, he went left, straight to a pair of black lacquer double doors. Without hesitation, he turned the knob and went right in.

The room within was a compact den with wood-paneled walls and expensive-looking furniture. To the left, a dark mahogany L-shaped desk stood squarely in front of a wall of shelves, half-filled with books. Much of the rest of the shelf space was occupied by golf trophies and framed photographs. The adjacent wall, opposite the doorway, featured drapery-covered windows. If I wasn't mistaken, they probably looked out upon the rear driveway and parking area near the back door. To the right, a pair of leather club chairs flanked a tall square end table.

Unlike the rest of the home I'd seen, this space had a surprisingly lived-in feeling. A folded, rumpled newspaper had been left on one of the club chairs, and a half-empty coffee cup rested on the desk. A suit jacket hung loosely over the back of the office chair. On one end of the desk, next to a laser jet printer, was a golden letter tray stacked full of what looked to be household mail. Balanced on top was an open cardboard box containing wedding programs.

I spoke in a hushed tone. "Are you sure it's okay for us to be in here?"

Nick gave me an indulgent smile as he sat at the desk and shook the computer mouse. "The door was unlocked, wasn't it? Don't worry so much."

Easy for you to say. "The computer isn't password protected?"

"Nah. Frank has another computer upstairs. This one is mainly for playing solitaire and reading the news. Anyway, it's not like we're going to open his email or anything."

While I hung back, Nick clicked open an internet browser, then stood up. "Here you go. Feel free to print your pictures, if you want. This thing is high quality." He pressed the button on the printer, and it whirred to life.

"Cool," I murmured. "Thanks." At the same time, I wondered how Nick knew all this. How long had the vendors been meeting in this house?

With a friendly nod, Nick left me alone in the mayor's home office. Pushing aside my lingering nervousness, I sat at the desk and shot off a quick text to Deena. Then I pulled up the Flower House website. At least we had a few nice photos in our online gallery. It could serve as a starting point.

I glanced at the printer. Did I dare use it? Printer ink was expensive. On the other hand, it seemed as if Frank and An-naliese wished to spare no expense for their daughter's wedding, and surely this would be only a drop in that bucket.

Swiveling in the chair, I looked at the photos on the shelf behind me. Apparently, Marissa was an only child, and her parents clearly doted on her. Besides a sweet family portrait, with a young pigtailed Marissa in the center, there were several pictures that proudly featured the girl alone: on horseback, at a dance recital, accepting an academic award. And another with a horse.

I picked up one of the more recent photos to get a closer look. It showed Marissa in a cap and gown, standing in front of a cake and surrounded by a group of friends. Based on their ages, I guessed this was from her college graduation. I wondered if one of the guys was her fiancé. Marissa seemed happy in the photo, with bright eyes and a sparkling smile. Nothing like the somber girl I'd met this morning.

The slam of a car door pulled me from my musings. Was Deena finally here? I moved toward the windows, planning to pull back the curtains for a look, when my phone buzzed. It was a text from Deena herself.

New plan. The photo files are too big to send, so I'll upload them to our website. As soon as I figure out how. Stay tuned!

Dang. Shaking my head, I could only laugh. I never believed in Murphy's Law, but this was getting ridiculous. Granny Mae would say I must've done something to attract misfortune. I tried to remember. Had I broken any mirrors lately? Did I cross the path of a black cat or walk under a ladder?

A ladder! The security guy had climbed a ladder this morning to install the cameras. At one point, I did sort of

step beneath it to reach for a screwdriver and hand it up
to him.

I scoffed to myself. *Ridiculous.* I don't put much stock
in Granny's superstitions. I believe we create our own luck.

With that thought in mind, I realized I'd better get out of
the den. Taz could be looking for me. Leaving the website
up and the door open, I jogged back to the dining room.

The room was empty. For a second, I eyed Regina's food
containers. I hadn't had supper yet and wouldn't mind trying an hors d'oeuvre or two. Or a cupcake. But I restrained
myself. I couldn't do that without asking Regina first.

Instead, I made my way to the kitchen. Maybe I could
help myself to an apple like Anton had. Or maybe I'd run
into Regina.

Finding the kitchen empty as well, it struck me how
quiet the house was. There were no voices, no strains of violin music. I headed toward the back door to peer outside,
but I didn't quite make it. A loud thud, from somewhere in
the house, made me pause. I turned my head and listened,
fully expecting to hear a string of curses and yelling. Either
someone dropped something or, more likely, Taz had lost
his temper and thrown something across the room.

However, there was only silence. And for some reason,
this bothered me more than yelling would have. A strange
feeling came over me. Retracing my steps to the empty dining room, then through the pocket doors, I entered the great
room and looked around. There was no one in sight. Fueled
now by a mixture of curiosity and low-grade dread, I glided
slowly across the long room and glanced up at the balcony.
Did everyone go up to the ballroom? Should I join them?

I moved toward the marble staircase, my eyes still flicker-
ing upward. It was only in my peripheral vision that I became
aware of a dark shape on the floor beside the stairs. Frowning,
I turned my head and stared. *What is that?*

In a heartbeat, I knew. The crumpled heap was a person . . . in a burgundy suit. It was Taz.

I clapped my hand over my mouth and gasped. *It was Taz!*

For a split second, I looked around wildly. Had he tripped and fallen? Why wasn't he getting up? And where was everyone else?

Coming to my senses, I rushed to his side and kneeled down. "Taz? Are you okay?"

It was a foolish question. He was clearly not okay.

He was lying on his side, his face turned away from me. With trembling fingers, I reached for his wrist to check for a pulse. The instant I touched him, he groaned.

I jumped. *Thank God!* Touching his shoulder, I spoke gently. "Taz, what happened?"

He didn't respond. I was afraid to move him, in case he had any broken bones, but I wanted to see his face. Moving with care, I stepped over him and wedged myself in the space between his body and the marble stairs.

"Taz? What happened? Should I call an ambulance?"

One look at his colorless face and closed eyes, and I had my answer. Of course I should call an ambulance. I fumbled to open my purse, then stopped as he made another sound. I leaned over him, lightly resting my fingers on his forehead. "It's okay," I said softly. "Don't try to move. I'm going to get help."

Suddenly, his eyes popped open and his body gave a jerk. In the next instant, I felt his icy fingers latch onto my wrist. I could only stare back at him, transfixed by his intense gaze. His mouth worked silently, his lips opening and closing like a fish frantic for oxygen. Then a sound bubbled through.

"Sss . . . ah. It was . . . uh . . ."

He wasn't making sense. I wondered if he was in shock. "Shh," I soothed. "It's okay."

"Sss . . . snake."

"Taz," I said. "I need to call for help. Try to . . ." I trailed off, as I became aware of something I hadn't noticed before. On the floor, beneath Taz's burgundy jacket, was a spreading pool of crimson liquid.

His fingers loosened their grip on my wrist. In horror, I looked from the floor back to his face, where his staring eyes were now blank. Vacant. Dead.

A scream shattered the silence, echoing throughout the great hall.

Chapter 4

I couldn't have said who arrived first. One moment I was alone with Taz, the next I was surrounded by people. There was a lot of shouting and screaming, crying and questioning. At first, I hadn't even realized it was I who had screamed first, alerting the others of the crisis. But as soon as I knew I wasn't alone, I'd backed away from Taz's body to let everyone else see for themselves what I'd seen.

After a few minutes of chaos, it was the women, Regina and Kendall, who had the presence of mind to call 9-1-1. I watched as they both placed the call, neither seeming to notice, or care, that the other was doing the same.

As for the men, Gordon had a hold on Anton's arms, evidently trying to keep him from getting too close to the body. Nick stayed on the periphery, looking as if he might be sick. I wasn't too far behind him. On shaky legs, I backed away from the group and dropped to a seat on the lowest step of the staircase.

And that's where I stayed, numb and confused, until I became aware of a person standing before me. She crouched down to my level.

"Sierra Ravenswood?"

I looked up into the inquisitive gray eyes of Officer Renee Bradley, *Captain* Bradley now, a woman I'd encountered before on more than one occasion. For no good reason, I felt a pang of guilt.

"What happened here?" she asked. As always, she had a pleasant, non-threatening manner—which belied the intractable toughness I'd witnessed firsthand. If I wasn't mistaken, she seemed tenser than usual, with a perceptible tightness about her eyes. Her short blonde hair now included strands of gray around the temples.

I shifted my gaze to the area beneath the balcony, where a cluster of first responders blocked my view of Taz's body. I swallowed hard. "I have no idea. I found him there, on the floor."

Returning my attention to the captain, I saw her press her lips together. In my imagination, I could almost hear her thoughts: *You found him? Of course, you did.*

But she was professional. She only said, "Who is he?"

"Taz Banyan. He's a wedding planner. *Was* a wedding planner."

"What was going on here? Who are all these people?"

"It was a vendor meeting, to prepare for Marissa Lakely's wedding." *So much for that.*

She seemed to consider this for a moment, then asked, "Was anyone with you when you found the victim? Or anyone in the vicinity at all?"

I shook my head. "Not that I know of. The room was quiet and empty when I came in."

Captain Bradley looked over her shoulder, where the other vendors were milling about.

"Okay, Sierra. I'd like to hear more, but first I need to get this scene secured and separate the witnesses. Please don't talk to anyone until—"

She broke off as the front door swung open. All motion in the room froze, as a bear-like man loomed into view. With the aid of a cane, he stomped slowly toward us. It was the gaunt, intimidating figure of Police Chief Walt Walden.

I shrank a little, hoping, irrationally, that he wouldn't notice me. I'd always felt small around Chief Walden, whether he was visiting my dad—his old college football buddy—or investigating the first murder at Flower House. *I still can't believe there's been more than one!* He'd been out on a medical leave and, as far as I knew, was at least semiretired now. Captain Bradley had been the acting chief in his absence. I gathered that was no longer the case.

With all eyes on him now, it was clear the chief was in charge. He didn't even have to raise his voice to start issuing orders.

"All civilians, line up against this wall, please, and don't say a word. I'll be with you shortly. Bradley, find some barrier tape, will you? Secure the core crime scene, then the whole house. EMTs, step back and let CSI get in there to do their job. Detective Bryant, after you photograph this room, spiral out. Anybody check upstairs yet? The mayor is on his way home, and I want to have some answers ready for him."

Everyone complied without question—though Bradley pressed her lips together again. As I moved to join the other vendors, I overheard the chief ask one of the paramedics about the apparent cause of death. Of course, he must've already determined he was dealing with a homicide.

The medical technician, a young man in a blue uniform, wrinkled his forehead. "Victim has a stab wound to the back of his torso, as well as visible fall injuries. It appears he came over the railing up there." He pointed toward the balcony. "At this point, I can't say if he was already dead when he hit the floor."

I spoke without thinking. "He wasn't."

Both men turned to stare at me. The others must have overheard—a second hush fell over the room as all murmured conversation died away.

The paramedic gave me a doubtful look. "He had a pulse?"

"He was conscious, at first. He spoke to me."

Someone made a noise behind me—something between a cough and a gasp. From the corner of my eye, I saw Captain Bradley step forward and hold out her palm, like a crossing guard stopping traffic. I also sensed the others closing in, creating a semicircle around me.

"What did he say?" asked Regina, her voice slightly breathless.

"Miss Ravenswood," began Chief Walden.

"I don't know," I said. "It was all jumbled. I think—"

"Miss Ravenswood!" barked the chief. "Hold up. I'll take your statement first." He moved toward the sitting room and pulled open the door. "This will do."

He beckoned another officer to join him and ushered us into the vacant room. I stood uncertainly for a moment, hugging my arms together, as they spoke in low voices. Then the chief asked me to have a seat on the sofa. The other officer, a young, earnest-looking patrolman, pulled up an armchair and removed a notebook from his pocket. I perched on the edge of a sleek, firm cushion and watched the chief, as he moved near the window opposite the sofa. He remained standing there, occasionally flicking a glance outside, as he questioned me.

"Go on," he said. "Tell me everything."

My words poured out in a rush. At this point, I was desperate to hand off all the knowledge I had, so I could be done and go home. I told them all about the wedding job and the meeting, as well as everything I knew about the other vendors. The chief interjected with a question now and then, but he was mostly quiet as he listened to my account. The note-taker didn't say a word, but I could hear his pen scratching furiously. When I reached the end, the chief limped toward me and pulled a small tape recorder from his jacket pocket.

"Do you mind repeating that last bit for the record?" He pressed a button and set the device on the coffee table.

I nodded in agreement and leaned toward the recorder. "Taz was struggling to speak. He made some sounds, nothing sensible at first. Then he said, 'It was the snake.' No, wait." I squeezed my eyes shut for a second before continuing. "I know he said, 'It was.' Then he made some other sounds and said 'snake.'"

"'It was snake'?" asked the chief.

"Yeah. I'm pretty sure."

He regarded me for a moment, then grabbed the recorder and snapped it off. With another glance out the window, he moved toward the door. "Okay, you can leave now. But I'd like you to come to the station tomorrow morning for a proper interview. If you think of anything else, you can tell me then."

I stood slowly and started to check my phone. The chief gave an impatient grunt. "Come along! The mayor will be here any minute, and I have to get through the other field interviews."

"Sorry." I scurried to the door, ducking my head apologetically.

As he opened the door for me, his manner suddenly softened. "Take care now, Sierra. Tell your dad hello."

"I will," I promised.

"Oh," he added, touching my arm. "And don't tell anyone else what you've told me tonight. Especially any of the other witnesses."

I nodded and left the room.

It was quiet in the great room. Captain Bradley and another cop stood watching over the vendors, who were now seated in folding chairs along the wall spaced several feet apart from one another. They were all glued to their phones. *What would keep them from texting one another?* I wondered.

Regina was next in line. As she stood and headed to the sitting room, she shot me a somber, curious look. I tried to give her a sympathetic smile, but it probably came out more like a grimace.

The paramedics were gone, and so was the body. A cordon of red tape marked an irregular shape around the spot where Taz had lain—apparently the "core crime scene" Chief Walden had mentioned. I shivered and rubbed the cool skin on my bare arms. *Where did I put my sweater? Oh, yeah. The ballroom.*

I headed upstairs to fetch my sweater. Halfway up the marble staircase, I paused and glanced over my shoulder. Was it okay for me to go up here? No one seemed to notice me. Captain Bradley and the other officer had their heads bowed over a pad of paper, probably showing the crime scene sketch. I hurried on. I'd be quick.

On the second-floor landing, I saw that the area in front of the balcony had also been sectioned off with red tape. I gathered that the red plastic must be used for inner barriers, while the usual yellow tape must be for outside. I thought of other times I'd seen that ubiquitous fluttering plastic, usually on TV or the news. Police Line. Do Not Cross. It was so cheap and lightweight, I reflected. Disposable. Yet so heavy in its import. Giving the protected area a wide berth, I trotted up the next flight of stairs.

My sweater was right where I'd left it. I didn't even bother turning on the lights. As I slipped my arm through the second sleeve, my phone buzzed. It was Deena. "Hey," I said softly.

"Thank goodness!" she said. "What in the world is going on there?"

"You don't know?" Usually, news spread though Aerieville faster than our internet service. It was uncanny.

"How would I know? There's all kinds of cop cars and emergency vehicles blocking the driveway. The guard at the entrance wouldn't let me through."

"There's been a . . ." I trailed off. I wanted to say "accident," but I knew that wasn't true. Yet I couldn't bring myself to say "murder."

"A what?"

I sighed. "A terrible thing. Taz is dead." Deena gasped, then plied me with questions, as I made my way out of the dark ballroom and toward the stairs. "I'll tell you all about it as soon as I get out of here," I said. "Where should I meet you?"

She told me she'd driven back to the road, but she would circle around and return to the estate. Maybe they'd let her come up to the house now. After all, she was my ride home. I said I'd hang out inside until she called me, rather than wait outside. We hung up, and I dropped my phone into my purse.

Once again on the second-floor landing, my eyes automatically found that hideous red tape again. *What happened up here? Someone stabbed Taz and pushed him over the rail? Why?*

I shifted my gaze to the dim hallway and recalled seeing Nick emerge from one of the rooms. Then I noticed something different. Just beyond the place where I'd seen Nick, one of the doors was ajar. A pale orange patch of light illumined the floor and opposite wall.

I couldn't help myself. I had to take a peek.

At first glance, the room appeared to be a combination den and storage room. To the left, a large L-shaped sofa faced a flat screen TV, and to the right, stacks of cardboard boxes and wedding decorations covered a table and the surrounding floor. Beyond this, a cased opening in the wall led to a tandem room. I drifted forward, propelled by my innate curiosity. The adjoining room was outfitted like a cozy guest room. Based on the bottles of hair gel and beard oil on the dresser, and the assortment of colorful neckties draped over the back of a chair, I realized this must have been Taz's room. The faint scent of sandalwood lingered in the air. I shook my head sadly, as I gazed around the room. *It's unreal. Here one minute, and gone the next . . .*

On a chest at the foot of the bed lay an open suitcase, half-full of neatly folded clothes. A laundry bin in the corner of the room was also half full. I guessed Taz must have been staying here at least a couple of days.

Moving closer to the suitcase, I noticed the inner pockets bulged with hidden contents. The smaller pouches might have held toiletries or pill containers. The larger pocket could carry papers or a notebook. My fingers itched to open the flaps. Of course, I didn't. I wouldn't dare . . .

What's this? My eyes landed on a threadlike tendril of hot pink, stark against a white T-shirt. It was a strand of hair. *Kendall's hair? Has to be.*

A creak from below jarred me to my senses. *I should get out of here.* I left the small guest room and moved swiftly through the den, darting a regretful look at the wedding decorations. *Such a shame.*

At the still open door, I started to leave the room, then froze at the sound of footsteps. Someone was coming up the hallway. *Dang!* How embarrassing to be caught snooping. It was probably Captain Bradley wondering what was taking me so long. Swallowing my pride, I took a step forward, ready to apologize and make excuses. Then I caught sight of the golden-haired woman at the end of the hall. *Marissa.*

I jumped back out of sight. She hadn't seen me. She'd been looking down at her phone, before pausing to gaze toward the taped-off balcony.

Biting my lip, I stood immobile just inside the doorway. I didn't know why I was hiding. She probably wouldn't mind that I was here. Still, something held me back. Maybe I was just afraid of startling her, or intruding upon her private pain.

I listened for further sounds, but there was nothing. No footsteps or anything—until I heard the click of a door opening. I hesitated two more seconds, then cautiously looked out, just in time to see the door shutting on the neighboring room. I breathed a sigh of relief. *Time to get out of here.*

As I tiptoed past the closed door, presumably Marissa's room, it occurred to me that this was where I'd seen Nick acting strange.

What was Nick doing in Marissa's bedroom?

Chapter 5

With no word yet from Deena, I decided to bide my time in the kitchen. I'd overheard Captain Bradley say it had already been searched and cleared. And it seemed like a safe, neutral zone, well away from all the buzzing police activity—not to mention the suspicious, fraught tension emanating from the waiting vendors. For something to do, I grabbed a dishcloth and wiped spilled coffee grounds from the counter around the cappuccino machine. My thoughts naturally shifted back to Taz and his demand that I make coffee. *What a bully.*

A bully somebody murdered.

I still couldn't believe it had happened.

In the midst of my ruminations, I heard the back door click open. Annaliese came inside in a noisy rush, letting the door slam shut behind her. Catching sight of me, she hurried over.

"Oh, you poor dear! Are you okay? What a dreadful situation."

"I'm okay," I said, somewhat startled. "I-I just feel bad about what happened. I'm sorry."

She rubbed her temple and winced slightly, before forcing a grim smile. "I know you feel bad. I'm sure everyone does. I don't understand what happened, but the police will get to the bottom of it. Frank is talking to the officers outside right now."

I murmured my agreement, not knowing what else to say.

"Are you hungry?" she asked, opening a pantry door. Without waiting for my response, she handed me a boxed coffee cake, her fingers trembling as she let go. "Would you be a dear and take this to the dining room? I'll put the coffee on. I have a feeling this will be a long night."

I wasn't going to argue. The truth was, I was famished. I might as well have a bite to eat as I waited for Deena.

When I pushed open the door to the dining room, I was surprised to find it occupied. Regina, Nick, and Gordon were sitting at the table picking at Regina's samples. The second they saw me, they jumped into action, Gordon pulling out a chair, Nick taking the cakebox from my hands, and Regina sliding over a paper plate stacked with three tiny triangle sandwiches. It was a far cry from the earlier reception I'd received.

"Thanks," I said, taking the proffered chair. "Annaliese is making fresh coffee."

"How are you holding up?" asked Nick. "You had quite a shock."

"I think we all did," I said.

"Yes, but you found him," said Gordon. "You were at his side when he took his last breath."

"Mm-hmm," I murmured. *He makes it sound so dramatic.*

"What did he say?" Regina asked bluntly.

"I don't know." I took a bite of the little sandwich and chewed self-consciously. All three were watching me.

"I wonder what he was thinking about," Regina said, more softly this time and not to anyone in particular. "He must have known he was dying. What must have been going through his mind?"

"You think his life passed before his eyes?" asked Nick.

Gordon sat back in his chair, looking pensive. "Famous last words. Deathbed confessions. It's quite fascinating, if you think about it."

Nick raised his eyebrows, then shook his head. "Come on, people. If he said anything, it was most likely one of two things."

We all looked at the DJ, waiting for him to go on.

He held up an index finger. "One—he said something along the lines of 'Ouch, my head hurts.'"

"Or his back," Regina put in.

"Two," continued Nick, "he named his killer."

Everyone turned to face me again.

"He didn't," I began, then stopped myself. The chief had warned me not to talk. Still, I felt compelled to say something. "He didn't make any sense. He just made some sounds." *Stop talking, Sierra!* I looked down at my phone. *Where is Deena?*

"I can't believe no one saw anything," said Regina. Addressing Gordon, she said, "Weren't you the last one with him?"

He puffed out his chest defensively. "I certainly was not. We were in the great room for only a minute or so before my A-string broke. I told Taz I'd replace it and be right back. I came in here, to the dining room, only to discover I didn't have extra strings in my case. So, I left my violin on the table and went out to my car. When I came back in, I heard screaming."

"Huh," said Nick. "I didn't see you. After leaving Sierra in Frank's office, I went out to my van to get my gear."

"I didn't see you either," Gordon said pointedly.

"I didn't see either of you," said Regina. "After visiting the powder room, I'd gone outside for fresh air."

For a moment, no one spoke. Then the pocket doors slid open, and Anton and Kendall came into the room.

"Oh, look," Anton announced cheerily. "It's all the suspects."

"Speak for yourself," said Gordon, standing up. He moved to close his violin case.

"We were just recounting our whereabouts," said Nick. "Anton, weren't you supposed to be shadowing Taz?"

The stylist scoffed. "What am I, an intern? No. I told him I'd wait for him to finish with everyone else. I took the opportunity for a little cat nap."

"Where?" asked Kendall, with a touch of surprise.

"On the couch in that TV room, where all the decorations are."

Glancing at my phone, I saw that Deena had finally texted me. She was waiting in the driveway outside. But now I didn't want to leave just yet.

"Where were *you*, Kendall?" asked Regina.

For some reason, Kendall glanced at Nick before answering. "In the ballroom, waiting for Taz."

Anton gave Kendall a cheeky look and opened his mouth to speak, but she swiveled toward me and spoke first. "So, what did Taz say when you found him? Any parting wisdom? A deathbed confession?"

I frowned, a little uncomfortable with her insensitivity. I also noted she'd used the same "confession" phrase Gordon had.

"Lay off, Kendall," said Nick. "Sierra already told us Taz didn't say anything. Just nonsense." He gave me a questioning look, as if asking me to confirm.

Anton snickered quietly. "Nonsense to the end."

"Poor devil," said Regina, almost as if talking to herself.

Like a magician, Nick suddenly produced a bottle of

scotch. He set it on the table with a thud. "How 'bout a toast to our old friend?"

Anton opened the sideboard and gathered some glasses, and Kendall helped pass them out. When everyone had a glass with a splash of liquor, Nick held his in the air. "To Taz."

"To Taz," we echoed.

As I sipped the smoky spirit, I regarded the others through narrowed eyes and felt like the outsider I was. That was fine. *One of you is a murderer*, I thought soberly.

Without saying goodbye, I slipped out of the room, breezed through the kitchen, and escaped from the manor.

Good riddance to you all.

Deena drove us back to Flower House and dropped me off beside my car, a bright orange Fiat I usually liked to think of as sunshine on wheels. I was feeling far from sunny now. I was exhausted, physically and emotionally. Still, Deena wanted to hear everything, every little detail, about what had happened after she left, and I obliged. I could relate to her sense of curiosity—not to mention her concern as a friend.

More than once during the telling, she'd shuddered and exclaimed in dismay. By the time she pulled up alongside my car, she was more perplexed than anything.

"It doesn't make sense," she said, shifting into Park. "It couldn't have been one of the vendors."

I pulled down the visor against the new security lights above the shop's back door. "Why not?"

"Because now they're all out of a job—an important, high-paying job. I assume the wedding is off, right?"

"I assume so, or at least postponed indefinitely." I stifled a yawn and peered across the dark lawn toward the faint glow of nightlights in the bakery next door. Flower House was located in a sleepy, mostly residential neighborhood, featuring quaint old Victorians and only a couple of other businesses. What it lacked in foot traffic, it made up for in charm.

"Are you sure there wasn't anyone else in the house?" asked Deena.

"Pretty sure." I squinted through the windshield. A car rolled down Oak Street, its headlights casting a wobbly beam on the trees nearest the curb. "I guess I can't know for sure," I amended. "Someone could've been hiding in one of the bedrooms. Or could've snuck in when we were all in the meeting." I shivered at the thought.

For a moment, neither of us said anything. Then I turned to my friend. "He was trying to tell me something, Dee."

"Something about a snake?"

"I think he was trying to tell me who stabbed him. It had to be someone he knew."

Deena gave me a worried look. "Do you want me to follow you home? Better yet, why don't you stay at my place tonight?"

Another car drove slowly past Flower House, going in the opposite direction this time. I couldn't tell if it was the same one as before.

"That's okay," I said. "I'm fine. I just want to go home, take a hot shower, and crawl into bed."

"You sure?"

I mustered up a wan smile. "I'm sure. Thanks, though."

I left Deena's car and got into my own, then made the short drive to my tiny cottage—dubbed "the dollhouse" by my mom based on its general cuteness as much as its size. I'd decorated the little starter home to suit my upbeat style, with fluttery curtains, brightly painted walls, and flowers on every table.

When I let myself in and flipped on the lights, I couldn't

help noting the vast contrast between my humble abode and the opulence of Bellman Manor. All in all, I preferred my house. My acoustic guitar waited patiently on a stand in the corner of the living room. Framed vinyl album covers made for quirky art above the apartment sofa—a plush, sky blue nest I often sank in to read. Stacks of books—mostly romance and mysteries mixed in with self-help favorites— shared surface space with the flowers. Motivational sticky notes inspired me at strategic locations in every room.

I had everything I needed here. Well, almost everything. Tonight something was missing—something in the nature of a four-legged furry friend.

Deena had told me she'd texted my brother while she was waiting for me outside Bellman Manor. Pal that he was, Rocky had said not to worry, he'd keep Gus overnight. And I'd agreed; it seemed like a good idea at the time. Now, walking through my empty house, I regretted both decisions— not picking up Gus *and* not accepting Deena's offer. It was far too quiet for my edgy nerves.

But it was too late to change my mind. I turned on some meditative music, popped a pill for my headache, and took a steamy shower. By the time I crawled under the covers, I still missed Gus—especially the way he kept my feet warm at the foot of the bed—but I was ready for sleep.

Unfortunately, it was a fitful sleep. I kept waking up from troubled dreams. At least once I was startled by a strange noise outside. I sat up, squinting toward the dark window. After a moment of silence, broken only by the faint creak of the wind through the eaves and the faint horn of a distant train, I dropped back onto the pillow. *It was probably just a cat or raccoon.* I pulled the covers up to my chin and rolled over. *I'm sure it was nothing.*

Chapter 6

I was awakened by my phone before my alarm had a chance to do the job. More accurately, it was my mother who woke me up. I grabbed the phone from my nightstand and answered groggily.

"Hi, Mom."

"Rise and shine!" My mom's peppy voice cut through the morning fog. *Once a cheerleader always a cheerleader.* "Hope I didn't wake you. I wanted to be sure to catch you before breakfast. I'm making omelets and yogurt parfaits."

I sat up and rubbed my eyes. "Sounds good. I need to pick up Gus from Rocky anyway."

"I know. I heard him barking at the crack of dawn. For a little guy he sure has big pipes."

I should've figured Mom knew already. Rocky lived in the apartment above our parents' garage. She probably knew all about my ordeal last night and wanted to hear more.

"Coffee's brewing," she said. "See you soon!"

One of the advantages of living in a small town was the short drive to just about anywhere you wanted to go. In less than twenty minutes—including the time it took to dress, comb my hair, and apply a smidge of makeup—I pulled up in front of my parents' gray-shingled two-story house. The early morning sun cast a soft golden light over the mature trees surrounding my parents' property. When I opened the car door, the shrill whistle of a robin echoed in the cool, clear air.

I'd barely stepped foot on the lawn before a loud string of excited yips met my ears. I looked over to see my brother rounding the corner of the house. As strong as he was, Rocky still appeared to be pulled along by mighty little Augustus, straining on the end of his leash. Then Rocky let go and Gus bounded straight at me, fast as the wind. I felt a smile broaden my face, even as I braced myself. Gus jumped on my legs, his stubby tail quivering with happiness. You'd have thought we'd been apart a month rather than a day.

"Hey, Buddy. I missed you too." Laughing, I crouched down to pet him, doing my best to deflect the kisses he tried to lavish on my face.

"Wow," said Rocky. "And here I thought he enjoyed hanging out with me."

"I'm sure he did," I said generously.

As we chatted, another car drove up and parked behind mine. It was our grandmother's familiar old Subaru Outback. When Granny Mae climbed out of her car, with bulky cloth bags draped over each arm, Gus emitted a sharp bark of welcome and ran over to her. So much for the touching reunion.

Granny hollered in greeting to us and fed Gus a treat she'd brought especially for him. Rocky took her bags, and we all went inside, Gus close to Granny's heels. Following the mouthwatering aroma of sautéed mushrooms and onions, we found our parents in the kitchen, where Dad was slicing a melon and Mom was setting the table.

As owners of a health club, my parents were naturally early risers. Fresh-faced and energetic in their matching Dumbbells sweatshirts, they looked like they'd been up for hours. *Yet another way I differ from my family*, I reflected as I headed straight for the coffee pot. I'd never been an early bird—until I found myself running a flower shop and had no choice.

Dad took his usual place at the head of the kitchen table, with mom at his right elbow. I sat down next to him, across from Mom. As Rocky sat on her other side, I noted, not for the first time, how my petite mother looked like a pop-star celebrity, flanked as she was between two muscular body-guards. Or maybe head of state was more apt, considering her current posture and the laser-like stare she directed at me. Then Dad turned to me too.

"Heard you had quite a time last night," he said, with a pseudo casualness that didn't fool anyone.

"That's one way of putting it." I took a sip of coffee, acutely aware they were waiting for me to elaborate. I bit back the urge to go on the defensive: *It wasn't my fault!* Even though they didn't say it, I often had a feeling my family thought I courted trouble. It was ironic, really, considering I actually made a concerted effort to attract positive things in my life.

Granny slid into the chair next to me and patted my hand, before reaching for the butter dish.

"What happened?" asked Mom. "People are saying there was a murder at the mayor's mansion. And that there was some kind of party there, with mostly out-of-towners— except for one person: a local florist. What were you even doing there?"

"It wasn't a party!" I protested. Hearing my reactive tone, I paused and took a breath. I sounded childish, and I'd worked so hard lately *not* to appear childish in front of my parents. "It was a meeting to prepare for the mayor's daughter's wedding."

"And someone killed the party planner?"

"Yeah." In a stiff, somewhat formal manner, I gave them a brief account of how I ended up at the mayor's home. "After the meeting, everyone dispersed to different parts of the house. I was busy trying to figure out how I was going to show Taz photos of my work. Apparently, someone else was busy stabbing him in the back."

My mom clapped her hand over her mouth. Granny froze in the midst of spreading strawberry jelly on a piece of toast. Dad cleared his throat, and Rocky looked thoughtful.

"It happened on the second floor," I continued. "Then he either fell or was pushed over the railing next to the staircase in the great room. That's where I found him. I tried to help, but . . ." I trailed off, suddenly finding it difficult to speak over the lump in my throat.

"Oh, honey," said Mom. "How awful."

"It was too late," I concluded. "He died." I reached down to scratch the top of Gus's head. He'd been sitting quietly at my knee. "There's not much more to tell. The police are investigating."

"Walt will solve it," Dad said firmly. "No doubt about it."

For a moment no one spoke. We concentrated on our food until Rocky said, "Any theories?"

I glanced over at him, and he gave me a sly little grin. "C'mon, sis. You seem to have a knack for sniffing out bad guys. Surely, you have an opinion or two."

"Rocky," said Mom with a sharp look.

"I don't have any theories," I answered. At the same time, my mind immediately started pondering the possibilities. "In fact," I continued, "it seemed like a lot of people might have had cause to be upset with the guy. But enough to kill him? I have no clue."

"'No clue'? Interesting word choice," said Rocky, a note of amusement in his voice.

"Could you pass the salt?" asked Dad, gently nudging my arm. It might have been his attempt to change the subject, but it didn't work. As I handed him the saltshaker, my thoughts were still at Bellman Manor.

"He tried to say something," I said quietly.

"Who did?" asked Rocky.

"Taz. When I found him, he tried to talk."

"Oh, Lord," said Mom.

Dad's eyebrows shot up. "He was still alive?"

I nodded and took another sip of coffee, narrowing my eyes as I remembered.

"What did he say?" asked Rocky.

"Something about a snake. 'It was the snake.'"

"He thought he'd been bitten by a snake?" said Rocky.

I shrugged. "He could have been referring to a person."

"Interesting," said Granny. "Snakes aren't always bad luck, you know. It all depends on what kind of snake it is and when and where you see it. Of course, it's true that they're rarely a good sign." She pinched off a piece of her crust and tossed it to Gus.

"Don't do that, Ma," said Mom. "You're only encouraging him to beg."

"He's a dog, isn't he? That's what they do."

And just like that, the conversation moved on. Mom hopped up to refill coffee cups, and Dad asked Rocky about his personal training schedule for the day. I sent off a text to Deena, letting her know I needed to stop in at the police station, and she replied that everything was under control at the shop.

As we finished breakfast, Granny told me about the wildflowers she'd brought for me down from the mountain. Listening to her comforting prattle, I almost started to feel normal again.

After breakfast, Granny offered to dog sit, while the rest of us headed downtown. We caravanned partway, through my parents' hilly neighborhood, across the railroad tracks, past the library, and down the street the locals called "Church Row," until we reached Franklin Street, just a block shy of the town square. This is where Rocky and my folks turned east toward Dumbbells, with a wave and a toot of their car horns. I continued on to Main Street, Aerieville's busiest thoroughfare. I knew parking wasn't allowed on the street in front of the police station, so I found a spot in the municipal lot a couple of blocks away. I didn't mind the walk. The sky was blue and the sun was warm on my shoulders. Here and there among the green leaves of the boulevard trees, I noted the beginnings of pale pink and brownish yellow around the edges. Autumn was in the air.

At a little after eight, traffic was nearing its peak, as people headed in to work and school. Some of the shops and offices I strolled past weren't open yet, but then I came to one place of business that had been open for hours: Nell's Diner. It was a 1950s-era eatery serving up breakfast, lunch, and copious amounts of gossip. This was thanks in large part to the overactive interest of the owner, Nell Cusley. She had her ear to the ground and her finger on the pulse of all Aerieville happenings, big and small. As I walked by, I averted my face and ducked my head, lest anyone recognize me. I half expected to be accosted by Nell herself. I was sure lips were flapping about the murder at the mayoral mansion—which, admittedly, had a salacious ring to it. What Nell wouldn't give for a first-hand tidbit from me. *Perhaps a generous slice of chocolate silk cream pie? Hmm.* Come to think of it, that might not be a bad trade after all.

I laughed at myself as I continued on my way, unnoticed and undetained. From somewhere behind me a high-pitched buzzing increased in volume like a rapidly approaching bee. I glanced around to see a black motor scooter zipping through traffic, dodging cars like they were orange cones on an obstacle course, before swerving off the road and disappearing into an alley. *Must be a racer*, I mused, considering the fast driving and shiny black and silver motorcycle jacket. The person had worn a large black helmet with tinted visor, making them appear rather mysterious.

Unbidden, a memory surfaced of the last time I'd seen someone ride a motor scooter. It was during a brief trip to Knoxville with Calvin. We'd stopped at the house where he'd lived before moving to Aerieville—a home still occupied by his ex-girlfriend. While he went inside, I'd waited in the car and happened to see her arrive on a sporty blue Vespa. It had been about the coolest thing I'd ever seen.

Calvin never did tell me much about the woman. He'd only said that they broke up partly because she'd thought Calvin wasn't assertive enough. It seemed like a rather skimpy reason to me.

Now that Calvin was on my mind again, I wondered why I hadn't heard more from him lately. Lost in thought, I approached the corner of Grant and Main and paused to look at the traffic lights. At the change of the signals, I crossed Grant, then turned to wait my turn to cross Main. Rush hour in Aerieville might've been tame compared to larger towns, but there was enough traffic to warrant obeying the law. Besides, only a fool would jaywalk this close to the police station.

As I waited, I looked at my phone out of habit. *I should*

*just text Calvin myself. What's my hang up anyway? So
what if he knows I miss him. It's true.*

A delivery truck rumbled past, followed by a yellow
school bus. The buzz of a motor sounded behind me, similar
to before . . . only much nearer. Suddenly, the noise pitched
to a roar. Before I knew what was happening, I felt a rough
shove against my lower back—and found myself hurtling
into the street, right in the path of the oncoming traffic.

Chapter 7

Time is a slippery devil. It has a way of speeding up or slowing down on its own, with no say from us mere mortals. In the split second I comprehended I was on a lethal trajectory, with no hope of stopping myself, time stood still. Suspended between stillness and motion, I was fully aware of only one all-consuming thought: *This could be it.* "It" being *the end. Finit. Caput.* I was also conscious of a curse on my lips, and not one I usually said. That's how stunned I was.

Then I hit the ground and was slammed with sensation— the painful bite of asphalt scraping my hands, the crack of my knees on hard pavement, the terrible screech of brakes assaulting my ears. I would later think of those shrieking brakes as a beautiful sound, since they had a big part in saving my life. But in that moment, I squeezed my eyes shut and braced for the inevitable.

It was the slam of a car door and shouting from multiple directions that made me open my eyes. And that's when time sped up. What followed was a blur . . . concerned voices asking me questions, kind hands helping me to my feet, an exchange of information with a stranger. Then, finally, a walk to the police station.

I sat in the lobby on a surprisingly soft chair and spoke with a nice young officer named Marina. She explained, somewhat apologetically, that the interview room was currently occupied. Someone else gave me a cup of water, and more than one person asked me if I wanted medical attention. I assured them I was fine. *More or less.*

The driver of the car that had missed me, a chatty senior citizen named Gary, had escorted me to the station. He was too excited to sit down, but his statement was brief.

"She just sorta fell into the street. At least, that's what it looked like. There were a coupla poles on the corner, for the traffic light and a streetlamp, and a garbage can, I think. My eyes were on the road. I didn't see anything besides her, coming out of nowhere."

Officer Marina looked conflicted. "You really should have stayed at the scene. Why didn't you call nine-one-one?"

"Well, the station was right here," Gary explained. "I thought we might as well go inside, let the young lady sit down. Besides, there wasn't really an accident. There was no impact."

"Were there any other witnesses?" she asked.

"Oh, sure," said Gary. "Several people stopped to help."

"Anyone you know? Can you give me any names?"

Gary wrinkled his forehead. "I don't think so. There was a jogger in a track suit, had a mustache, I think. The guy in the car behind me got out for a minute. And the lady from a car on Grant Street. And another lady, I think."

The officer frowned and made a note on her form. As I listened to this exchange, I tried to remember if I had anything helpful to add. I was so stunned at the time, it was hard to think straight. The only face I could recall from the scene was Gary's, since he was the first one at my side. And when others started arriving, there had been so much confusion, with much overlapping of voices. Then I remembered one thing.

I turned to Gary. "Did you see a motorcycle? Or did someone say something about a motorcycle or a motorbike?"

He nodded slowly. "Yes, I believe the lady coming from Grant said she saw a small motorcycle or scooter speed away. I don't know that she necessarily said it was involved, though. I thought she was just miffed it didn't stop."

"I heard it," I said, sitting up straight in the chair. "I heard the motor. I think it came right up behind me on the sidewalk. The driver must have pushed or kicked me."

Officer Marina took a look at my back. "I don't see any marks."

"Maybe it just spooked you," Gary suggested.

"No," I insisted. "Somebody either ran into me or gave me a shove. I'm certain of that."

Gary shrugged apologetically. "Sorry. I didn't see anything like that."

The officer finished her paperwork and asked both Gary and me to sign the report. Then Gary left.

"Is there someone I can call for you?" asked Marina. "Somebody to come and pick you up?"

I checked my phone and was surprised to see this whole incident had cost me only about twenty minutes. Shaking my head, I said, "I was actually on my way here to see Chief Walden. He asked me to stop in."

She told me she'd see if he was available. While I waited, I leaned back in the chair and closed my eyes. *Whew. What a close call.* I still couldn't believe it had happened. Before I could stop myself, my memory returned to Taz Banyan, on the floor at Bellman Manor. In a way, we'd both had the rug pulled out from under our feet. We'd both had an awful shock, a sudden thrust into danger, followed by a moment

in limbo, on the razor's edge . . . but only one of us had sur-
vived.

"You can come in now."

I started at the voice. With a nervous chuckle, I stood up
and joined Officer Marina where she stood holding open an
inner door off the lobby.

"You can go on in," she said, pointing to a glass-windowed
office at the rear of a large office space, divided into half a
dozen cubicles. Glancing around, I noticed at least one familiar officer among the cops seated at their desks—a
ginger-haired policeman named Officer Dakin. In the past,
he'd often partnered with Captain Bradley. I was hoping I'd
see another cop I knew, the boyfriend of a friend of mine,
but Davy was nowhere to be seen.

As I made my way toward the chief's office, a door
opened from a side room, and a woman walked toward me.
Looking over, I saw that it was Annaliese Bellman Lakely,
wearing a smart off-white pants suit and wiping her fingers
on a tissue. She recognized me at the same time.

"Hello, dear," she said mildly. "Miss Ravenswood,
wasn't it?"

"Yes, ma'am. Hello."

She gave me a tired smile and started to say something
else, when we were both distracted by a loud voice. The door
to the chief's office had just opened, and someone stood in
the doorway, apparently not ready to leave. Although her
back was to us, I soon realized it was Captain Bradley.

"With all due respect," she said heatedly, "I don't think
that's the right approach."

The chief's response was low but still audible. "It goes
to motive, Captain. You know I wouldn't waste your time."

"I didn't say that! But motive is irrelevant if we can
pinpoint who had the means and opportunity. If we can
establish—"

"Irrelevant?" he interrupted.

"You know what I mean. It's secondary. I think we should—" She broke off suddenly. I imagined it was a look or gesture from the chief that had stopped her. Spinning around, she stalked out of the office and left through a back door without so much as a glance toward anyone else in the room. All the other officers seemed to be intently focused on their computers or files and didn't look up. Annaliese and I looked at each other with raised eyebrows. Then I heard my name.

Chief Walden now stood framed in the doorway to his office. "Come on in, Sierra."

For all the trouble I went through to meet with the chief, the interview turned out to be a letdown. I said as much to Deena back at Flower House. We were arranging flowers together in the converted kitchen that served as our workroom. Granny and Gus were in the backyard, where Granny appeared to be giving Toby a lesson in gardening, showing him how to cut back the spent plants. She always stopped by when she was in town to look in on us and offer her help, and I was glad to see Toby spending more time with the plants. This time, besides dropping off Gus, she'd brought some of her homegrown herbs and vegetables for us to use in the café.

Today I was doubly glad she was here, since she'd fussed over my scraped hands. Lucky for me, she had with her one of her homemade folk remedies, a healing salve made from calendula and beeswax. She'd slathered it on my palms and wrapped them up, from the base of my fingers to the heels of my hands, with a first-aid bandage. I still had good use of my fingers, though I was slower than usual as I trimmed flower stems and poked them in a vase.

"So," said Deena, turning a pitcher of multicolored zinnias on the table in front of her, "the chief wouldn't share any information about the murder investigation?"

"He wouldn't answer any of my questions, Dee. Not a single one."

"Well, that's hardly surprising. Weren't you there to answer *his* questions?"

"In theory." I picked up a cut sunflower and some roses, peach and red, and held them together to judge the effect. "He mostly wanted to know about Taz and the other vendors. Since I'd only just met them all, I wasn't much help."

"What did he have to say about your accident?"

"I didn't tell him about it."

She looked at me in surprise. "You didn't?"

I shrugged. "I'd just gone over the whole thing with another officer. I assume he'll hear about it. I guess I was ready to move on."

I picked up some shears and tried to cut through the thick stem of the sunflower, but the bandage on my hand made it difficult to squeeze hard enough. Deena took the tool and snipped the stem for me.

"Thanks," I said, placing the sunflower in the forefront of my arrangement. "So, tell me what I missed here this morning."

Our conversation turned to business matters, as Deena filled me in about some calls we'd received, including one from a woman who wanted to reserve a table in the café for her book club meeting. That got us to thinking about other ways we could make use of the flower-themed café.

"We could run an ad," Deena suggested, "promoting the café as a place to hold showers—both baby showers and bridal showers."

"You mean rent out the whole place?" I asked. "That's

not a bad idea. It could be a nice space for any kind of small, low-key party, really."

As we chatted and dreamed, Granny came inside to wash her hands and fill Gus's water bowl. I told her what we were talking about and asked for her opinion.

"Sounds dandy to me," she said. "These days folks are finding all kinds of reasons to throw a party, from kindergarten graduations to divorce celebrations. Why, somebody was just telling me she recently went to a *menoparty*."

"What's a 'menoparty'?" I asked.

"It's a party to celebrate menopause!" Granny cackled merrily. "Can you believe it?"

"Goodness," said Deena, with an amused smile.

Granny picked up the teakettle from the stovetop and gave it a shake. "Or the *end* of menopause, I should say. Come to think of it, that *is* something to celebrate."

I laughed too. "I'm sure it is." I placed my completed arrangement in the cooler, then gave Granny an impromptu hug. "Every day's a party when you're here, Granny."

Considering this, she nodded. "Every day's a blessing. Every morning we wake up to a new day—that's cause for celebration in my book."

"Mine too," I said, chuckling.

Deena nudged my arm playfully. "Now I see where you get your positivity."

"No doubt," I agreed.

We took a break to have lunch in the café. Then Granny left to deliver her "herb bags," homemade sachets filled with various healing concoctions, to her customers around town. I spent much of the rest of the day repotting orchids and filling orders. At five o'clock, we closed the shop, and I sent Allie and Toby home. Deena offered to stay and help tidy up, but I insisted that she leave too. She'd also had a long day, not to mention a late night yesterday.

Gus and I retreated to the office—me with a cheese and tomato sandwich and him with a chew toy. I wanted to count the day's sales and update our inventory spreadsheets. Felix's old bookkeeper, Byron Atterly, still handled accounting and payroll for the shop, but I knew I wouldn't be able to rely on him forever. He'd surely up and retire one of these days. I tried to stay on top of our finances as best as I could.

Sometime later, Gus began to whimper. Glancing at the clock, I was surprised to see it was almost seven. "Sorry, buddy. Where *does* the time go?" It seemed like eons ago that I'd arisen early to have breakfast with my folks. Yawning, I shut off the computer and picked up my purse.

We left through the back door. Outside, the air was still pleasantly mild, even as the sun sank behind distant trees in the west. The golden glow of twilight made for a pretty sky and left the yard and garden in a blanket of deepening murky darkness. I opened the back door on the Fiat, and Gus jumped right in.

Instead of going straight home, I made a quick detour to the drive-through ATM to make a deposit, then stopped off at the pet store to pick up dog food and more treats. The cashier knew Gus and kept him entertained while I found what I needed. Then we were finally on our way.

By that time, it was completely dark. As we left the center of the village, the streetlights and lit-up restaurants of Main Street gave way to darker residential roads. On two quaint blocks, old-fashioned streetlamps cast intermittent spheres of orange light. In between, pools of darkness stretched backward, engulfing trees, homes, and whatever else lay quietly hidden in the shadows.

Usually, I'd have the radio on, but this evening I savored the quiet. It was almost meditative—the soft rumble of the small car, the lonely song of crickets chirping in the blackened trees. Gus was curled contentedly in the back seat, apparently enjoying our moment of Zen as much as I was.

The faint buzz of a motor told me I wasn't alone on the road. At first, I didn't think much of it—until the sound grew closer and, glancing in my rearview mirror, I saw a single white headlight. From the size and shape of the vehicle, it seemed to be a motor scooter.

I tightened my grip on the steering wheel. Was it the scooter from this morning? Had the black-clad stranger come to finish the job?

Seconds passed and nothing changed. The grating motor grew neither louder nor quieter but remained steady at about a car's length behind me. I paused at a stop sign, and my follower stopped too—at a respectful distance. They were too far away for me to make out any identifying features in the mirror.

At the next corner, I turned left. The scooter turned in kind. I took in a breath, trying to keep my nerves in check. At the next intersection, I turned again, even though it wasn't the right way to my house. Again, the scooter followed.

What should I do?

I thought about going to my parents' house, but they lived in a quiet, secluded neighborhood. Besides, I was reluctant to lead this person to their home. By now, there was no question that they were tailing me. I zigzagged my way back toward the town square. I had half a mind to stop at Deena's apartment on Main Street, but then I had a better idea. I drove straight to the police station and pulled right into the no-parking zone.

Slowing to a stop, I reached for my phone, prepared to call 9-1-1 if a cop didn't come out right away to tell me to move. But the scooter didn't follow me. It continued down the street and out of sight.

Now that we weren't moving, Gus perked up from the back seat and looked out the side window. I waited a moment, debating whether to go inside or call someone. A minute passed, then another, and I began to relax. The scooter was gone, and I was beat. I shifted into Drive and headed for home once more, this time without any unwanted company.

In the back of my mind, I was aware that my follower could be hiding somewhere, just waiting for me to drive off again. But my intuition told me otherwise. I felt sure they'd moved on. Nevertheless, I kept a sharp eye on my mirrors the whole way home. Once we reached the dollhouse, I let Gus out, grabbed my things, and fairly flew up the walk, dashing into the safety of home in no time flat.

Chapter 8

In the light of day, I could almost imagine it had never happened. Stepping outside with Gus into the cool September morning, I gazed at the vivid azure sky. No one had pushed me into the street yesterday, at least not on purpose. No one had followed me on a motor scooter. (A motor scooter! Was there any *less* intimidating vehicle this side of a moped?) And no one had murdered a wedding planner in the middle of the planning meeting. And I hadn't witnessed his death.

Except I had. And someone did. But that didn't mean I needed to dwell on it.

I headed to the shop and opened the café like it was any regular old Wednesday morning. I chatted with Deena and Allie and greeted customers. I arranged a basket of flowers and gave Toby the delivery instructions. I answered calls and kept an eye on Gus. From the outside, I probably looked the same as always. I was my usual smiling self, intent on spreading joy through flowers and conversation.

But inside I was struggling. I could feel the façade cracking. As a rule, I believed in focusing on the positive, but I also believed in honoring my feelings. And right now, I felt unsettled. The instant the front door closed behind a departing customer, I let my smile fall away. My denial—or whatever it was—gave way to melancholy.

It didn't feel right to carry on as if nothing had happened. Taz was dead. I barely knew him—*didn't* know him, really—but I still felt bad.

Gus was out of sorts too. Maybe he was picking up on my mood, or maybe he was just bored, but he seemed unsatisfied with his usual toys and treats. When he wasn't whining to go outside, he was chewing on the fringe of the area rug.

Sighing, I found his leash behind the counter. "Okay, buddy. We'll go out again. Let's just tell Deena first."

Deena was in the café showing Allie one of our many edible flower guides. (We made a point to keep all nonedible flowers well away from the café.) They looked up as I approached, and Deena handed Allie the book. "Hey, Sierra. Want a cup of tea? I was thinking of having one."

"Actually, I'm going to take Gus for a little walk. I won't be gone long."

"Take as long as you want," said Deena. "Go clear your head and try to relax. In fact, go home, if you'd like. Take a self-care day. I can handle things here."

I looked at her in surprise. "A self-care day? Do I look that bad?" I said it in a jokey way, trying, again, to mask my emotions.

"You look fine, but you've been through a lot."

I started to protest, falling right back into my knee-jerk optimism. Then I caught myself and nodded. "You're right. I could use a little break." I held up my thumb and forefinger, half an inch apart. "Just a tiny one."

She smiled. "Right. Now go on and take your tiny break, and don't worry about things here. Allie and I have everything under control."

I gave her a mock salute. "Yes, ma'am. Call me if you need to." Then I looked down at the corgi. "Ready, Gus? Want to go for a ride in the car?"

He ran to the back door, helpfully leading the way.

At first, I wasn't sure where we'd go. Part of me wanted to leave town and drive into the mountains. But I also wanted to be outside, under the open air, as soon as possible. There were several places to hike around Aerieville without needing to go very far.

"I've got it. We'll visit your old stomping grounds. I need to look in on Felix's cabin anyway."

Before he left, my former boss had lived in a modest one-bedroom cabin in the forest on the edge of town. From there, it was a short hike to the Nolichucky River along a well-worn dirt trail. Felix was a dedicated fisherman—in recent years more so even than he was a florist. But his passion for fishing was rivaled by another singular interest: treasure hunting.

He'd long been an enthusiast of geocaching, the outdoor game whose reward was the thrill of the hunt more than any actual treasure. Yet, somewhere along the way, Felix had become enchanted by the tale of a *real* treasure—an alleged stash of gems and other valuables hidden by an eccentric collector known only as "Arwin." I'd just learned about it after Felix took off, quite abruptly, last spring. Evidently, he had solved one of the more perplexing clues left by the mysterious Arwin and sped off to pick up the trail somewhere out West. This was how I'd ended up in charge of not only Flower House, but also Felix's puppy, Gus.

I glanced at my four-legged passenger, sitting quietly but expectantly in the back seat, and grinned. I'd never known how much I'd been missing before this little guy came into my life.

"You're good company, Gus," I said. "And a good excuse

for getting outside." He tilted his head, making me smile even wider. "Not to mention a great source of entertainment."

I turned onto the secluded lane leading to Felix's property and parked on the gravel driveway next to the cabin. We got out of the car and looked around. While Gus sniffed the bushes and overgrown weeds, I noted how dark and dingy the cabin looked, with grimy windows and a coating of dust on the front-porch railings. The desolation made me shiver.

I wasn't responsible for this place. Felix hadn't left it to me, or to anyone else for that matter. He'd given me a spare key ages ago because he was prone to forgetfulness. I'd asked Byron Atterly what he thought we should do, and he said he suspected Felix would be back, if only to ride out the winter. Byron continued to pay the utility bills to keep the water and electricity on. I took it upon myself to look in on things every now and then.

I peeked in the mailbox to confirm it was empty—as it should be, since I'd redirected all Felix's mail to the shop. Then I grabbed an old broom to sweep off the porch and knock down an empty wasp's nest from under the eaves.

Replacing the broom in the corner of the porch, I caught sight of a blue jay, its vibrant feathers dazzling against the brown branches of an oak tree. I watched it for a moment, until Gus barked loudly next to me, making me jump. He had his eye on a bushy-tailed squirrel and evidently felt the need to assert his dominance.

"Alright," I said laughing. "Enough of this dusty old cabin for now. Let's go tramp in the woods."

We went around to the back side of the cabin and found the trail to the river. It was a quiet walk. Aside from the twittering of birds and buzzing of insects, my own footsteps were the loudest sound around. A few minutes in, the trail split into three, one footpath that continued to the river and two that forked to the left and right. We took the left-hand path, which ran roughly parallel with the riverbank. The trail was fairly wide and clear as it meandered through the dense woods. It was easygoing, especially at the leisurely pace I imposed. With every step, I felt my energy and mood lift in equal measure.

I didn't think much as we strolled. I didn't try to problem-solve or sort through any issues. Instead, I idly observed all the interesting textures and shapes hidden in the dense thickets all around us. I took the opportunity to practice a little mindfulness. Breathing deeply, I allowed myself to be present in the moment, to soak up nature's healing vibes, and to just *be*.

After about half an hour, we came to an outcropping of rocks above a gentle slope to the water's edge. I stopped for a moment, keeping a tight hold on Gus's leash, and watched the river flow lazily by. *Go with the flow*, I thought. *Enjoy life, take it as it comes. Accept the things you can't change. What a perfect way to be.*

With these mellow thoughts in mind, I headed back the way we'd come, noting the new view from this direction. I was feeling blissfully peaceful and calmer than I had in quite some time—which made the sudden commotion that much more jarring. I froze, listening. A few yards off the trail there came a noisy rustle of leaves and crackling of twigs. It sounded as if someone were bushwhacking a new path through the forest.

Gus barked sharply and tugged on his leash. I held tight and waited. Whatever it was, it sure sounded bigger than a squirrel. If it was a larger animal—a deer say, or a bear— would it flee from the little dog? Or would it remain un-daunted, aware that Gus was no real threat? On the other hand, if it was a person, wouldn't they call out to announce themselves and say hello?

Gus finally quieted down, and I realized the noise had

stopped too. No one came out from the trees. After a moment, I exhaled and urged Gus to move on. Maybe it was only a squirrel after all. They could be noisy.

We resumed our hike, but my carefree attitude had evaporated. Just like that, the pleasant woodland no longer felt like a sanctuary. Now I felt vulnerable, exposed to whoever, or whatever, might be lurking in the tangled woods. Granted, I'd been known to have a wild imagination. Still, considering recent events, it was probably wise to be wary.

With my eyes roving from tree to tree, I wasn't paying attention to the trail in front of us. When Gus suddenly halted, I almost tripped over him. I looked at the pup in surprise.

"What is it, buddy?"

He stood stock-still, practically bristling with tension. A low, soft growl rumbled from his throat.

A second later, I saw why. Coiled thickly in the middle of the path was a sizable tan-colored snake with distinctive reddish-brown markings. A copperhead.

I gasped and felt my eyes widen to saucers. Biting my lip to keep quiet, I inched backward. I tried to remember what I knew about snakes, and about this species in particular. Copperheads were poisonous, I knew that. But they weren't necessarily aggressive, were they? I didn't think they were likely to strike out unless threatened. And I had no intention of threatening it. Our best bet was to go around it.

Gus didn't seem inclined to move at all. Some instinct kept him back, his short legs trembling beneath him.

"It's okay," I said quietly. "We'll go a different way."

Still walking backward, I pulled Gus along and stepped off the trail. With one eye on the snake, I cast about for a big stick—just in case. A few feet away, near a fallen tree, I spotted a straight, sturdy branch that would serve nicely as a trekking pole. I picked it up, then forged ahead through the trees.

I wasn't afraid of getting lost since the river still peeked in and out of view. Hidden creatures were another matter. Besides that, now that we were in the thickets, we had to watch our step so as not to trip or twist an ankle. Gus's fur quickly picked up bits of leaves and burrs, but he was much happier now. I moved along gingerly, with one hand on my walking stick and the other on Gus's leash. My mind, however, didn't slow down.

How funny that I saw a snake. I haven't seen one that big in a long time. It was *a copperhead, wasn't it?* When we were kids, Mom and Dad had always warned Rocky and me to watch out for rattlesnakes and copperheads, the only two venomous snakes found in the Smokies. *That was surely a copperhead.* But how funny to see a snake when Taz's last words were about a snake. What could he have meant? And what did it mean that one had quite literally blocked my path? *It has to mean* something . . .

I couldn't help seeing signs and omens in nature. Maybe this was partly due to Granny's influence, or maybe it was all from my own observations. Either way, it was interesting to contemplate. I wasn't able to reach any conclusions, though. After a few minutes of tromping through the mud and leaves, our detour came to an end. We cut back to the beaten trail at the point where it intersected the path to the cabin.

Whew! I was relieved on more than one count, ready to put this little excursion behind us. Moving swiftly now, we approached the cabin from the rear. I planned to go inside just long enough to get Gus a drink of water and conduct a quick walk-through. Gus seemed as eager as I was. Rather than acting tired, he marched ahead at a fast clip, pulling me along toward the cabin.

A few yards away, I stopped short. *What the heck?* The back door of the cabin was standing open. As I stared, a flicker of movement crossed the window. Someone was inside.

Chapter 9

They say bad luck comes in threes, and I'd had three alarming surprises in the space of a single hour. Hopefully, that meant that this one was the last. However, the problem remained: *What should I do?* I seemed to be asking that of myself a lot lately.

I couldn't fathom who would be in Felix's cabin—short of Felix himself, returned from his trip. As far as I knew, I was the only one with a key, and I was sure I'd locked up last time I was here. With the place empty for so long, I'd been afraid it might attract squatters. Was that what had happened?

Treading lightly, I started to skirt the house. I wanted to see whose car was up front—and be near my own car in case I needed to make a quick getaway. Unfortunately, Gus had other ideas. In a sudden burst of energy, he pulled the leash from my grip and bounded up to the cabin and right inside the open back door.

"Gus!"

I had no choice but to follow him. Holding my walking stick aloft, I ran up to the back door, heart thudding in my chest. At the threshold, I hesitated. *Gus?*

The kitchen was empty. Then I heard Gus's high-pitched yip, followed by a man's laughter. Familiar laughter. Lowering my stick, I walked through the kitchen and into the small living room. And that's where I found Gus, wriggling with joy as he jumped all over the legs of a sandy-haired guy, lean and tan in khaki pants and a short-sleeved button-down shirt.

Calvin.

He looked up, his blue eyes sparkling. "Hey, Sierra."

My initial shock transformed instantly into a giddy sort of delight. I'd missed him so much. And seeing him now, he looked even better than I remembered. Working outdoors at his parents' farm had given the bookish botanist a more rugged appearance—reminding me, for all the world, of Professor Indiana Jones. I had a strong urge to throw myself into his arms, until a sudden rush of shyness held me back.

What if he doesn't feel the same way?

"What are you doing here?" I asked.

"Looking for you. I went to Flower House first, and Deena told me you'd taken Gus on an outing. I had a feeling you might come here."

"Really?" I frowned, feeling slightly confused. There were a lot of other places I could've gone. And why didn't he just call me? For that matter, why hadn't Deena called or texted me? I had so many questions. "How did you get in?"

Still scratching Gus behind the ears, he looked up at me and grinned. "I got a key from Felix."

"You saw Felix? When? Where?"

"In South Dakota, two days ago."

My mouth must've fallen open, because Calvin laughed. "Don't worry. I'll tell you all about it. I want to hear what's going on with you too, and how things are going at Flower House. Have you had lunch? Wanna go with me to Nell's Diner?"

"Uh, yeah. I mean, no. Lunch sounds good, but not at Nell's. How about Bluebird Café?" I didn't feel like subjecting myself to the attention I knew I'd get at gossip central.

"Great idea. They have outdoor seating, right? That means Gus can come along." He patted Gus on the side, clearly as pleased to see the pup as Gus was to see him.

"Cool. Just give me a sec."

I set out a bowl of water for Gus, then used Felix's small bathroom to pick the leaves from my hair and wash up. When I came out, I found that Calvin had swept up the mud we tracked in. After a hasty look around the cabin, I locked the back door and shut off the lights.

On our way out the front door, Calvin picked up a binder from the end table and tucked it under his arm. Whatever it was, I was pretty sure it hadn't been there the last time I'd checked on the cabin. Either Calvin had brought it in or, more likely, had taken it from Felix's bookshelf. He must have set it on the table before Gus came running in.

Is that why Felix gave him a key? Or did Calvin have his own reasons for coming here? Either way, Calvin sure had a lot of 'splaining to do.

Bluebird Café was a small, bright glass-fronted restaurant a few blocks off the square. With its assorted juices, salads, and gourmet wraps, it was the closest thing Aerieville had to a health food store. It was also a popular lunch destination for local business professionals. I shouldn't have been surprised, then, to find all the outdoor tables were taken. Calvin and I took turns going inside to buy our food, then walked across the street to Weller Park and found a picnic table near the ball field.

"How's your dad?" I asked, as I removed the paper from my wrap. "All recovered from his hip surgery?"

"Yeah, he's doing well. He's able to get around and pretty much do everything he needs to do."

"That's good." We chatted lightly for a few minutes, until I could no longer stand the suspense. "So, tell me about Felix. How is it that you met up with him in South Dakota? I thought he was in Colorado."

"He was. He drove up to the Badlands a couple of weeks ago. He said it was partly to work on another Arwin riddle and partly to shake some of his followers."

"By 'followers,' you mean competitors, right? How many does he have?" I knew of at least two fellow treasure hunters who'd followed Felix out West: a former Flower House employee named Jim and an acquaintance of Calvin's I'd never met.

Calvin nodded and started to answer, but stopped as an older man approached us. Looking over, I recognized Gary, the friendly senior citizen who'd almost run me over. He gave me a tentative wave.

"Miss Sierra? I thought that was you. I was just dropping off my granddaughter at tennis practice and thought I'd pop over here and see how you're doing. Still sore, are you?"

"I'm fine, thanks." I showed him my palms and smiled. "Barely a scratch left, thanks to my granny's healing salve."

Calvin raised his eyebrows. "Sore from what?" he asked.

I shook my head, as if to say "It's nothing."

"Glad to hear it," said Gary. "When I told my wife what happened, she asked if you're the same Sierra who runs Flower House. I told her I didn't know, but odds were for it. *Sierra* isn't a very common name."

"That's me," I affirmed.

"Then you were at the mayor's house when that business went down the other day? That's what my wife said. She said she heard folks talking about it at Nell's. You were the only local there, were you?"

My smile slipped a notch, but I nodded pleasantly. "Unfortunately, yes."

"What business?" asked Calvin.

"Didn't you hear?" answered Gary. "A man was murdered at the mayor's house. An event coordinator, or some such. It's the talk of the town."

"Ah," said Calvin. "I bet it is." He turned to me with an incredulous look and leaned forward, propping his elbow on the table and his fist on his chin. The expectant look he gave me was so exaggerated I almost laughed.

Gary scratched his gray head thoughtfully. "The cause of death has been a source of some debate. Some folks say he was stabbed, others say he was hit on the head." He turned to me with a look that matched Calvin's.

I shrugged. "I couldn't say. I guess we'll have to wait for the coroner's report." I took a big bite of my wrap, hoping Gary would take the hint. Instead, he directed his comments to Calvin.

"Supposedly, the mayor and his family weren't home at the time, but I'm not sure I buy that. I mean, they *would* say that, wouldn't they? Seems a little too convenient. Who has that many people in their house without being home?"

"There were a lot of people, were there?" said Calvin, with visible interest.

"I believe so. At least ten, from what I heard. Of course, Miss Sierra would know better."

I finished chewing my sandwich and took a sip of iced tea. Then I picked up my lunch bag and stood before answering. "It was less than ten, and it's true that the mayor and his family weren't home. It was a meeting of the wedding vendors in preparation for Marissa Lakely's wedding. I really don't know what happened, but it sure is awful for everyone involved."

Gary looked a smidge contrite but still curious, as he took a step back. "Oh, it sure is. Very awful."

I shouldered my purse and reached for Gus's leash. "And now, if you'll excuse us, we need to get back to the flower shop."

Calvin checked his watch. "Yeah, I guess we should." Standing up, he gave Gus his last bit of sandwich. Gary nodded at us and headed toward the parking lot. As soon as he was out of earshot, Calvin grabbed a hold of my hand. His amusement was gone, replaced by an air of concern. "You were involved in another murder?"

I sighed. "Yeah. I kinda was." With a quick glance to make sure Gary was really gone, I dropped back onto the bench and told him everything.

By the time we made it to Flower House, it was after three o'clock. We parked side by side near the back door, and Calvin popped his trunk. When he'd arrived earlier in the day, he hadn't brought his luggage in. Gus and I met him at his car as he started unloading it.

"Need some help?" I glanced in the rear window and noticed the binder he'd taken from Felix's cabin. It was lying on the back seat next to a folded blanket and a rumpled jacket. I'd forgotten to ask him about it, but now didn't seem to be the time.

"Sure," he said, handing me a backpack. With Gus at his heels, he headed to the back door with a suitcase in each hand. I hurried to open the door for him, and he preceded me into the kitchen.

Allie was removing a bouquet from the refrigerated case and looked up, apparently startled to see us. Though she'd never met Calvin, she knew about him from Deena and me.

Still, the way she gaped at him now, you would've thought she'd caught a glimpse of a movie star.

"Hello," he said pleasantly.

I shooed Gus indoors and shut the door. "Hey, Allie. This is Calvin. Calvin, this is Allie Johnson. I think I told you we hired her and her brother?"

"Right. Nice to meet you, Allie."

"Hi," she said softly, still staring.

I pointed at the bouquet in her hand. "Is that for a customer?"

"Huh?" Dragging her eyes from Calvin, she looked at me with a brief glimmer of confusion. Then she laughed nervously and shut the refrigerator door. "Oh, yeah. Also, there's a woman waiting for you in the café."

"For me?" I asked.

"Yeah. She's been here a while. Deena told her she could leave a message, but I guess she didn't want to."

Calvin pushed open the door to the hallway. "I'll just take my stuff upstairs, then you can put me to work." He set his suitcases on the floor, where Gus sniffed them curiously, as he unlocked the door leading to his upstairs apartment.

"Take your time," I said. "I'm sure you're tired after your long drive."

I followed Allie to the front of the shop and said hello to the customer who was waiting for her at the cash register. I felt a little self-conscious about my appearance. My boots were dirty from my hike in the woods, and my hair was windblown. *Oh, well.* Tucking it behind my ears, I proceeded to the café.

When I saw who awaited me, I felt even more schlumpy. It was Annaliese Bellman Lakely, polished and elegant in denim trousers, a white blouse, and fashionable kitten-heeled shoes. She was the sole customer in the café, seated at a table near the front windows with a slice of flower-petal cake and a cup of oolong tea.

Deena was behind the counter refilling the teakettle. She looked up as I entered and appeared relieved to see me. I waved at her as I approached Annaliese.

"Hello again," I said.

"Oh, Miss Ravenswood. Good. I was told you might not come back today and couldn't be reached, but I decided to take my chances. Won't you sit down?"

"Call me Sierra." As I pulled out the chair across from Marissa's mother, I felt a strange sense of déjà vu. Here was another woman in need, about to ask me for a favor. I was sure of it.

"This cake is delicious," she said, piercing it with her fork. "And so lovely with the colorful petals. I've ordered one for my mother's birthday next month."

"Oh? How nice." I glanced at Deena, as she walked over with the teakettle and handed me a cup. She gave me a slight shrug and a smile, knowing, as I did, that we usually didn't sell entire cakes.

"Can I get you anything else, Sierra?" she asked. "Something to eat?"

"I'll just have tea, thanks. Peppermint." To Annaliese, I said, "What can I do for you, Mrs. Lakely?" Something told me she wasn't here to discuss funeral flowers.

She folded her hands on the table. "I'll be blunt, if I may. I'd like to go forward with the wedding."

"Go forward? You mean, on the same date?" I crinkled my forehead, thinking I must've misunderstood.

"Yes. Practically everything is in place already. It will be easier to carry on as planned, rather than reschedule. I understand the vendors may have qualms, which is why I intend to double everyone's fees."

"But—"

She cut me off, with a raised hand. "Please don't think me disrespectful of Taz. I've given this a lot of thought, and I believe this is the best way to honor his memory. He put a lot of work into planning this wedding."

"Yes," I said slowly. "I see what you mean. But maybe *now* isn't the best time?" Did I really need to spell it out for her? The vendors were all suspects. She was talking about inviting a murderer back into her house.

"I realize my home is a crime scene," she said, frowning on the last words. "Which brings me to the second part of my request. You see, Frank and I are aware of the assistance you've provided to the police force in the past, and it seems they could use your help again."

Now I was really surprised. Also, I was quite sure the police wouldn't characterize my past involvement in their cases as "assistance," so much as "interference."

"Um," I said, "I've already told them everything I know."

"Let me rephrase." She lowered her voice and leaned forward. "I wouldn't say this to just anyone, but I know you won't repeat it. The truth is, I don't have a lot of faith in the Aerieville Police Department at the moment. There's some internal squabbling going on, as you and I both witnessed yesterday."

"Well," I began, but Annaliese didn't let me finish.

"Frank feels he can't call in the county or state without upsetting the local police force. So, what I'm proposing is a parallel inquiry. While the police are taking their time, doing whatever it is they're doing, I'd like to hire you to conduct a private investigation."

"Me?" I touched my chest, taken aback. "I'm not a private investigator. I think you need a license for that."

"True." She tapped the side of her teacup with ruby-colored nails. "Alright, then. I won't hire you as a private detective. But I'd still appreciate it if you'd conduct an *unofficial* investigation. Perhaps poke around and ask questions. You'll be well-compensated, of course."

Deena had been hovering nearby, apparently not wanting to interrupt. I beckoned to her now, and she handed me a tea infuser filled with dried peppermint leaves. I placed the tea in my mug and poured hot water over it—stalling, since I didn't know what to say to Mrs. Lakely. In truth, part of me was flattered. Still, I hesitated.

She watched me closely. "I really hope you'll help me," she said. "As you're decorating for the wedding, I think you'll be in a good position to listen and watch . . . and, hopefully, figure out who did this terrible thing."

"I don't know," I said doubtfully. "I'm sure Chief Walden and the other officers are doing everything there is to do. It's only been two days, after all."

"I wish I shared your confidence," she said. "The fact that it *has* been two days, with no arrest and no apparent leads, is quite worrisome." She lowered her voice even further. "People are talking, you know. I'm not trying to make this about my husband and family, but, well, this is very bad press."

"I know." My sympathy for her was real. I definitely knew people were talking.

"At least say you'll still provide the flowers. You can think about the other bit."

I stirred my tea and sighed. *Yep. Just like I thought. Déjà vu all over again.*

Chapter 10

What I needed was a sign. An omen, one way or another. I was a big fan of writing things out, listing pros and cons and creating "mind maps" to help sort through problems. I also believed in listening to my gut. But none of that seemed to be helping this time. After Annaliese left, I undertook a wrestling match in my mind.

Should I say yes, or should I say no? On one hand, the extra money was tempting. And the prestige of working such a lavish, high-profile wedding was just as compelling as before. On the other hand, would it be safe? If all the original vendors returned, as it appeared they would, wouldn't I be placing myself in the presence of a killer?

Then there were the two motor scooter encounters. I couldn't help feeling they were connected to the murder. Perhaps I was targeted since I was the one who'd heard Taz's last words. But did that really make sense? I'd already told the police what Taz had said. Besides, there had been no scooter sightings today.

And so my internal dialogue continued:

Marissa and her family need my help.

My own family will never approve.

I'd be a fool to turn down such a rare opportunity.

I'd be a fool to voluntarily reenter a lion's den.

Granny had taught me about reading signs in nature—watching out for peculiar behavior in animals and birds and looking to the stars or clouds for direction. In my own experience, I'd often found meaning in unlikely coincidences and synchronicities. But sometimes looking too hard could be counterproductive. It was like watching a pot of water to make it boil, or staring at a phone to make it ring. *Signs can't be forced. Sometimes you just need to let it go and carry on.* So that's what I tried to do.

For the rest of the afternoon, I divided my time between the office and the workroom. Calvin busied himself in the greenhouse, while Deena worked in the café. If anyone came into the shop asking for me, they were told I wasn't available. If they hoped to pick up a tidbit of gossip along with their flowers, they had to leave disappointed.

By closing time, I still hadn't made a decision, and it started weighing on me again—for more than one reason. This was Wednesday, the day my parents closed the gym early and expected me for supper. It would be hard to get through an evening with them without talking about my dilemma, and I already knew what they'd say. What I needed was a more objective perspective.

Deena had been no help. She'd waffled as much as I did. And all of my other friends and family would surely tell me to err on the side of caution. At this point, I was almost ready to flip a coin.

After Deena, Toby, and Allie left, I puttered around the shop for a few minutes. While Gus napped in the office, I carried pails of cut flowers from the front of the shop to the back room and changed the water. Before placing the restocked buckets in the refrigerated case, I removed a few flowers that had begun to brown. They were too pretty to toss, so I grabbed a vase from the cabinet and made myself a small arrangement to take home.

With my quandary still in mind, I contemplated the petals of a week-old daisy. I had just plucked the first petal, when the back door opened and Calvin came inside, carrying a pail of roses. He saw what was in my hands and grinned.

"Why don't you just ask him?"

"Him who? Ask what?"

He nodded toward the petal between my fingers. "Whoever you're asking the flower about. 'He loves me, he loves me not.' Isn't that the game?"

For some reason, I felt a blush warm my cheeks. "That's not what I was doing," I said, tossing aside the daisy. *Does he think I'm thinking of him?*

"If you say so." There was a teasing glint in his eye, but he let it go.

If I was being honest with myself, the Lakely wedding wasn't the only subject on my mind this afternoon. Ever since our picnic in the park, my thoughts kept returning to Calvin. What *was* the nature of our relationship? Before he left, we'd only just begun dating. And although we'd started becoming pretty tight, we never discussed where things were headed, or even if we were going to be exclusive. So what now? Were we just going to pick up where we left off? Let things evolve in their own time?

I almost voiced these questions out loud, when Calvin

set the roses on the worktable and removed his gloves. "I'll come back and clean these in a minute. There's a van on the street that seems to be having engine troubles. I'm gonna go see if they need help."

I stood up with a sigh. *Another interruption.* Wasn't that just par for the course for Cal and me?

There was a bark from the office. Gus must have heard us talking. As Calvin went out the back door, I retrieved the pup, attached his leash, and headed out the front door. Sure enough, in the street at the end of our driveway—blocking our egress—was a colorfully painted van. I recognized it immediately by the stylized rattlesnake. It was DJ Nick's van. He was standing at the front of the vehicle next to the raised hood and frowning at a cloud of steam.

As Calvin walked over, Nick looked up and flashed a beleaguered smile. "Seems to have overheated. . . . Again."

"Need some coolant?" asked Calvin.

"Nah, I have some. But I have to wait for the engine to cool down first." Nick spotted me then and waved. "Hey there. I *almost* made it to your shop."

"I see that." I introduced Nick and Calvin and let Gus greet the newcomer. As Nick obligingly let Gus sniff his hands, I pointed to the front porch of Flower House, where we had a couple of painted metal chairs. "Want to have a seat while your van cools off?"

"Yeah, sure." We strolled across the grassy front yard and sat down. Then Nick cut right to the chase. "Did you get a call from Annaliese?"

"I got a visit," I said. "You too?"

"We all did. And I gotta say, I have mixed feelings about her offer."

"Me too!" At last, maybe here was somebody who could help me make up my mind, somebody in the exact same predicament—or, nearly so, anyway. Presumably, I was the only one asked to investigate the other vendors.

Calvin gave me a questioning look, so I told him about the bride's mother wanting to go forward with the wedding.

"Personally, I think it's a bad idea," said Nick.

I nodded. "Yeah."

"But it's hard to turn away so much money." He gestured toward his van. "Especially when it's really needed."

"Yeah," I repeated. "I can relate." I'd had to borrow money to remodel, decorate, and stock the café, and I was fast realizing how long it was going to take to pay off the loan.

"I also wonder," continued Nick, "how it would look to say no."

"What do you mean?" I asked.

"I mean, if everyone else agrees, I wonder if somebody not agreeing would make them look guilty." He scrunched his face uncertainly, as if trying to sort out the logic of his own theory.

"Have you talked to any of the others about it?" I asked.

"I've talked to Kendall and Regina, and they've spoken with Anton and Gordon. I'm not sure if everyone's made up their mind, but I think they're all leaning toward saying yes."

I stroked Gus's fur and thought about how odd this whole conversation was. Here we were calmly discussing whether or not to go back to a job that had been interrupted by a murder—and the murderer was most likely one of us.

"They're not scared?" asked Calvin.

Nick tilted his hand back and forth, as if to say "so-so." "I think we all assume the police will have to make an arrest before the wedding date, you know, if it's really gonna go forward."

I imagined how that might play out. What if the arrest

were made only a day or two before the ceremony? If Annaliese didn't line up some substitutes, she could wind up
without a caterer or photographer—or DJ—et cetera, at the
last minute. I decided to keep this thought to myself.

"It's tough," I said. "Everyone will have business decisions
to make." I paused, gazing down the trafficless street, before
continuing. "I gathered Taz was staying at the manor. Were
the other vendors staying in town too?"

Nick shook his head. "Not more than a night or two, if
that. Except Monday night, of course. Everyone had to stop
in at the police station yesterday, but then most of the vendors went back to Nashville. All except Kendall. She has a
photo shoot in the area tomorrow."

"And you," pointed out Calvin. His tone was friendly,
but I noticed how closely he was regarding Nick.

"And me," admitted the DJ. "I'm working a private party
in Knoxville on Friday, and I have friends who live there.
So, I decided to stick around for a couple of days."

That made sense to me, since Knoxville was less than
an hour from Aerieville. In fact, everything Nick had said
sounded reasonable. Still, for some reason I couldn't help
feeling he was holding something back.

"So," I said thoughtfully, "if the wedding can't proceed
unless an arrest is made, then why do you have mixed feelings? Is it because of the uncertainty?"

He stared across the street, toward the closed antique
store. "Yeah, I don't know. It's just weird, I guess."

"That's for sure," I agreed.

He eyed me then, as if an idea had just occurred to him.
"You know, if *you* were to say no, I don't think anyone
would bat an eye. No one really thinks of you as a suspect,
since you didn't know Taz before."

"Hmm," I said noncommittally. I wasn't sure what else I
was supposed to say—thanks?

"And maybe," he went on, "if you say no, Annaliese will realize she should postpone the wedding. That would probably be for the best."

Calvin had been following our exchange without saying much, but now he spoke up. "I would think so. What's the harm in postponing? Someone ought to talk some sense into that woman."

I smiled at Calvin, touched by his concern. He was right, of course. Except he didn't know about Annaliese's other motive for bringing the vendors back together—and for asking for my participation, in particular. Maybe it was obstinance or even curiosity on my part, but the more I spoke with Nick, the less afraid I felt. And the more inclined to accept Annaliese's offer.

Glancing over at his van, with the fierce-looking cartoon rattlesnake, I was struck with a sudden observation. This morning a snake had blocked my path in the forest, and now a snake was blocking my driveway. And Taz's final words were something about a snake.

Perhaps this was the sign I'd been waiting for. I wasn't going to be able to move on until I solved the mystery of the snake.

Is that a stretch? I asked myself. *Maybe.* But it was good enough for me. I'd made my decision.

After Nick got his van started, Calvin and I stood beside the road and watched him drive off. Then Calvin turned to face me. I expected him to say something about the murder or the wedding, but instead he patted his stomach.

"I'm famished and my cupboards are bare. Want to come along as I rustle up some grub?"

"I'm supposed to go to my parents' for supper tonight.

Why don't you come along? My mom always makes enough to feed an army."

He brightened like a kid at a carnival. "Love to!"

We quickly took care of the roses he'd brought in from the greenhouse, then locked up the shop and headed out in our separate cars. On the way, I called my mom (using my car's hands-free tech, of course) to give her a heads-up that I was bringing a guest—and to urge her and Dad to be cool. Although they'd both met Calvin, he'd never been to their home, and I really hoped they wouldn't make a big deal of it and embarrass us both. She assured me they'd do no such thing.

Luckily, she was true to her word. Mostly. She welcomed Calvin into the kitchen with the same enthusiasm she'd show any of my friends, serving him a generous portion of Tex-Mex casserole with a side salad and cilantro-lime vinaigrette. She chatted the whole time. Probably no one besides me picked up on the definite twinkle in her eye or the plethora of questions she asked about Calvin's family.

On second thought, Rocky probably noticed too. This was why he rarely brought girlfriends home anymore. I caught him rolling his eyes at least once. And he grinned extra wide when Mom asked Calvin if his parents were eager to become grandparents.

I almost spit out my water. "Mom!"

"What?" she asked, the picture of innocence. "Too personal?"

"It's okay," said Calvin. "They actually *are* excited about being grandparents. My sister is expecting her first child in January."

"Oh, how nice!" gushed Mom.

Rocky shot me a significant look, and I slid down a few inches in my chair. I couldn't really blame our mom, though.

She'd grown up in a big family and always seemed happiest with a houseful of people. Luckily, Dad changed the subject and started talking about rock-climbing and other adventurous sports. By dessert—blackberry cobbler and homemade vanilla ice cream—I finally started to relax. Calvin was holding his own, and Mom had stopped mentioning babies.

After dinner, Calvin offered to help clean up—earning him bonus points in Mom's view, but she'd have none of it.

"Why don't you two go sit outside on the porch swing? Hardly anyone uses it anymore. Go enjoy the pleasant air while you can."

Calvin took his plate to the sink and smiled at Mom. "Thank you for dinner, Mrs. Ravenswood. It was delicious."

"You're quite welcome," she said. "I hope you come again."

"Me too," he said.

I called Gus over and led the way out the kitchen door and onto the back deck. I was feeling quite content and pleased with how the evening was going. By unspoken agreement, no one had brought up the murder; Calvin was being particularly charming; and now I finally had a chance to ask him about his recent encounter with Felix. Or not. Maybe we'd talk about other things.

We sat down next to each other on the wooden swing and looked out into the dark grove of trees behind my parents' house. Gus barked once, probably to warn away any night critters from his domain, then settled down at our feet. With the sun long gone, I was feeling a little chilly. I unrolled the sleeves on my blouse and contemplated moving closer to Calvin.

Then I made a stupid mistake. I looked at my phone.

"Jeez," I muttered, staring at the loathsome device.

"Something wrong?" asked Calvin.

"I have five missed calls and twice as many text messages. I guess word of my recent adventures finally trickled through the grapevine."

I scrolled through the messages, dashing off quick replies where appropriate—*Thanks* to well-wishers and *Doing okay* to those who asked. Two of the texts were from my friend Richard, owner of a local B&B and sometime handyman. His first message made me chuckle.

Sorry for all the phone calls. Got a little excited when I heard the news—you're decorating for Marissa Lakely's wedding! So cool! (Except for the murder part.)

His second message, however, really got my attention.

BTW, you might be interested to know you have something in common with one of my current guests—the photographer for said wedding. (Should I be worried?)

"Huh," I said.

"Anything good?" asked Calvin.

"Um, maybe." I heard my distracted tone and immediately felt like a heel. Looking up at him, I said, "I'm sorry. I'm being rude."

He waved away the apology. "Don't worry about it. You have people who care about you. That's a good thing." From the faint light shining through the windows of the house, I saw him quirk his lips into a small smile.

"Yeah, but I don't need to do this now." I tapped a finger on my phone, then glanced down at the screen in surprise. The display showed an incoming call—which I'd just inadvertently answered. I widened my eyes in dismay. *Oops.*

A woman's voice, sounding uncertain, said, "Hello?"

I shot Calvin an apologetic, and somewhat sheepish, smile as I lifted the phone to my ear. "Hello?"

"Sierra Ravenswood? This is Annaliese Bellman Lakely."

"Oh! Mrs. Lakely! Hi." I glanced at Calvin again and shrugged. *How did she even get my number?*

"I'm sorry to bother you, but there's been a development . . . and there's something I'd like to show you. I don't suppose—is there any possibility you could stop by the manor tonight?"

"Tonight?"

"Yes. I'm afraid it's urgent. You see, I've learned that Marissa is now a suspect. And it seems she's disappeared.

Chapter 11

Calvin and I headed to Bellman Manor in his car, an old gray compact sedan. He'd offered to drive, and I was happy to let him. It felt good to be at his side again, in the dark intimacy of the car, as we traveled to the hilly outskirts of town. Plus, his vehicle was a lot less conspicuous than my bright orange Fiat. Something told me "discretion" ought to be our watchword tonight.

We hadn't even told my family where we were going. I'd just asked Rocky if he would watch Gus while Calvin and I went for a drive. He'd agreed without question. In fact, he seemed almost eager to see us go, making me wonder if he might be expecting some company of his own.

When we arrived at the mayor's estate, I directed Calvin to the rear of the house. Annaliese was waiting for us at the back door, still surprisingly chic under the circumstances. Only her bare lips and slightly smudged eye makeup indicated this was the end of a long trying day. She greeted us warmly and ushered us into the kitchen.

"Can I get you anything to eat or drink? Coffee or wine? Seltzer water? Tea—"

"No, thanks," Calvin and I said at the same time. If we didn't cut her off, she might've kept naming beverages all night. "Have you heard from Marissa?" I added.

She sighed. "No. I think she's run off, but hopefully not for long. She didn't take her luggage. The only thing missing, as far as I can tell, is her purse, a backpack, and a few toiletries. And her car, of course."

I wasn't sure what to say to that. The fact that she took a backpack instead of a suitcase *could* indicate Marissa didn't intend to stay gone long. It could also mean she left in a hurry.

"You said the police think she's a suspect?" I prompted.

"It's ridiculous, really." Annaliese moved toward a wine rack and placed her hand lightly on a bottle of cabernet. "Are you sure you wouldn't like a small drink?"

"No, thanks." When she didn't go on, I decided to switch gears. I had a hard time believing Marissa was a serious suspect anyway. "You said there was something you wanted to show me?"

"Oh, yes, Taz's room. It's upstairs."

She pulled herself away from the wine and moved toward the short hallway leading to the great room. There she opened a panel door, revealing a narrow staircase. I hadn't seen it before, though it figured there would be a second staircase in a home this size. I imagined it might have been for the servants' use when the house was originally built. Or maybe it was just for the residents' convenience. What did I know about mansion living?

At the second-floor landing, we entered the main corridor. Passing what I presumed were bedrooms, Annaliese led us to the den where the wedding decorations were being stored—and which connected with the room Taz had occupied. Before entering, she paused and looked across the hall.

"Would you like to see where it happened?" By her hushed, somber tone, there was no doubt what "it" was.

Calvin frowned, but I was curious. Hadn't it happened next to the railing in the balcony area?

She crossed the hall and opened another door, standing back to let us enter. "This is my sewing room."

It was a relatively small, square room, with old-fashioned feminine décor, including ruffled curtains, rose-patterned wallpaper, and an upholstered bench with rolled arms and a matching pouffe. It seemed to be a functional space as well. A fabric-covered worktable blocked the windows, and an ironing board stood open next to a dressmaker's dummy. There was nothing to indicate a crime had occurred in here. If anything, it appeared exceptionally clean.

Annaliese must have read my mind. "You should have seen it before Gretchen cleaned up. Fingerprint powder everywhere, evidence bags. . . . It was a mess."

"And—" I began.

"And a drop of blood," said Annaliese matter-of-factly. "Earlier, my sewing shears had been lying on the table. The killer must have grabbed them and taken Taz by surprise. There was no sign of a struggle."

"Only a drop of blood?" asked Calvin. He now seemed as curious as I was.

"It must have happened quickly," said Annaliese. "We speculate that Taz was already on his way out of the room, perhaps with his hand on the doorknob, when he was stabbed. From there, he must have run or stumbled forward, perhaps thinking he'd go for help. There was a short trail of blood in the hall—all cleaned now, thank heaven."

"And then he fell over the railing?" I asked.

"It seems likely," she said. "The killer probably saw Taz go over and fled the scene."

"Any sign of the shears?" I asked. I didn't recall seeing them in Taz's body, and I was sure I'd notice something like that.

Annaliese nodded and inclined her head to the left. "The room next to this one is a bathroom. They were in the sink, the handles rinsed clean."

She didn't mention the blades, and I wasn't going to ask. I was more interested in what happened next. I stepped out of the sewing room and looked to the left and right.

Did the killer run down the back stairs and out the back door? Or go up to the ballroom? Or did they slip into one of the bedrooms to compose themselves and wait for the inevitable scream? With half a dozen people at various locations in the house, they could have run into anyone anywhere. *It's a wonder they got away with it. At least, so far.*

Calvin placed a gentle hand on my back. "What are you thinking?" he asked.

"I'm trying to remember where everyone came from, when I was downstairs . . ." Trailing off, I walked over to the balcony and looked down. I closed my eyes and envisioned myself back in the moment when I'd realized Taz was dead. I'd screamed, and people had come running.

I spoke softly. "I think Gordon and Regina might have arrived first, from the side door in the great room. Kendall and Anton came down the grand staircase, more or less at the same time. Nick came in last, also from the side door, or possibly from the dining room." I turned to look at Calvin and shook my head. "None of this helps."

"You never know," said Annaliese, a note of hope in her voice. She'd been watching me carefully.

I glanced down the hall. "Do you mind if I look around a little?"

"Please do. That's why I asked you here." She swept her arm wide, indicating I should take the lead.

First, I took a peek inside the hall bathroom. Like the sewing room, it was spotless, with the added touch of rose-scented potpourri. The tile floor gleamed. The waste basket stood empty. Next to the sink, a ceramic dish held a brick of unused pink soap, with a carved blossom in the center. *Where's the handwashing soap?* This bar looked too precious to get wet.

With Calvin and Annaliese hovering behind me, I next moved to the den across the hall. The boxes of wedding decorations stood against the wall, their flaps hanging open. It appeared as if they'd been examined, then cast aside. In the adjoining room, I saw at once that all of Taz's personal belongings had been removed. No doubt confiscated by the police. Still, I crouched down to look under the bed and behind the furniture. There was nothing to be found.

Back in the den, Annaliese stood near the fireplace, staring into space. Calvin had taken a seat on the oversized plush sofa and was looking at his phone. I wandered across the room, drawn to a large potted plant, a bird-of-paradise, to the right of the doorway. The glazed Japanese design on the container was lovely, but it was the giant leaves that attracted my attention. They were browning at the edges. Out of habit, I pressed two fingers in the soil and found it was slightly damp. Under-watering wasn't the problem. Probably the plant was too close to the cast-iron radiator against the wall. Holding my purse out of the way, I leaned down to pull the plant away from the heat source. That's when I noticed the gap between the radiator and the wall.

Hmm. Might as well take a look.

I leaned over the radiator and peered into the dark crevice below—and spied a bulky object resting on the floor against the baseboard. *What do you know?* The skin on the back of my neck tingled. I pulled out my phone, turned on the flashlight, and shined it behind the radiator.

"Is there something back there?" Calvin asked from the sofa.

Annaliese looked up sharply and strode to my side.

"Probably a lot of dust. I doubt Gretchen cleans back there, at least not more than once or twice a year."

By the light of my phone, I observed what looked to be a black, rectangular book. It was thick and leather-bound. *Not a book. An organizer.* Just like the one that had held Taz's master agenda.

I started to reach for the book, then stopped myself. I turned to Annaliese, who wore an eager, questioning expression.

"Do you happen to have any gloves I can borrow?" I asked. "If this is what I think it is, I don't want to leave any fingerprints on it."

She clapped her hands together. "Good thinking! I'll be right back."

As soon as she left, I told Calvin about Taz's planner and handed him my phone. He took a look for himself and whistled under his breath.

"Amazing. Do you think he hid it back there?"

"More likely, he probably set it on top of the radiator and it fell. Maybe he was in a hurry." *Which means he was here, in the den, right before he met his killer in the sewing room.*

Annaliese returned and handed me a pair of white satin evening gloves. I slipped them on, reached behind the radiator, and retrieved the book. The second I saw it, I knew I was right. A small silver monogram on the front cover said T.B.

Taz Banyan.

Annaliese let out a girlish squeal. "I *knew* I could count on you! Come, have a seat. There might be clues in there!" She reached out a hand, as if she wanted to pull me forward.

"We need to let the police know about this," I said. Still, I didn't protest when Annaliese beckoned me to have a seat on the sofa. I was dying to have a look.

"I'll turn on more light." Annaliese moved toward a lamp in the corner.

Calvin sat down next to me. "Are you sure about this?" he whispered. "Why is she putting this on you, anyway?"

I shook my head. "She thinks I'm some kind of private eye or something. And she doesn't think the police are working fast enough."

"This is crazy," he muttered.

"I know. But . . ." I left my excuses unsaid, as my eyes slid to the planner on my lap. I couldn't help feeling like Alice in Wonderland. I'd fallen down a rabbit hole, and everything kept getting "curiouser and curiouser."

Annaliese circled the sofa to stand behind me. Avoiding Calvin's scrutiny, I tightened the gloves and opened the book.

The entire planner was dedicated to Marissa and Michael-William's wedding. There were tabbed pages, color-coded notes, lists, and more lists. Every detail was meticulously recorded. With Annaliese looking over my left shoulder and Calvin leaning in from my right, I slowly turned page after page. After about a minute of this, I started flipping faster and stopped reading every word. It seemed unlikely this exercise would bring us any closer to understanding Taz's murder.

Then I came to the daily calendar pages. *Now we're getting somewhere.* With one page per day, there was plenty of room for Taz to record appointments and phone calls, and—most interestingly—his commentary. In some places, it read almost like a diary. I read a few of his notes out loud.

"Listen to this. 'Anton is on board, as I knew he would be. Riding my coattails as usual, but he'll do a good job.'"

"Had an ego, did he?" remarked Calvin.

"A little bit," I said. "Oh, here's another note about Anton. 'Make sure he keeps his focus and doesn't get distracted by his side hustle. Gotta get him away from his cousin's influence.'"

"Wonder what his side hustle is," I mused.

"No idea," said Annaliese. "He's a wiz of a stylist, though." Leaning over me, she pointed to an annotation in smaller print. "What does that say about Regina?"

"'Regina is on board,'" I read. "'Said she'll behave.'"

"'Behave'? What does that mean?" asked Annaliese.

"Your guess is as good as mine," I said.

Annaliese paced to the front of the sofa, her brow furrowed in puzzlement. "Regina has been quite courteous and professional to me. In fact, when I spoke with her this morning, she offered to take over as wedding planner. She told me she has some experience with event planning, in addition to catering."

Now that *was* interesting. If Regina was also a wedding planner, did that mean she and Taz were competitors?

Returning to the daily calendar pages, I said, "It looks like he lined up all the vendors pretty quickly. 'Gordon and Tammy are on board—at least he knows what's good for him.' Wonder what he meant by that? . . . 'Kendall's on board. . . . Sidewinder's on board.'" I glanced at Calvin. "That's Nick. 'DJ Sidewinder.'"

"Right." He met my eyes and spoke evenly. "A sidewinder is a kind of rattlesnake, isn't it?"

"Yeah," I said. "But I don't think . . ." I trailed off, refocusing my attention on the planner. I knew what Calvin was getting at. I'd thought it myself. Could Taz, in his dying breath, have been referring to Nick? Was Nick the "snake"? I wasn't convinced. If Taz had been trying to identify Nick as his killer, why not just say "It was Nick"?

"It's a stage name," said Annaliese, oblivious to Calvin's point. She didn't know about Taz's last words, and I wasn't sure if I should tell her.

I turned the page, and then the next. For a few days, Taz's notes were limited to wedding business. Then I paused, as the word "disaster" caught my eye.

Again reading out loud, I said, "'Disaster averted. Tailor flubbed the measurements and cut Marissa's gown way too small. She thought it was ruined, but I talked to him myself. It will be fixed.'"

"That's right," said Annaliese. "Poor Marissa was so upset." She picked up a cell phone from the shelf, looked at it a moment, then held it between her palms. As if talking to herself, she said, "I wish she would get back to me."

It occurred to me how worried Annaliese must be. "Does she have any friends you could reach out to?" I asked gently. "Or maybe her fiancé?"

She looked up at me with a slightly dazed expression, but her face quickly cleared. "I'm sure she'll call tomorrow. Marissa is a good girl. It's just—we need to solve this murder as soon as possible."

A good girl who's now a suspect. I wanted to ask Annaliese to explain why she thought the police now suspected her daughter. But then I remembered something else. When I'd first met Annaliese, she'd said something about Taz managing to prevent a number of "crises." I asked her what she'd meant.

"Oh, yes," she said. "The gown was one. There was also a mix-up with the invitations. The printing company got the date wrong. Luckily, Taz caught the error before they were mailed out." Sighing, she pulled up a rocker from the corner and sat down. "The worst, though, was the fire alarm incident."

"Fire alarm incident?" echoed Calvin. He glanced up at the smoke detector on the ceiling near the door.

Annaliese nodded slowly. "It started when we had an unexpected visit from a state building inspector. I still don't know who called him. He took one look at the ballroom and said it wasn't up to code. Something about the exit and size." She waved her hand dismissively.

"Those rules apply to a private residence?" asked Calvin.

"Evidently, they apply wherever fifty or more people assemble. For a minute, I thought we were going to have to uninvite thirty guests! But then Frank told him the manor is a certified historic building, which has different requirements. The inspector still made some recommendations, which, of course, we took care of. Frank had an electrician out the next day to convert our smoke alarms to a hardwired system."

Must be a perk of being mayor—no waiting for contractors. Out loud, I said, "That's good." I would've been worried if they'd decided to circumvent any fire codes.

"Ultimately, it is, I suppose," she said. "Except that it led to the smoke alarm incident."

"There's more?" asked Calvin.

"Unfortunately, yes. You see, Taz had a vendor meeting planned the next day. But something malfunctioned in the new system. The smoke detectors kept going off, blaring all day. In every room." She rubbed her temple, as if the memory gave her a headache. "Every time it stopped, you'd breathe a sigh of relief, thinking it was surely over—until they blasted again, giving you another jolt."

"That would be . . . alarming," said Calvin.

I elbowed him gently and tried not to smile. I sensed that his tiredness threatened to bring out his natural goofiness. I probably wasn't too far behind.

"Very," said Annaliese, seemingly oblivious to the wordplay. "At one point, the florist, Tammy, was standing right beneath an alarm in the great room. She was so startled when it went off that she dropped a heavy vase on her toes. The way she howled, I thought for sure she'd broken every bone in her foot. Of course, Taz had to cancel the meeting after that. He's the one who got the electrician to come back."

"Is that why Tammy quit?" I asked.

"I don't think so. At least, she didn't say anything about quitting for another ten days or so after that." She creased her forehead. "I don't believe Taz ever gave a reason for her departure."

I skimmed through the next few pages of the planner, wondering what he'd had to say about "the smoke alarm incident." When I reached the calendar page for that day, I saw that he'd drawn a line through the words "vendor meeting." Beneath that, he'd written, "Canceled due to noise and lunacy. Is someone trying to sabotage this wedding?"

I grinned at the first sentence, but my grin quickly dropped away. For a long moment, I stared at the second sentence. *Sabotage? I'm beginning to wonder the same thing.*

Calvin nudged my leg. "It's getting late," he said softly.

Annaliese stood up and looked at her phone again. "Goodness, it's after ten. You two should stay here tonight."

"Oh, we couldn't do that," I said, glancing at Calvin. He regarded Annaliese with a mixture of surprise and amusement.

"We have plenty of room," she said. "And everything you could possibly need."

I saw Calvin raise his shoulders in a slight shrug, as if he actually wouldn't mind spending a night at Bellman Manor. Well, he didn't have a family to answer to like I did.

"That's kind of you," I said. "But I'm almost to the end of this book."

I quickly perused the last few pages, searching for any further clues in Taz's written notes. When I reached the entry for last Sunday, the day before the final vendor meeting, something jumped out at me: a boldly drawn asterisk. Beside the star, Taz had written, "Note to self: Keep an eye on Kendall. She's up to something."

Hmm. What could she possibly have been up to? I remembered the pink hair I'd found on Taz's suitcase. Had she been searching his things? For what?

Still lost in thought, I turned the page. Looking at the date, I realized I'd reached Taz's final day. I felt goose bumps prickle along my arms. *Poor guy.* Then I read what he'd written.

"Six o'clock—meet with new florist. Some yokel Marissa found. Lord help me."

I scowled. Calvin, reading over my shoulder, laughed. "I guess that's you, huh?"

"Yeah, that's me. Just a small town 'yokel.'"

Annaliese covered her mouth to hide a yawn. "Is there anything else of interest? Any clues to the murderer?"

I closed the planner. "I'm not sure what to make of Taz's notes. Some of his comments do seem suggestive. I'm sure Chief Walden will want to follow up on several of them."

"Do you want to take pictures of any of the pages?" she asked. "Or copy down any of the notes? I could get you some paper."

I looked into her tired, worried eyes and felt a pang of guilt. She'd asked for my help, and what did I do? I came over here and spent an hour looking through evidence and asking her questions. I was acting as if I thought I could help her.

"I'm sorry. I'm not really a detective." I handed her the book and pulled off the white gloves. "We should leave this to the pros." I felt my cell phone buzz in my purse beside me. Pulling it out, I saw it was a text from Rocky.

Hey, Sis. Gus is asleep and I'm heading to bed. I'll bring him to FH on my way to work tmw. :)

Huh. There went my two biggest excuses for leaving: Gus's bedtime and Rocky's third degree.

I showed Calvin the message, then dashed off a quick reply. *Thank you and sorry! I didn't expect to be gone this long. I owe you one!*

I felt Calvin watching me as I returned my phone to my purse. He spoke in a low voice. "I can give you a ride home, if you don't want to pick up your car tonight. I'll pick you up in the morning too. It's not a big deal."

Annaliese still regarded me with a tinge of hope. "Are you sure you won't stay? The guest rooms are already made up. And, to be honest, I feel a bit uncomfortable being in the house alone tonight."

"Alone?" I said, surprised. I hadn't realized her husband wasn't home.

"Frank stayed in the village," she explained, "as he sometimes does when he has a late meeting and too much to drink." Smoothing her hair self-consciously, she added, "It's just as well. He doesn't know Marissa is a suspect, and I don't want to tell him."

I raised a finger at that. Maybe now I could ask the questions I'd been holding back all evening. "I'm sorry, but I'm a little confused. When did *you* find out Marissa is a suspect? And when did she leave, anyway?"

"When?" Annaliese echoed. "She left earlier today. I was at the police station again, speaking with Captain Bradley. When I got home, I realized Marissa was gone."

"Do the police know she took off?"

Annaliese shook her head. "I don't think so. I'm hoping she'll come back, and they'll never even need to know."

Something didn't sit right about this whole thing. "I still don't understand why Marissa is a suspect. Did she have something against Taz?"

Annaliese stood up abruptly. "Listen, it's late. Why don't we call it a night and regroup in the morning? I'll answer all your questions then."

Biting my lip, I shot a questioning look to Calvin. He shrugged again. "Whatever you want to do is fine with me."

I turned to Annaliese and smiled uncertainly. "I guess we could stay after all. I do have to get up early, though."

Annaliese brightened. "Wonderful! All the more reason to stay over, right? Breakfast will be ready at seven, and we can talk more then. We'll have a council of war, as they say." Smiling now, she headed to the door. "I'll show you to your rooms."

Chapter 12

It always comes back to trust. Who can you rely on? Who can you believe? With whom can you let down your guard?

I pondered these things, as I stood in the steamy shower, letting hot water wash over me and breathing in the heady floral scents of luxury bath soaps I could never afford. They were made in France, according to the labels, and sported exotic and puzzling names: *Le Cynique Fleur, Le Beau Chien*.

The cynical flower? The beautiful dog? I giggled to myself as I sudsed my hair. I trusted Annaliese wouldn't stock her guest bathroom with dog shampoo—especially since this was the room she said her mother would be staying in.

I was beginning to learn my way around the manor. On the second floor, from front to back, the right-hand doors led to Marissa's bedroom, the den, and the master bedroom. On the left side were the sewing room and powder room (together comprising the approximate size of one of the bedrooms), then two guest bedrooms—one across from the den and one across from the master suite. I knew this, because Annaliese

had said she'd be right across the hall if we should find that
we needed anything.

I couldn't imagine that I would. Annaliese had been true
to her word on this point. My room was a richly appointed
retreat, with thick carpet, polished antique furniture, and a
soft blue and white quilt on the pillow-topped queen-sized
bed. Before saying good night, Annaliese had urged us to
avail ourselves of everything we could find in the guest ac-
commodations.

"Thank you so much," I'd said. "That's very generous. I
think I'll just take a shower before going to bed."

Calvin had said he'd do the same, then gave me a jaunty
salute before retiring to the room next to mine. I grinned at
the memory. How many guys would be such a good sport
about this whole thing?

Rinsing off now, I contemplated how natural it had felt to
be with him again after two months apart. And I wondered
where we stood, relationship-wise. I found myself staring
at the logo on the French bath products, a small daisy-head
design. It reminded me of the daisy oracle. *He loves me, he
loves me not.*

Are we dating? It had started to feel that way this evening. On the question of trust, he'd earned mine—in spite of
a rocky start in that department last spring. At a minimum,
I counted him as a true friend.

I switched off the water and dried off with a fluffy, fresh-
smelling towel. After slathering on some rich French body lo-
tion, I wrapped myself in an equally fluffy floor-length white
robe. *Is this what it feels like to stay in a five-star hotel?*

As for Annaliese, I *wanted* to trust her. In fact, I didn't
really have any reason not to. But I also knew myself. I
sometimes had a tendency to be more trusting than I should
be, and I'd been duped before—most embarrassingly by a

scoundrel of a boyfriend back in Nashville. Of course, I was a few years older now, and, hopefully, a few years wiser.

I'd just finished brushing my teeth (with a brand-new packaged toothbrush provided on the vanity), when I heard a tap on the door. As I crossed the room, my phone buzzed on the dresser. Grabbing it up, I saw a text from Calvin.

Still up? It's me in the hall.

Grinning, I opened the door and ushered him in. "Were you out here long?"

"Not at all. It just occurred to me after I knocked that I ought to text first." He quirked his lips in a shy half smile. "I don't know the etiquette here. I don't think I've ever been in such a weird situation—and that's saying something."

"Me either."

We stood looking at each other for a beat. I noticed his hair was still damp from his shower, and he smelled delicious, like he'd used the spicy, masculine version of the French bath soaps. He'd put his jeans and button-down shirt back on.

There was an upholstered straight-backed chair in the corner. He pulled the chair away from the wall and gestured for me to sit on the foot of the bed. I sat down, making sure my robe was securely closed, as I tucked my legs beneath me on the bed. Calvin sat on the chair facing me.

"I've been thinking," he said.

"Do tell."

"You have an adventurous spirit, right?"

That was unexpected. "Uh, sure. I like to think so."

"You have a curious mind. You enjoy solving problems and uncovering truths?"

"I do," I said slowly and with growing suspicion. "Why do you ask?"

"Because I have an idea. Instead of getting mixed up in police business—in possibly dangerous criminal investigation stuff . . ." He paused, his eyes sparkling. "Why not join me on a treasure hunt?"

My shoulders slumped. "Felix's treasure hunt?"

"Felix doesn't own it," he replied. "The hunt belongs to everyone. But only the smartest and the most determined have a shot at it: the legendary Arwin Treasure. It's a trove of rare coins, precious gemstones, golden relics—just waiting for a savvy detective to solve the puzzle and find the hiding spot."

"It sounds like a myth," I said. "A pipe dream. Haven't people been searching for years?"

"It's real," he said. "Arwin published photos before he hid it. And some of his hidden clues have been found already."

"Mm-hmm," I said.

"Take a look at this," he said, reaching into his pocket. He pulled out a folded piece of paper and handed it to me.

Unfolding the paper, I saw that it was a typed poem.

<u>First Things First</u>, by Mr. Arwin
It's not a Legend, it's not a trap;
There is no door, there is no map.
It's Nature's game, as real as life;
Play along, cause no strife.
What's on a map? A Compass rose.
How many ways? The Cardinal knows.
Now go Forth, and seek the truth
Find and learn, as in your youth.

I skimmed the lines. "What is this?"

"It's the first clue. The invitation and the call. What do you make of it?"

I read it again. "It sounds like a riddle."

"Bingo. Anything else?"

I sighed. "Well, it sounds like this Mr. Arwin is having fun. He uses the words 'play' and 'game.' Perhaps it's all one big joke. He's having fun at the expense of all the treasure hunters."

Calvin leaned back and laughed. "I think you're partly right. It is like a game, and he is having fun. But so are the seekers. Does anything else jump out at you?"

Knitting my brow, I studied the poem. The truth was, I did love a good challenge, and this was starting to pique my interest.

"Random words are capitalized," I said. "Or maybe not so random. 'Legend,' 'Compass.' 'Cardinal' could refer to the cardinal directions. These are all items on a map . . . but he says 'there is no map.' Is he speaking metaphorically? Or spiritually? As in, 'There is no spoon, Neo.'"

Calvin chuckled again. "*Matrix* reference. I love it."

I looked again at the paper. "There are also references to numbers. It's called *First Things First*. He asks 'How many ways?' And the word 'Forth' is capitalized—though it's spelled differently than 'fourth,' as in the number."

"You're good," said Calvin, sounding impressed.

I re-read parts of the rhyme, muttering under my breath. "'Legend,' 'no door,' 'how many.' A legend on a map is also known as a key. But not to a door. . . . There are four cardinal directions . . ." Something clicked in my mind, and I looked up.

"Is he saying there are four keys?"

Calvin broke out into a pleased grin. "Wow! You got that in, like, five minutes. Very good!"

"So, I'm right? That's it?"

"You're right. Four keys to the treasure chest. People speculated that's what it meant for a long time, but there wasn't any proof—until now. Felix found the first key."

"Ah." I refolded the paper and handed it back to Calvin. "Did he call you? Is that how you knew where to find him in South Dakota?"

"Not at first. Remember that geocaching message board, where Felix and I first met?"

"Yeah."

"After ignoring it for months, Felix—aka "Flower Man"—made an appearance. He couldn't resist sharing a picture of his find."

"As if he doesn't already have enough people breathing down his neck?"

"I know. He really needs to watch his back. I told him as much when he called. He used the message board to reach out to his old friend 'Plant Prof'—yours truly—and ask for my number."

"So, he called you and asked you to meet him in the Badlands . . . so he could give you a key to his cabin? Why not mail it? Or, better yet, why not just contact me?"

Calvin fiddled with the folded paper, tapping it from palm to palm. "He wanted to talk, get my opinion on a few things. He didn't know I was in Iowa at the time. I decided to drive up and see him in person, because I figured it would be easier. He's so distractible. It's kinda hard to hold a phone conversation with him."

"That's true," I acknowledged. In my experience, it could be challenging to have a conversation with Felix in person too. I regarded Calvin for a moment, wondering what he was trying to tell me. I was afraid I knew.

"So, this Arwin guy," Calvin continued, "is a lover of science. Felix figured that out. He found the first key by unraveling a string of botanical clues. Now he's working through some geological puzzles to find the second key. He thought I might be able to help."

"But you're a botanist, not a geologist. Right?"

"Right. But I've studied a little geology too—anyway, that's not important. Bottom line, Felix asked if I'd partner up with him to find the treasure."

My heart sank at the news. Dropping my eyes, I pleated the belt on my robe. "I see."

"All kinds of alliances have been formed," Calvin went on. "With four keys, the treasure will likely have to be shared anyway. So far, Felix has been approached by more than a few people wanting to partner with him. He's refused them all."

"You should feel special then," I said dryly.

Calvin snickered lightly. "I suppose so."

For a moment, neither of us said anything. It was so quiet, I could hear the bedside clock ticking past the seconds. Finally, I looked up and met his eyes.

"Why did you come back, Calvin?"

He cocked his head slightly. "Don't you know?"

"To get something from Felix's cabin?"

He gave me a funny look and shook his head. "No. I came back because of you. I missed you."

A rush of warmth coursed through my veins, but my doubting mind wasn't ready to accept it. "Really?"

"Yeah, really." Setting the paper on the dresser, he reached for my hands. As our fingers intertwined, he gave me a questioning look. "Didn't you miss me?"

I couldn't help smiling. "More than you know."

Our eyes locked, and he leaned toward me. Like a magnet, I leaned forward in kind. Our lips were inches apart, my eyelids closing—when a sharp blast from the fire alarm wrenched us apart.

Chapter 13

Calvin used a pillow to swat at the smoke detector. After two tries, the device fell blessedly silent. I rubbed my ears, which continued to ring—until I realized the ringing came from outside the room. Calvin opened the bedroom door, and it soon became apparent that smoke alarms were going off all over the house.

The door across the hall swung open, and Annaliese rushed out. She wore a long satin robe and backless slippers, looking, somehow, as if she'd stepped off the cover of a high-end catalogue. "Where's the fire?" she demanded.

"Isn't this another malfunction?" I asked.

"It shouldn't be. That was fixed. The alarms are all connected. We have to find the one that went off first." She made for the back stairs, leaving Calvin and me to look helplessly at each other.

"I think I should go with her." I tightened my robe and stepped into my loafers.

"I'll check this floor." He squeezed my shoulder, and we parted.

I raced after Annaliese, catching up with her in the kitchen.

"Oh, this is maddening!" She had to yell to be heard over the piercing alarm. It beeped incessantly, like a frantic, electronic heartbeat.

Trying to keep a level head, I said, "I don't smell smoke. Maybe it's a false alarm after all."

She threw up her hands, as if it didn't make a difference. Spinning on her heel, she headed for the great room. "This house is so blasted big!"

I started to follow, then hesitated. On an impulse, I opened the cabinet beneath the kitchen sink and found a small fire extinguisher. Taking it with me, I went in the opposite direction from Annaliese, to the hall leading to the dining room. That's when I smelled smoke.

It seemed to be coming from the end of the hall, and the mayor's home office. For half a second, I stood motionless. *Why didn't I grab my cell phone?* Collecting my wits, I charged ahead, then stopped short. *Safety first.* I put one hand on the door to check for heat. It was cool. Of course, it was also thick. Taking a deep breath, I turned the knob and pushed it slowly open.

I saw the flames right away. I probably would have heard them crackle as well, if the alarms hadn't been so loud. The fire was coming from a wastepaper basket next to the mayor's desk. Flames shot from the metal bin at least two feet high, singeing the edge of the desk and the base of a table lamp. Acrid smoke billowed from the lampshade.

I can do this. With no time to spare, I pulled the ring from the fire extinguisher and directed it at the flames. Squeezing with all my might, I emptied the canister, dousing the entire area with white foam. Thankfully, the fire went out.

I lowered my arms, shaky from the exertion, and set the extinguisher on the floor. Breathing heavily, I staggered to the window to let in some fresh air. Only, when I pulled the curtain aside, I saw that the window was already open, raised to its full extent. At the same time, the blaring alarm abruptly ceased, leaving me in a resounding silence.

Slowly, I turned around and surveyed the room. How had the fire started? Had someone come in through the window, set the fire, then left? I moved toward the blackened waste basket, now spattered with white, powdery residue. Whatever it had previously contained was now nothing but ash and foam. I frowned. If this was a case of arson, wouldn't the miscreant have been more likely to ignite the curtains or furniture, rather than start a small trash fire?

I scratched my head, trying to figure out what was going on here. One thing seemed clear: this was another crime scene, and the police should be called. I was lifting the receiver on the desktop telephone, when Annaliese burst into the room.

"Oh, you found it! And put it out! Thank goodness." She took in the scene at a glance and visibly relaxed. "And there doesn't seem to be too much damage."

"It was mostly confined to the trash can," I said.

Like me, she started toward the window. "It smells dreadful. I wonder if the odor will ever come out."

"Better not touch anything," I said quickly. At her look of surprise, I added, "This fire wasn't an accident. I'm calling the police."

"What? Don't do that!" She looked more upset now than when the alarms were blaring.

"Annaliese, the window was open when I got here. Someone must have climbed in and set the fire."

"Please," she said. "No more police. Not tonight. I-I'll lock the window and leave everything else untouched. We can call them in the morning."

"But the intruder could still be out there! I really think we should call the cops now."

Annaliese took a deep breath and pressed her hands together. "I'm sure whoever it was is long gone. Don't you think? They probably fled the second the fire alarms went off. There's nothing the police can do tonight that they can't do tomorrow."

I looked at her doubtfully, not liking this one bit. Finally, I said, "I'm going to call Calvin and let him know where we are." *Maybe the two of us together can talk some sense into her.*

I knew his cell phone number by heart. Turning to the mayor's landline once more, I made the call. Calvin was relieved to hear from me and said he'd be right down—as soon as I explained how to find the study. In the meantime, Annaliese paced the floor, tracking white powder across the carpet. I stood in one place, looking closely at the mayor's desk.

Something's missing. Last time I'd been in this room, I'd noticed how full the mail tray was. It was still full now ... but the box of wedding programs was gone. I peered into the burned-out trash can, wondering.

"Annaliese, do you know where the wedding programs are? I happened to see them in here on Monday." In case this concerned her, I added an explanation. "I was told I could borrow the printer, but I never did."

She looked at me, then at the mail tray. "They *were* in here, last I knew." Her look of bewilderment turned quickly to comprehension, and she joined me beside the trash can. "You've *got* to be kidding me."

I heard footsteps behind us and turned to see Calvin hurry in.

"Whoa. So, there really *was* a fire. Everybody okay?"

"Yes, thanks to Sierra and her quick thinking," said Annaliese. She gave me a strained smile. "I owe you a huge debt of gratitude."

"How did it start?" asked Calvin.

"That's what we were discussing." I filled him in, including my belief that we should call the police. Annaliese immediately repeated her belief that we shouldn't.

Calvin strode over to the window and looked outside. "It's too dark to see anything from here," he said. Then he faced Annaliese. "If there was a burglar in your house, that has to be reported to the police."

She wrung her hands and answered in an agitated, raised voice. "I *will* report it! Just not tonight. Please."

Calvin and I exchanged a cautious glance. I was beginning to wonder if she knew who set the fire.

He took Annaliese by the elbow and gently guided her to one of the club chairs. I sat in the other one, feeling a deep fatigue setting in. We both fixed Annaliese with expectant stares.

Calvin spoke kindly. "Perhaps we should all leave. Do you have a friend you could call? Or maybe just find a hotel room for the night?"

She shook her head tiredly. "I don't think that's necessary. However, I can call Dennis. He's a private security guard we sometimes hire, and he lives nearby. I'll ask him to come over right away."

I decided to try one more time. "Why don't you want to call the police, Annaliese?"

She clenched her fists and laughed without humor. "I just need a little more time. They don't know Marissa left. And Frank doesn't know anything. I don't *want* him to know about the chief's suspicions." She looked up at us with a defeated sort of embarrassment. "You see, the chief thinks I had an affair with Taz, and that Marissa found out and did something drastic."

For a moment, her words hung in the air, as senseless as a foreign language. I thought I must have misunderstood her.

"Of course, it's not true!" she said. "None of it is true. I told you it was ridiculous." She rubbed her hands over her eyes. "The police have it all wrong."

I finally found my voice. "Can't you just set them straight then? Why do they have it wrong?"

She sighed, and, without meeting our eyes, spilled forth her story. "I met Taz at a charity event a couple of years ago. I decided he'd be perfect to plan Marissa's wedding, so I met with him, several times, to talk and go over ideas. He was fun to be around, I admit, and always very flattering. Some of my friends began to tease me. I was aware there were rumors. And . . . I didn't deny them."

"Your husband didn't know about the rumors?" asked Calvin.

"No. This was in Nashville. I made frequent trips to the city without Frank. But, I swear, there was no dalliance. I was just having a little fun, leading my friends on."

"So, the police learned about the rumors," I said. "How does that implicate Marissa?"

She shook her head. "To be honest, I don't fully understand. When the police confronted me about my so-called relationship with Taz, one of the officers, Captain Bradley, told me it was Marissa who had 'spilled the beans.' I had no idea Marissa even knew about it."

"Captain Bradley said Marissa was upset about this?" I guessed.

"She implied she was. And then she made much of the fact that Marissa was late in meeting Frank and me at the restaurant for dinner on Monday night. I knew why, of course. Marissa had returned to the house, at around seven, to get something she'd left in one of our cars. She only went to the garage and never into the house. Supposedly, this was enough to make her a suspect in the eyes of the law."

At this point, my head was spinning. A little voice in the back of my mind tried to tell me that we ought to just gather up our things and leave Bellman Manor. But the helper in me wouldn't allow it. The idea of leaving Annaliese alone seemed heartless.

Calvin cleared his throat. "Mrs. Lakely, maybe you should call that security guy you mentioned."

"Yes, of course." She stood up and went to the phone. Apparently, the man picked up right away. After a brief conversation, she hung up and told us he was on his way.

I reached my hand up to Calvin, and he helped me to my feet. "I'm beat," I said.

"It's been quite a day," he agreed.

Yielding to our host's wishes, we told her good night and went up to bed.

The next morning, we found coffee and a hot breakfast awaiting us in the breakfast nook, courtesy of Gretchen the housekeeper. But no Annaliese. Gretchen informed us that Mrs. Lakely was under the weather, and that she sent her apologies for not seeing us off. As soon as Gretchen left the room, Calvin and I looked at each other with matching smirks.

"So much for our 'council of war,'" I said.

"And so much for her calling the police," pointed out Calvin. "At least, not anytime soon. What now?"

I gripped the handle of my coffee cup. "Now, I need to think." Sipping the coffee, I let my eyes wander around the spacious kitchen, from one end to the other. I had so many unanswered questions.

Who set the fire last night? Was there any connection to Taz's murder? And was Marissa really a viable suspect?

After a moment, Calvin checked his watch. "We should probably go soon."

"Yeah," I agreed. "I just need to run upstairs and get my purse. Then I want to take a quick look outside, around the office window, before we leave."

Calvin cleared off the table, taking our dishes to the sink, while I dashed up the back staircase to the guest room. After grabbing my purse, I stepped out into the hallway and paused.

Annaliese's door was shut tight. The whole floor was quiet and still. *Gretchen must be working in another part of the house.* Almost without thinking, I gravitated to Marissa's room. Was it really so strange that the bride-to-be took off? Maybe she needed space to process what had happened.

On the other hand, why wouldn't she tell her mother where she was going?

I tried the knob and, finding it unlocked, let myself in. After all, I rationalized, Annaliese *had* invited me to look around the night before. And I wouldn't be *too* snoopy.

The room was tidy, with a neatly made queen-sized bed and polished furniture. In some respects, it looked more like a guest room than a lived-in bedroom. Of course, this wasn't Marissa's permanent residence anymore. She would have moved away for college and probably only came home for occasional visits.

Without touching anything, I gazed around, taking note of the few personal details in the room: a bookcase filled with YA fantasy novels and horse-themed knickknacks, a cluster of framed photographs on the bureau. The photos included the same family picture I'd seen in the mayor's office, as well as a novelty photo-booth series featuring a young Marissa with another girl, both laughing and making silly faces. The rest of the pictures were of horses.

Where's the fiancé? There was no engagement photo or couples photo of any kind. Maybe she took it with her? Or maybe she hadn't displayed any recent photographs in her old room.

I took a quick peek in the closet and the en suite bathroom. Nothing struck me as having any particular significance.

Oh well. I let myself out of the room and headed back downstairs.

Calvin was no longer in the kitchen. I figured he already went outside to do some looking around of his own. I started for the back door, then had another thought. Since I was here anyway, I might as well take a quick walk-through of the dining room. I recalled Taz referring to it as his "command center." He'd probably spent a lot of time in there.

Pushing through the door, I was startled to find Gretchen sitting at the dining table. She was polishing the silver, a full-length apron over her maid's uniform and rubber gloves on her hands. She gave me a questioning look.

"Did you need something, miss?"

"Oh, hi," I said. "No. I'm good. I was just looking around. Mrs. Lakely asked for my help with, uh, sorting things out." That was essentially true. Not that I knew what I was doing.

Gretchen nodded, apparently satisfied, and resumed her task. I walked over to where Taz had stood on Monday evening, issuing his wedding prep instructions. One glance, and one peek under the table, told me there wasn't a crumb of evidence left behind. If there ever had been, Gretchen would have cleaned it up already.

On a whim, I sat down across from her and propped an elbow on the table. "Poor Annaliese," I said. "She's been through a lot. No wonder she doesn't feel well."

Gretchen gave a slight nod but didn't look up. She dipped her cloth in a dish of polish and rubbed it on a silver teapot.

"I know she was worried about Marissa last night," I continued. "Do you know if she's heard from her?"

"No, miss."

No, you don't know? Or, no, she hasn't heard? The maid was obviously not inclined to chat. Undaunted, I kept talking. "Do you have any idea where Marissa might have gone?"

She shook her head. "No, miss."

Of course not. I glanced over my shoulder, toward the hallway. "Did Mrs. Lakely tell you about the fire?"

She nodded again. "She told me not to clean Mr. Lakely's office until the insurance inspector comes out."

That was good. Maybe Annaliese had made some phone calls this morning after all. "And the police too, I imagine," I said.

Another nod.

I sighed. Gretchen was certainly a loyal employee. I had to admire her unwillingness to engage in idle gossip. I could have asked her about Marissa's relationship with her parents, about how she'd been acting, about any number of other tidbits, but I could tell it would be of no use. Still, there was one more question I could ask.

"Gretchen, did you have much interaction with the wedding planner?"

I fully expected her to shake her head in the negative. Instead, she raised her eyes. "Not much. He only spoke to me when he needed something. But he was pretty busy when he was here. And he was on his phone a lot."

His phone. This reminded me of my first encounter with him, in the great room. He'd taken a phone call from Kendall. Then he'd gotten a message, or perhaps seen a missed call, and gone into the sitting room to "deal with something."

"I don't suppose—did you ever hear him arguing with anyone, by chance?"

She set down her cloth. "I did once."

I raised my eyebrows and leaned forward. "What did you hear?"

"I was walking past the den upstairs. The door was open, and he was in there on his phone as usual. He seemed . . . exasperated. Like he was tired of repeating himself."

"Did you catch any specifics?"

She nodded, and this time she met my eyes. "He said, 'I'm not going to jail over this.'"

"Jail?"

"That's right." She picked up her cloth again and reached for a silver candlestick. "That's all I heard."

"Did you mention this to the police?"

She shrugged. "Yes, and I almost wish I hadn't. They kept me for an hour, asking me over and over to pinpoint the exact time, and I couldn't remember. I couldn't even remember for sure which day it was."

I smiled ruefully, feeling sympathy for both Gretchen and the police. With Taz's cell phone in their possession, they could trace all of his recent calls. But considering how much he was on his phone, it would be difficult to identify the call Gretchen had overheard without knowing the precise time it had occurred. Presumably, the police would question everyone about the jail comment. But if one of those people was the murderer, they'd surely lie and deny any knowledge of the matter.

Which begged the question—what was Taz involved in that could lead to jail time?

I found Calvin outside, waiting for me beside his car. He'd already examined the window that had been left open after the fire. Although I trusted his powers of observation, I wanted to see for myself. Yet, five minutes later, we were back at the car. There were no clues to be found.

Before leaving, I gave my brother a call to let him know I was on my way to pick up Gus and get my own car. I asked if he'd meet me outside, since I wouldn't have much time. In truth, I was also hoping to avoid an inquisition from Mom and Dad.

As Calvin pulled up to the curb in front of my parents'

house, we saw Rocky coming up the sidewalk, returning from a walk with Gus. Before getting out of the car, I turned to Calvin.

"Thanks for . . . everything." I smiled ironically at the absurdity of the situation.

"Thank *you* for a very entertaining evening. We should totally do it again sometime."

"Oh, totally," I agreed, with mock seriousness. We'd never had a chance to continue our discussion about the Arwin Treasure, or what Calvin planned to do about Felix's offer. But, funny enough, it didn't trouble me at the moment. I was just happy to know he cared about me. Laughing lightly, I opened the car door. "See you at the shop."

I waved as he took off, then turned to greet Gus and Rocky. I fully expected to get an earful from Rocky. To my pleasant surprise, he didn't say a word about last night. There were no questions and no teasing. In fact, he seemed to be in a hurry. He only gave me a quick grin and a knowing wink as he handed me Gus's leash and said he needed to get to work.

Thankful for the extra time, I made a quick trip home to change. I even made it to Flower House before we were scheduled to open. I didn't see Calvin's car, so I figured he must've had errands to run. When I came in the back door, I found Deena in the kitchen talking with Toby. At my entrance, she stopped mid-sentence and gave me her full attention.

"Hey, girl," she said, with a note of amusement.

"Hiya. What's up?" From the way she was looking at me, I thought there was something wrong with my outfit, so I looked down. I was dressed in typical attire—jeans and a brightly colored shirt, today a long-sleeved lime green T-shirt with Love in cursive lettering across the front. *Hmm, maybe I had dressed with romance on the brain . . .*

"Have a good time last night?" she asked.

I narrowed my eyes. "Uh, yeah. Why do you ask?"

"No reason. You just seem extra *sparkly* this morning, that's all." Turning to Toby, she said, "Doesn't Sierra look sparkly?"

He turned rose red and shifted his feet. "I don't know. She looks nice, I guess."

"Thank you, Toby." I moved past him to fill Gus's water dish. Gus, meanwhile, sniffed Toby's and Deena's legs, per his usual custom.

"I don't know," said Deena, in a playful voice. "I see a little something extra. I thought it might have something to do with your date last night."

I put one hand on my hip and stared her down. "Hang on a minute," I said. "How do you know about my date? What did you hear?"

"Not much," she said nonchalantly. "A little birdy told me you spent some time with a certain someone. A good deal of time—perhaps making up for lost time?" She tore off a piece of floral paper from a roll on the wall and began to wrap a richly hued harvest bouquet.

"You sure say 'time' a lot," I retorted, smiling in spite of myself. "I think it's about *time* I ask you a few questions— like how you've been spending *your* time. Because there's only one 'little birdy' who knew about my . . . date, for lack of a better word. Only he's more of a *big* bird."

Laughing, Deena handed Toby the wrapped bouquet and told him to wait for a second one. As she quickly put together a twenty-four-rose vase arrangement, I picked up a floral knife to help her strip the leaves. But that didn't mean I was ready to let her off the hook.

"Deena Lee, have you been holding out on me?"

After she and my brother had seemed to grow chummy over the summer, they'd suddenly stopped mentioning each other—at least to me. And I hadn't pursued the topic. In truth, I'd been a little worried that if they did start a relationship, and if it didn't end well, then my friendship with Deena could suffer as a result. I probably should have given them more credit. I now realized they must've decided to be discreet—likely because Rocky wanted to spare Deena the kind of grilling Calvin had received from our mother.

She grinned noncommittally. "I'll dish when you do." Turning to Toby, she asked if he needed a box.

"I have one in my car," he said, grabbing up the second bouquet. He appeared eager to escape, lest we try to draw him into our personal conversation.

I held open the door for him. "Thanks, Toby. Have a nice morning!"

No sooner had he left, than Allie came into the kitchen to let us know we had customers in the café. We got to work and didn't have a chance to chat—or dish—until they left an hour later. Calvin had made a brief appearance to let us know he'd be in the greenhouse. He took Gus with him to give the pup a change of scenery.

Deena and I cleaned up in the café. Then she set out the ingredients for another batch of pansy sugar cookies, one of our signature treats. Toby had picked the last of the blossoms yesterday, and they were best used fresh. While Deena mixed the dough, I shared the highlights of my evening. She was enthralled.

"I can't believe you spent the night at Bellman Manor! Was it . . . strange?"

"Oh, it was quite strange. Interesting, though." When I told her about Taz's day planner, she wanted to hear every detail. While she rolled out cookie dough on the work surface behind the counter, I recounted what I could remember.

"I can't believe you didn't take notes," she said. "You're usually all about writing stuff down."

"I know. But I was wearing gloves and trying to hurry

and be careful at the same time. Anyway, I'm pretty sure the most salient parts are emblazoned in my brain."

"It sounds like a lot to keep straight, though," she persisted. "Especially when you factor in all those mishaps Annaliese told you about."

"Yeah, well, it's not like I'm officially investigating or anything." Yet, even as I made excuses, I started formulating lists in my mind. I grabbed a notebook from a shelf under the counter. "Maybe I'll just jot down a few things right now."

"Good idea," said Deena. "Wish I'd thought of it."

Smiling absently at her joke, I sat down at the nearest café table and began writing. For starters, I listed the names of all the wedding vendors, roughly in the order in which I'd met them: Regina, Nick, Anton, Kendall, and Gordon. To the right of each name, I wrote a few words based on my own observations, as well as on Taz's comments.

"Regina (caterer): Seemed irritated with Taz; he was condescending to her. He wrote 'said she'll behave.' She offered to take over as wedding planner."

After each note, I read Deena what I'd written, and she offered her own impressions. "Regina seemed nice," she said. "But maybe overly serious."

"Yeah, she seemed to have a history with Taz. But then again, I think they all did." I returned to my notebook.

"Nick (DJ): Said he's learned to put up with Taz's ways . . . but he sometimes seemed irritated. Seems to know the house well . . . was sneaking in Marissa's room? Professional name is Sidewinder—a snake."

"I didn't meet him," said Deena. "But you said he was friendly. Didn't he try to help you find a printer?"

"Yeah. He also came by Flower House yesterday." I frowned for a moment, then continued writing.

"Anton (stylist): Taz was angry/impatient with him for

not being serious; he seemed blasé. Taz wrote that Anton 'rode his coattails, as usual.'"

"I didn't meet him either," said Deena. "Does he do both hair and makeup? Or does he have a staff he supervises?"

I shrugged. "If he has any staff, they weren't there."

"Kendall (photographer): Seemed irritated with Taz's demands; pink hair found on his suitcase. He wrote that he should watch her, because she was 'up to something.'"

"It sounds like a lot of people were 'irritated,'" pointed out Deena. "That's hardly a motive for murder."

"I know. But that was just the surface. I imagine the feelings ran deeper for all of them."

"Gordon (violinist): Seemed uptight, unfriendly . . . Taz wrote that he 'knows what's good for him.'"

I paused. Was I projecting my own opinions? I hadn't really observed Gordon being unfriendly to Taz. It was me he seemed hostile to.

For a moment, I tapped my pen on the notebook. As an afterthought, I added Marissa's name at the bottom of the list. From what Annaliese had said, her daughter was apparently on or near the premises at the time of the murder.

I looked up at Deena, who was now using cookie cutters to cut circles in the dough. "What do you know about Marissa Lakely?"

"You mean besides the fact that she's the mayor's daughter, heir to the Bellman fortune, beautiful, privileged . . . what more do you need to know?"

"I don't know. From my limited interaction with her, she seemed a little down."

"Poor little rich girl?"

I glanced out the window, my gaze caught by a single yellow leaf floating downward in a breeze. "I have no idea. Maybe she was just stressed or missing her fiancé." I closed my notebook and rejoined Deena to help her press pansy blossoms onto the cut-out cookies. "She's probably our age or close to it. Had you ever met her before Monday?"

"Yes, actually," said Deena. "When we were children, we had a mutual friend, so I saw her at birthday parties. But then her parents sent her off to a boarding school in Knoxville. I'm sure she doesn't remember me."

"Hmm. Well, according to her mother, Marissa ran off yesterday because she's supposedly a suspect—in the murder of her own wedding planner. Bizarre, right?"

Deena looked up and frowned. "I don't buy it. Marissa would never *stab* anybody. That's way too messy."

"Maybe so, but she did take off. Speaking of which, do you know anything about her fiancé, Michael-William Princely?"

"Not a thing. He must not be from here. Why don't you look him up?"

"Good idea." I wiped my fingers on a napkin and found my phone. When I started typing the groom's name, a number of results popped up immediately. "Well, he definitely has an online presence. Mostly relating to his political stuff."

"What does he look like?" asked Deena, leaning over to see my phone.

"He looks . . . kind of like a middle-aged Ken doll. Tall and broad-shouldered. Pleasant, but in a slightly artificial way." I turned the phone so Deena could see.

She snorted. "Good description. He's older than I expected. That side part is so low it's bordering on a comb over."

I laughed. "Yeah, I'm guessing they didn't meet in college. I'm pretty sure he wasn't in the picture I saw of Marissa's graduation party."

I scrolled through Michael-William's social media profiles. There were a few pictures of him and Marissa, usually at fancy dinners, but no recent mention of the wedding. His last post was about a political fundraising event he'd managed a few nights ago—on Monday night.

"He's got a rock-solid alibi," I said, showing Deena a photo from the event. "Not that he's a suspect or anything."

"Maybe Marissa flew to Washington to be with him," suggested Deena.

"I don't know," I said doubtfully. "Annaliese seems certain she'll be back soon. And equally certain that the murder will be solved in time for the wedding to proceed as planned."

"And what do you think?" Deena asked.

"I think Annaliese is assuming a lot. In reality, there's a whole lot of uncertainty."

Deena slid the cookie sheet into the café's small oven and started filling a second tray. I helped myself to a purple pansy blossom and nibbled the edge of the petal. It was cold from the refrigerator and mildly sweet, with a faint lettuce-like flavor. It would be delicious with the buttery sweetness of the cookies.

What to do next? If I were a real investigator, I'd probably want to question the suspects—which isn't practical, considering they're all out of town. Nick is probably in Knoxville, and the others are presumably in Nashville. That is, all except for one.

I knew where Kendall was staying—thanks to my friend Richard. And, I suddenly remembered, I had a perfect excuse for going there.

Chapter 14

Richard Wales ran a charming farmhouse inn, aptly called Mountain View Bed & Breakfast. He'd been a couple of years ahead of Deena and me in high school, but I hadn't known him well—other than as a cute older boy I'd wished I'd known better. We'd become more acquainted over the past year, bonding over flowers and shared troubles, and I now counted him among my closest friends. He was also a customer of Flower House and liked to keep his home amply decorated with fresh arrangements year-round.

He waved from his front porch as I pulled up, then joined me at the Fiat. I opened the hatchback and handed him a crate of wrapped flowers.

"I've been hoping you'd stop by," he said. "Excitement follows you around, and I could use a vicarious fix."

Laughing, I grabbed another crate and followed him inside. "Doesn't your boyfriend share any exciting tidbits from the police department?"

He made a derisive sound with his lips. "Davy leaves work at work. That's usually fine with me, considering crime in Aerieville is normally of the petty kind. And I've no interest in the inner wrangling of department politics."

We walked through the homey mountain-lodge-style living room and into the large, sunny dining room. The long, oval table was covered with empty vases and fading flower arrangements.

"I gathered these up the minute you called," he said, making room for the crates we'd brought in. "Thought I'd save time, so you can get right to work . . . on filling me in."

"What do you want to hear about first?" I asked. "Marissa, the mansion, or the murder?"

"Ooh, sounds like a great title for a made-for-TV mystery movie. *Marissa, the Mansion, and the Murder.* Or *The Mansion, the Murder, and Marissa.* Or—"

"Or," I interrupted, "I could tell you about Calvin."

"Calvin's back?" Richard's eyes lit up.

"He's back." As I disassembled the old flower arrangements, I brought Richard up to speed on the events of the past few days. The only thing I left out was the information Annaliese had spilled about her supposed relationship with Taz, and Marissa's decision to skip out. Even though I'd told Deena, it now felt a little too gossipy to spread around.

Richard helped me dispose of the old greenery and wash out the vases. "Not to speak ill of the dead, but that wedding planner sounds like a real snot. He had no call to be so rude to you. . . . You're not a suspect, are you?"

"Not that I know of. Chief Walden knows me, and I had no real ties to the victim."

"Let's hope the state feels the same."

"What? What do you mean?"

He pulled out a chair and sat down. "Never mind. I don't want to worry you. Are you hungry? As soon as you finish up, we'll have lunch."

"Richard! Worry me about what? What have you heard?"

"Well, maybe I have heard a few things from Davy," he confessed. "There's some tension at the station. Too many cooks in the kitchen, as they say."

"Yeah, I kind of gathered that myself. Between Chief Walden and Captain Bradley, right?"

Richard nodded. "And those who ally with them. Walden wants to prove he's not a has-been, and that he's still the chief. And Bradley, who was in charge for six months, isn't too keen on giving up the power. Especially when she doesn't see eye to eye with the chief's methods."

I turned the vase I was working on and inserted a vibrant tiger lily, one of my favorite focal flowers for a late summer/ early autumn bouquet. "You mentioned 'the state.' Are the state police involved now?"

"They're trying to be. Neither Walden nor Bradley wanted to call them—that's one thing they have in common: matching outsized egos. Davy said the Tennessee Bureau of Investigation is asserting its jurisdiction. The local cops should be grateful for the help, but apparently there's some resentment. It was made worse when an agent implied the Aerieville force bungled the forensics process."

"Yikes. What a mess." I added one last accent flower and slid the vase toward Richard. "What do you think?"

"Gorgeous. You're such a pro."

I smiled, grateful for the compliment—especially since I'd been a "pro" for such a short amount of time.

"I'll take this one to the living room," he said, leaving me as I finished up the other arrangements.

When he returned, he went into the kitchen, and came out shortly with a glass of iced tea, which he placed on the table near me. "I have egg salad sandwiches and stoplight corn salad, whenever you're ready."

"Sounds great. I take it your guest isn't here?" I'd noticed there were no strange cars parked out front when I'd arrived.

"You mean the Berkleys? They left early to go hiking."

"Berkleys?" I said, confused.

"Yes. Retired couple from Georgia, sweet as peaches. They wanted to avoid the crowds in Gatlinburg, so they drove out of their way to stay here during their visit to the Smokies."

Smirking, I shook my head. He was teasing me. "I believe you have another guest. You told me so yourself."

"Oh, you mean the photographer, Kendall Waite." He winked cheekily. "She's not here either. Had a morning photo shoot out at the lake."

"Have you talked to her much?" I asked.

"A little. Oh! That reminds me. What time is it? I still need to make up her room." He got up abruptly, checking his watch. "Those small bouquets are for the bedrooms. Ready to bring them up?"

He helped me carry the small vase arrangements upstairs, one for his own room and two for the rented guest rooms. Saving Kendall's for last, he quickly dashed in and out of the other two rooms. Then he unlocked Kendall's door and went right in. I hesitated half a second, then followed.

Of course, I wouldn't dare touch anything. But I let my eyes roam, as Richard made the bed and fluffed the pillows. The room was tidy and spare, with not much to see beyond the pretty country-style furnishings and décor Richard had arranged. The only evidence the space had been occupied was the closed suitcase against the wall, a dangling cellphone charger from an outlet, and a few small items on the dresser: a menu from the Bluebird Café, a bottle of hair gel, and a round brush with pink hair caught in the bristles.

"Where should I put the flowers?" I asked.

"Here on the nightstand," he said, moving over a clock radio.

"She's neat," I remarked.

"No complaints here." He popped into the attached bathroom and came out with a handful of crumpled towels. "Be right back." A moment later, he returned with fresh towels and an empty plastic garbage bag and entered the bathroom again.

I wandered over to the bathroom doorway, as he hung up the towels and emptied the trash can. "You said you spoke with her a little bit? What's she like? I only met her briefly."

"She seems cool," said Richard. "Kind of serious and intense. To be honest, I got the impression she'd rather take gritty, artistic photos than wedding shots, but she knows where the money's at."

"She didn't say anything about Taz, did she?"

"No, and I was afraid to ask."

Finished in the bathroom, Richard took his garbage bag to the plastic waste bin near the bed. As he lifted it up to empty the contents into the bag, I glimpsed a handful of candy wrappers—and something else.

"Wait!" I said.

He froze and raised an eyebrow at me. "Why?"

"Could I just . . ." Trailing off, I reached into the trash can and plucked out what looked to be a business card. "I'm just curious."

"There's a surprise," he said wryly. He tapped the bottom of the can to dump out the wrappers, then placed it back on the floor. "Anything good?"

"Maybe." I stared at the business card, my wheels turning. It belonged to a person whose name kept cropping up: Tammy Reynaldo—Floral Designer—Nashville, TN.

Did it mean anything that Kendall had this card, and had

thrown it away? Not necessarily. In fact, probably not. It was probably perfectly innocent.

But it meant something to me. It meant it was high time for me to give this woman Tammy a call.

I placed the rest of Richard's flower arrangements on tables throughout the B&B, then joined him for a bite of lunch in the dining room. We chatted about mundane things, but my mind was never far from the mystery. What were the police doing? Did they now have Taz's planner in their possession? And why, oh why did I not take pictures of it while I had the chance?

"Don't you agree?" said Richard.

I gave a start. "Hmm? Oh, sorry. My mind wandered off for a minute."

Richard was grinning. "I just said, 'We ought to throw a party for your birthday. Don't you agree?' You clearly need a distraction from all this murder business."

"Aw, you remembered. I'd almost forgotten. But, yeah, a party sounds fun. We could hold it at the Flower House café."

"Perfect! What's the capacity there?"

"We have seating for twenty. That should be plenty."

Richard looked thoughtful. "Yeah, I suppose. I'll talk with Deena."

"Of course, I may be working a wedding that weekend. My birthday's on Sunday, and Marissa's wedding is supposed to be that Saturday." At Richard's doubtful expression, I shrugged. "I'm just saying."

He reached over and patted my arm. "That's my Sierra. Always the optimist. Don't go changing."

I threw my napkin at him. "You either, Richard."

A short while later, I helped him clean up, then gathered

my empty crates and said goodbye. As I stowed them in the Fiat and closed the hatchback, I heard a car pull into the driveway. I looked up to see whether it was the retired couple back from their hike or Kendall back from her photography job. Glimpsing Kendall's pink hair, I decided to wait a moment before leaving. She took her time gathering up her camera gear, then finally shut her car door and walked toward the house.

Upon seeing me, her face registered surprise, followed by suspicion. "You! What are you doing here?"

"Hi," I said, slightly taken aback. "I was just replacing the flowers and visiting with Richard. How are you doing?"

"Oh. I'm fine." Rearranging her features, she flashed a cold smile. "Sorry for being rude. You took me by surprise."

"That's okay," I said brightly.

She darted a glance around, as if to ensure no one else was nearby. "So, did you ever figure out what it was Taz was saying before he died?"

"Uh, no."

"Well, what did it sound like? Just because it didn't make sense to you, doesn't mean it wouldn't make sense to someone else." She leaned forward with a look so intense I felt compelled to take a step backward.

"There's nothing to tell," I said. "But I did want to ask you a question. You agreed to shoot the wedding, if it goes forward next weekend, right?"

"Yes. So?"

"I agreed to come back too. I guess everyone did. I'm just wondering if it's a good idea. I heard about all the mishaps, all the things that went wrong even before the—the tragedy with Taz."

Kendall narrowed her eyebrows, looking even more severe than before. "What are you saying? Do you think the wedding is cursed or something?"

"Cursed? No." I tried to laugh. Surely she was joking. "I was thinking more along the lines of sabotage."

I watched her closely, remembering what Taz had written in his datebook. He'd thought Kendall had been up to something. Now, she only acted bemused.

"Sabotage? Why would anyone sabotage a wedding? What would they have to gain?"

"Good question," I said. "Maybe to hurt Taz? Or Marissa?"

She gave me an odd look, like a cross between disbelief and pity. "You shouldn't go around saying such things. It could be dangerous."

Before I could reply, she brushed past me, trotted up the porch steps, and disappeared into the house.

I stared after her, more baffled than ever. *What was* that *all about?*

And was it a threat?

Chapter 15

I wasted no time in calling Tammy the florist. I wanted to know exactly why she'd quit such a lucrative job, and whether she knew anything about the other vendors—especially concerning Taz.

I first called from my car, before I even left Richard's driveway. A young-sounding woman answered the phone. When I asked to speak with Tammy, she requested my name and told me to hold. A minute later, she said Tammy wasn't available and offered to take a message. I gave her my number and asked for a call-back as soon as possible.

All afternoon, I anticipated that call. It never came. I assumed Tammy was busy, but I was still disappointed. The following morning, first thing after turning over the Open sign in the shop door, I called again. No one answered. An hour later, seated in the shop's office, I tried yet again. This time, someone picked up.

It was a woman's voice but not the same person as before. When I asked for Tammy, there was a pause, and then a short "She's not here," followed by a click.

Huh.

I stared at my phone for a moment, then set it on the desk and turned to the computer. Maybe I could find an email address for Tammy on her business website. A few clicks later, I found the site—a gorgeous, sophisticated webpage, featuring gallery-worthy images of elegant bridal bouquets. There was no email address, only a generic contact form. I was debating whether or not to send a message, when Calvin tapped on the doorframe.

"Hey," he said. "Happy Friday."

I looked up at him and smiled. "Hey."

I hadn't seen much of Calvin in the past twenty-four hours. We'd both been occupied with work—which wasn't necessarily a bad thing. But I'd been hoping for a chance to talk with him. Now that it was the weekend, I thought we might make plans to do something together.

"I've finally caught up with the greenhouse maintenance," he said. "I was going to update the website, but I see you're using the computer now."

"I'm finished." I closed the contact form, deciding in that moment that I would just try calling again later. I preferred a more direct approach, anyway. "Take a look at this site. Do you think we should model ours after this one?"

He placed one hand on the desk and leaned over me to peer at the computer screen. "Hmm. We could do something like this. Looks expensive, though. I wouldn't want to scare away any of your local customers."

Distracted by his close proximity, I found myself studying his profile instead of the webpage. When I didn't respond, he turned to face me. I swallowed.

"Uh, yeah. Good point."

A slow smile crept over his lips. For a moment, we looked into each other's eyes. I flashed on our last almost-intimate encounter, interrupted so rudely on Wednesday night, and felt myself leaning toward him.

As if on cue, Gus scurried into the office and made a beeline for Calvin. He barely had time to straighten up from the desk before Gus jumped on his legs. Then Deena poked her head into the office.

"Hey, Sierra," she began. Seeing the two of us, and my faint blush, she grinned apologetically. "Sorry about this, but there are a couple of cops here to see you."

I felt a pang of alarm. "Are there any customers in the shop?"

"Not at the moment. Do you want me to send them back here instead of the café?"

I glanced around the small, cozy office and shook my head. "No, I'll meet them up front. There's no hiding their patrol car, anyway."

Gesturing for Calvin to take over my seat at the computer, I headed to the shop front with Gus at my side. Captain Bradley stood admiring our window display, lush with late summer dahlias in hues of mauve, burnt-orange, and honey-gold. Next to her was a plainclothes officer I'd never seen before. He wore navy trousers, a white dress shirt, and a gray-striped tie. With his neatly trimmed hair and pleasantly neutral expression, he could have passed for any average businessman. It was the badge on his belt that gave him away: TBI, our state's version of the FBI.

Captain Bradley smiled at Gus and offered her hand for him to sniff. The other officer took a step back and stuffed his hands in his pockets. *Strike one, in my book.*

"Sierra," said Captain Bradley, "this is Agent Collins. He has a few questions, if you don't mind."

"Sure. Would you like to sit in the café?"

They sat side by side, with me across from them, as if we were engaged in a job interview rather than a homicide inquiry. Deena asked if they'd like coffee or tea, but they declined, saying they wouldn't take long. I sincerely hoped that would prove true.

Collins folded his hands on the table and affected a casual, friendly expression, presumably to put me at ease. "Miss Ravenswood, I understand you were brought on as florist the same day the incident occurred at Bellman Manor."

"Yes, that's correct," I said.

He nodded, then asked, as if he were merely curious, "Had you ever been to the mayor's home?"

"No. That was my first time."

"You didn't know the Lakelys, outside their role as the town's *first family*, so to speak?" He grinned at his own word choice, as if he'd made a clever joke.

"No. I'd never met any of the family before Monday."

"Alright. And what time did you arrive that day?"

"Six o'clock."

"Six exactly?"

"Yes. I know because Taz had asked me to meet him at six o'clock, and I didn't want to be late."

"Good, good. Had you ever met the victim, Taz? Or heard of him?"

I shook my head. "No." *So far, so good.* I was grateful for the softball questions, but I still felt on edge. Something about the agent's demeanor made me feel like I was on the witness stand, about to be trapped by a clever cross-examiner.

"Okay," he said. "Now, could you please walk me through your movements after you arrived? You entered through the back door, I assume?"

"Yep." I gave a brief account of my arrival and introduction to Taz, the tour he provided of the great room, and my quick walk-through of the ballroom. I concluded with the meeting in the dining room.

"Where did you go after the meeting?"

"Nick showed me to a home office with a printer I might borrow. He left me in there, and I texted with Deena for a couple of minutes." I gestured toward Deena, who pretended to be working behind the café counter. She waved in response. "Do you want to see our phones to verify the time?" I asked.

Agent Collins stretched his mouth into a fleeting closed-lip smile. "Maybe later. Go on, please."

"Okay. Well, next I went into the kitchen. I planned to step outside, but I heard a noise, so I went into the great room to see what was going on." I expected he would want to hear about how I found Taz on the floor beside the grand staircase, but apparently he had something else in mind.

"You didn't go upstairs?"

"No."

"Hmm." He cocked his head, as if he found my answer puzzling. "You didn't go up to the second floor?"

"No," I repeated and pushed up my sleeves. *Is it warm in here?*

"How, then, do you explain the fact that your finger-prints were found on the doorknobs of more than half of the second-floor rooms?"

Uh-oh. "Um. I don't understand."

"I don't understand either, Miss Ravenswood. You told me you walked through the first floor and that you went up to the third-floor ballroom. When were you on the second floor?"

"When?" I echoed. I glanced at Captain Bradley. Her face was impassive. Agent Collins stared at me patiently, as if he had all the time in the world.

I thought fast. The only second-floor rooms I'd entered the day of the murder were the den and its tandem guest room. If my fingerprints were found on any other doors, the prints must have been taken . . . yesterday. The TBI must have conducted its own belated search of the manor.

"Ohh," I said, as it clicked into place. "I thought you were talking about Monday. I returned to the house on Wednesday night, at Mrs. Lakely's invitation."

He narrowed his eyes, clearly not pleased with this revelation. If I wasn't mistaken, a flash of amusement crossed Bradley's face, before she quickly reverted to stoic-cop face.

"Why did you return?" he asked. "I thought you didn't know the Lakelys before Monday."

I gave him an innocent shrug. "I make friends easily?"

A twitch of his jaw undermined his smooth exterior, but the agent kept his cool. "Are you aware that there was a fire at the manor on Wednesday night?"

I felt my eyes widen, but I kept mum. *Of course, I'm aware. I put it out!*

"Miss Ravenswood?" he prompted.

I was unsure how much I should say. *Probably the less, the better.* Clearly, Annaliese hadn't told the cops I was there Wednesday night. I wondered how she explained the fire. I just knew Collins was going to ask me why I didn't report the incident to the police. He'd probably also ask if I knew about Taz's day planner—assuming Annaliese had turned it in, like she said she would.

At this point, I was on the verge of requesting permission to call a lawyer. Then the front door jingled. *Saved by the bell?* A moment later Flo Morrison, from the bakery next door, stepped tentatively into the café.

"Hi there," she said. "I hope I'm not interrupting anything." She lasered in on Agent Collins with unabashed interest.

He gave her a polite smile, then nodded at Officer Bradley, and stood up. "Miss Ravenswood, we have several more questions, but we've taken enough of your time today."

"Oh! Okay." *So, that's it? They're letting me off the hook?*

"Would you come to the station on Monday, so we can complete our interview?"

"Monday? Uh, sure. I suppose I can do that." I wasn't thrilled, but at least I'd have time to prepare.

"Wonderful. And, just to let you know, we'll be administering polygraph tests to all our interviewees that day."

"Polygraph tests?" I was starting to sound like a parrot, but I didn't know what else to say.

"It's voluntary, but highly recommended. And, of course, it's potentially beneficial for the innocent. Like you, right?"

"Right," I said weakly.

Flo stood by with her mouth gaping, as the two officers left the café. At the archway, Bradley murmured something to Collins and he grunted in reply. Then he continued to the exit, and she came back.

"Could I order a chamomile tea to go?" she asked.

"Of course," said Deena. "Coming right up."

While Deena prepared the tea, Flo said she suddenly remembered something, and left the shop. Bradley turned to me with a stern look.

"Sierra, I know what you're doing, and you need to stop."

"I'm not—" I began, but she didn't let me finish.

"Listen. *If* you're trying to play detective on this case, don't. Back off before you get yourself into trouble."

Deena placed a paper cup of hot tea into a cardboard sleeve and set it before the officer. "On the house," she said.

Now Bradley directed her disapproving gaze to Deena. "No," she snapped. "I'll pay."

"Sorry," Deena said meekly.

After Bradley left, Deena gave me an apologetic look. "I thought I was being nice. Now she thinks I was trying to bribe her!"

I waved away her concern. "You're fine. I'm the one in hot water."

And now I had a lie detector test to look forward to.

The visit from the police had cast a pall on my happy weekend vibes. I told myself I shouldn't worry about the polygraph test. I was an honest person by nature. I had no intention of lying to the police—nor should I have to. After all, I hadn't done anything wrong.

Had I?

Of course, Captain Bradley was right. I *had* been poking my nose into the investigation. What was worse, I didn't intend to stop. Now, more than ever, I felt I had to do whatever I could to get some answers.

But what could I do? As I worked in the back room, filling orders and arranging flowers, I stewed over the problem. I was doubly frustrated because no one would call me back. Tammy obviously didn't want to talk to me. And now it seemed that neither did Annaliese. I'd tried and failed to reach her more than once since the officers had left. I wanted to know what she'd told them—and whether she'd heard from Marissa.

I was cleaning up the trimmings from a cheerful get-well bouquet when I heard the shop phone ring. Though it was a welcome sound, often indicating another order, I didn't expect it to be for me. Tammy and Annaliese had my cell phone number.

Allie peeked into the room. "Sorry to interrupt. There's a call for you. A Nick Siden."

"You don't have to be sorry," I said automatically, wiping my hands on a towel. "I'll take it in the office."

Calvin had gone back out to the greenhouse, so I sat

again in the swivel chair in front of the computer. Like much of what Felix had left me, the computer was a relic and would probably have to be upgraded soon. The telephone, an old rotary, was practically an antique.

"Hello?" I said, tucking the receiver on my shoulder, as I reached for a pen and a piece of scrap paper. Something about being on a landline always made me want to doodle.

"Hi, Sierra," said Nick. "I'm glad I caught you. I'm heading to Knoxville, but I wanted to give you a heads-up. State investigators are looking into Taz's murder now."

"I know. I just met one of them."

"Have you had a chance to speak with Annaliese?"

I felt a slight twinge of guilt. Nick had wanted me to talk Annaliese into postponing the wedding. I'd been so sidetracked at her house, the wedding barely came up. And now, for some reason, she wasn't calling me back.

"I spoke with her a little the other night," I said. "She still seems determined to go forward with the wedding."

"Oh," he said, sounding disappointed.

"Nick, can I ask you something? Why did Tammy Reynaldo really quit?"

"Tammy? I don't know for sure. All I know is that she and Taz argued a lot. He was really demanding, and she didn't like to be bossed around. She even said something to that effect. Something like, 'You don't own me.' Or 'You can't make me.' Crazy, if you ask me. That pride cost her a lot of money."

"Yeah, maybe," I said vaguely. Drawing circles on the scrap paper, I wondered if that was really all there was to it. I also realized Nick might not be the most reliable source of information about Taz. If I wanted to learn more about the wedding planner, I'd do well to speak with someone who wasn't a suspect in his murder.

"Anyway," Nick was saying, "I guess we'll have to wait and see. I'll see you—"

"One more thing," I said, cutting him off. "Sorry. I think you mentioned Taz mopping floors a few years ago. Do you know where that was?" If I could track down any of Taz's old co-workers, maybe I could get some insight into why someone would want to kill him.

There was a pause on the other end of the line. Then Nick said, "Uh, yeah. Nashville. Place called Spa'Dae."

"Spa Day?"

"One word, and it's spelled like 'ice cream sundae,' with an 'ae' at the end. And there's an apostrophe after 'spa,' for no apparent reason."

I chuckled. "Fancy."

"I guess. I only know about it because Anton mentions it a lot. That's where he works."

I thanked Nick and hung up, then stared down at the doodle-filled paper on the desk before me. I'd drawn over-lapping circles, vine-like curlicues, and elaborate question marks. Lots of question marks.

Chapter 16

The idea had been building for a while. Like a slow-moving train rumbling in the distance, it had finally rolled from the back of my mind to the foreground—and the noise and heft of the notion could no longer be ignored.

I should go to Nashville.

All through my lunch of café leftovers, and well into the afternoon, I kept mulling over the idea. It seemed crazy, so I kept it to myself and focused on work. But the idea persisted.

About an hour before closing time, I ran out of orders to fill. Deena was restocking the tea in the café, and Allie was perched on a stool behind the cash register, reading a book—an epic fantasy from the looks of it. Calvin had taken Gus for a walk. Feeling restless, I took a broom outside and swept the porch and front steps.

The swishing of the broom became a meditation, keeping my body busy as my mind fussed to itself. *Most of the suspects are in Nashville. Taz was from there. Tammy's there. Maybe the answer is there.*

I liked Nashville, quite a lot. I'd made it my home for

a time, back when I'd dropped out of college to chase my dreams of music and stardom. Some good things had happened to me there. And some not so good things.

Calvin and Gus sauntered up the sidewalk. I leaned on the broom handle and regarded them with affection. *No regrets in returning to Aerieville. Lots of good things have happened here too.*

Deena came out to the porch and stood gazing at the sky. "It's chilly," she said, pulling her sweater closed.

Gus ran up to jump on my legs, and Calvin sat on the porch steps. "It feels great to me," he said.

I looked at each of them in turn. "Guys, I've been thinking."

"I'm sure you have," said Deena. "Did you tell Calvin about the grilling you got—and what awaits you on Monday?"

"What awaits?" he asked.

"The cops want me to take a lie detector test. Can you believe it?"

His face registered surprise and concern. "Why? You're not a suspect. Are you?"

"I guess they're covering all bases. Or grasping at straws."

"So, what have you decided?" asked Deena. "And is there anything I can do to help?"

"Actually, I think there is." I threw her a hopeful smile. "How would you like to take a road trip?"

Once the decision was made, our plans came together quickly. Calvin wanted to go with us, but I convinced him it would be more helpful if he'd keep Gus and mind the shop. What I didn't say was that he'd also be a distraction. Considering the romantic tension between us, I knew I'd be able to focus on the mystery better without having him so near.

Deena and I each ran home to pack a few things, and I gassed up the Fiat. We hit the highway before dark.

As we headed west toward the setting sun, I couldn't help thinking of Marissa. She'd run off with little more than I'd stuffed into my own overnight bag. I asked Deena if she had any theories on the matter.

"A runaway bride?" she said. "It smacks of cold feet, doesn't it? And you did say she seemed despondent, even before Taz died."

"Yeah." I tapped an idle rhythm on the steering wheel. "That could be it. Only, I don't know, that almost feels a little too cliché. I mean, how many people about to be married run off without telling anyone where they're going?"

"You'd be surprised," said Deena, with a touch of tartness in her voice.

I slapped my hand to my mouth. "I'm sorry! That was stupid of me." How could I have forgotten? Before returning to Aerieville herself, Deena had been engaged twice and didn't make it to the altar either time.

"It's okay," she sighed. "It's ancient history now." Then she flashed me a grin. "Your doubts don't surprise me. You've been shot with Cupid's arrow."

"Who, me?" I smirked without meeting her eyes. I couldn't deny it. My heart felt light. I was about to tell Deena about Calvin's treasure hunt invitation, but then I thought of something else. "Maybe there *is* a more romantic angle to Marissa's flight. She could have eloped. She probably met up with Michael-William, and they jetted off to Hawaii or the Caribbean." I indulged in a moment of dreamy speculation, recalling my old fantasies of intercontinental romance and adventure.

"Or maybe she's just creeped out," Deena said flatly. "I wouldn't want to stay at the site of an unsolved murder."

So much for my rose-colored fantasy. "That's valid. Though you'd think she'd at least talk to her parents about it."

"Maybe she did," said Deena. "Annaliese may not have told you everything."

"True. But she *was* open about her past with Taz, and about Marissa supposedly being a suspect—which, of course, could be the real reason Marissa left."

"You mean, because *she* killed Taz?"

I shook my head. "I don't know. It doesn't exactly look good for her, running off like she did. I can't believe she did it, though."

Pushing my sunglasses to the top of my head, I concentrated on the road. Dusk had settled over the valley, blurring the details in the scenery. I knew I was in the dark about what had really happened at Bellman Manor. And Deena was right that Annaliese might be holding something back. She still hadn't responded to the messages I'd left her after my visit from Agent Collins. But I didn't let these things bug me. The truth was out there.

We pulled off at the next exit for a quick bite to eat. For the rest of the drive, we turned our conversation to lighter topics. Deena surprised me by announcing she'd decided to take up running. She planned to sign up for the Turkey Trot in November. Then again, I probably shouldn't have been surprised. Training for the race gave her a handy excuse to spend some time with Aerieville's most popular personal trainer. I suspected I wasn't the only one who'd been shot with Cupid's arrow.

As we neared Nashville, my pulse quickened with the multilane traffic, and my heart soared at the sight of the twin spires of the tallest building. The bright city lights gave me a thrill of complicated emotions—nervous excitement chief among them.

Deena had used her smart phone to book us a room in a modest downtown hotel. She was a more experienced traveler than me and knew how to find the best deals. As soon as we checked in, we plopped down on our side-by-side double beds and formulated a game plan for the following day. I spread open a map I'd picked up in the hotel lobby. Deena looked up addresses on her phone.

"Tammy's flower shop first?" she asked.

"Yeah. I want to accost her as she's going in. In a nice way, of course."

"Of course."

"After that, we'll head to the salon, Spa'Dae, and try to gather some intel on Taz. Then let's check out Regina's restaurant. We can grab lunch there."

Taking a purple gel pen from my purse, I circled our targets on the map. Our plan was foolproof. Easy-peasy. Pop in, ask a few questions, pop on out. What could go wrong?

Chapter 17

I slept surprisingly well, considering the unfamiliar bed—my second one this week. We rose early, helped ourselves to the continental breakfast in the lobby, and checked out. This was going to be a quick trip.

Hopping in the Fiat, we took to the streets of Nashville, bustling with Saturday-morning energy. As when I'd returned to Aerieville, the city was both familiar and strange at the same time. Time had marched on, and so had I.

I pointed out places I remembered as we navigated to Tammy's flower shop. I'd never been there, but it was easy to find. We arrived early enough that parking wasn't a problem. Nothing was open yet.

Sipping coffees from hotel to-go cups, we settled in for our morning stakeout. I was fiddling with the radio, trying to choose some music to fit the occasion, when Deena grabbed my arm. "There she is!"

"Let's go!" I jerked open my car door and scooted up to the sidewalk. Tammy wasn't going to avoid me this time.

"Hello! Good morning!" I called.

Startled, she darted her eyes from me to Deena. The way

she clutched her purse, she must've thought we were going to mug her. She was younger than I expected, with mousy brown hair and small features. She reminded me a little bit of Allie.

"Tammy?" I said, already doubting.

"I'm Shelby. And we're not open yet. You'll have to come back." At least she looked a little less frightened.

I backed up a smidge to give her breathing room and copped a friendly attitude. "We're not customers. We're sister florists."

"You're sisters?" She gave Deena a sidelong glance, evidently puzzled by the idea that I could have an Asian American sister.

I resisted the urge to roll my eyes. Making a circle with my hand to encompass all three of us, I said, "No, I mean *we're* sisters—fellow florists. Compadres."

She still looked confused. Deena spoke up. "We're here to see Tammy about a job. Will she be in soon?"

"Oh. She won't be in today. She's out decorating."

"All day?" I asked.

"Yeah. She's got three weddings and a fundraiser event." Deena whistled. "Busy lady."

Guess she really didn't need Marissa's wedding, I thought.

Undaunted, I asked if she could share the locations of any of the events. "I'd love to see her work."

Shelby wrinkled her little nose in a disapproving frown. "I don't think I should. It's not like they're public affairs."

"We wouldn't stay," I said. "Honest, I only need, like, five minutes of Tammy's time."

"Can't you just come back on Monday?"

"We're from out of town," said Deena. "And we have to leave tonight."

"We drove all the way from Aerieville," I added.

Something changed in Shelby's expression. "Aerieville? Is this about the Lakely wedding?"

"Yes!" I jumped on her interest. "Exactly. Do you know why Tammy quit the job?"

"No, and I wish I did. I spent a lot of hours prepping for that wedding. I wrote up all the supply lists and planned the wholesale orders for all the bouquets and everything. What a waste."

"Did she say anything about it?" I asked.

"She just said the wedding planner was impossible to work with. It was odd, if you ask me." She pursed her lips, looking thoughtful. "You know, if you really want to talk to Tammy today, I can tell you where she'll be tonight. She's been talking about this concert she's going to at Orchestra Hall. Some kind of philharmonic something-or-other. That's partly why she's not coming back to the shop this evening. She's got to be at the hall by six o'clock."

"Good to know!" I could've kissed the girl. "Thank you, Shelby."

Our next stop was the day spa and salon so cleverly called Spa'Dae. From the moment we stepped into the lobby, luxurious and pristine with white oak floors, overstuffed sky blue chairs, and silvery water-inspired decor, I felt a sense of calm and longing. *Wouldn't it be nice to afford the services in a place such as this?* Ah well, that wasn't why we were here.

I was about to ask the young woman behind the counter if she knew Taz, when Deena placed a hand on my arm. To the woman, she said, "Do you have any openings today for any nail or facial services?"

The woman looked up from her computer and gave us a welcoming smile. "Normally we don't take walk-ins, but we had a last-minute cancellation this morning. So, you're in luck!"

"Well . . ." I began, but Deena cut me off.

"Terrific!"

Five minutes later, we were ushered into the nail studio and led to a row of leather chairs. Off came our shoes and socks, and in went our feet into hammered copper bowls of steamy rose-scented water. The receptionist handed us fluted glasses of sparkling wine.

Deena and I sank back into our chairs and sighed at the same time. "*Ahh.*"

I swiveled my head to look at my friend. "Why do I feel like we're shirking our duties?"

"Relax. This can be part of our mission. We're infiltrating the organization, or something like that. Also, this is my treat. For your birthday."

"Aw, you don't have to—" I stopped myself mid-protest. Deena's earnest expression reminded me that sincere gifts should be sincerely received. Besides, I knew she could use the break as much as I could. "Thank you. This is awesome."

Relaxing deeper into the cushy chair, I subtly cased the room. *So, this is where Taz mopped the floor. Wonder if anyone here knew him back then?* When I'd asked the receptionist, she said she'd never even heard of him.

We were the only customers in the pedicure area. Nearby, two other ladies were receiving manicures by technicians wearing cloth face masks. Through an open doorway in the center of the nail studio, I had a partial view of a bright and spacious hair salon. In the one occupied chair I could see, a middle-aged woman with foil-wrapped hair sat flipping through a magazine.

According to the menu in the lobby, the spa offered a host of services, from every kind of waxing to every kind of massage—many of which I'd never heard of. As intriguing as they sounded, they weren't part of the cancellation we were filling. We'd have to settle for whatever we could learn on the beauty side of the place.

After a short soak, two young men sat on stools at our feet and gave us the royal treatment: exfoliating salt scrub, hot stone massage of our feet and lower legs, and a slathering of aromatherapy cream. My tootsies had never felt so soft. The technicians were intent on their work and apparently not inclined to chat. I kept trying to engage mine with small talk, but he only gave me polite one-word answers and silent nods. As he applied the final coat of polish (poppy red in honor of my last sleuthing adventure), I tried one more time.

"Have you worked here long?"

"Mm-hmm."

"Do you know Anton Cooley?"

He shrugged noncommittally.

Okay. "Did you know Taz Banyan?" At his blank look, I addressed Deena's technician. "How about you? Did you know Taz Banyan? He worked here a few years ago."

He shook his head. Another negative.

An older woman passed by, carrying a stack of towels. With short gray-and-black ombré hair and a large-pocketed white apron with assorted makeup brushes sticking out, she looked like a master beauty artist. She glanced at us curiously before stowing the towels in a cabinet along the wall. On her way back, she walked over. Our technicians left, and she introduced herself as Maeve.

"Did I hear you mention Taz Banyan?"

"Yes!" I sat up straight in my chair. "Did you know him?"

"I sure did. He was hard to miss." At my encouraging nod, she went on. "He started out as a janitor here. He worked nights, but sometimes he would come in early, wearing these flashy expensive suits. People kept mistaking him for management." She chuckled at the memory.

"Expensive suits?" I said. "Did he have a second job?" Spa'Dae was certainly upscale, but I couldn't imagine it compensated its janitors *that* well.

"I don't think so. Taz was a student, studying hospitality. It sure paid off for him too. He was still in school when he planned his first event." There was a note of pride in her voice. "He got popular real fast. Written up in the papers and everything."

"Did he get along with everyone?"

"Get along?" The question seemed to puzzle her.

"I heard he could be somewhat demanding and . . . a little gruff sometimes."

"Ah. Maybe so. He was certainly confident. Besides the flashy suits, he liked to wear gold bracelets and such. He bought a nice car too, before he quit here and joined the big time."

"Smart," I said. "It sounds like he dressed for the part he wanted, and got it." It was a philosophy I followed myself.

"Yeah." She smiled wistfully. "Taz Banyan." She said his name as if he were a legend. It struck me that neither of us had mentioned his death. If she didn't already know he'd passed away, I sure didn't want to be the one to break the news. Before I could ask her about Anton, we were summoned to the manicure stations. Maeve left, returning to the adjacent hair salon.

As with our pedicurists, the manicurists weren't very helpful to our fact-finding mission. They were chatty enough, but they hadn't known Taz. As for Anton, they knew him but didn't have much to say. He was good at his job and had a loyal client base, and that was about all they were willing or able to share. In Aerieville, gossip flowed like water. Here at Spa'Dae, discretion was apparently more important.

While the technicians applied our polish—a sparkly pale pink for my short fingernails and a sophisticated garnet red for Deena's longer nails—our conversation bandied from topic to topic. Deena asked me questions about my stint in Nashville. I'd been a hardworking musician back then, performing everywhere that would have me, from street corners and coffee shops to, at the height of my experience, the stage. It was a tough business, though. And, as Deena had said of her broken engagements, it now felt like ancient history.

As we chatted, I continued to gaze around the salon. A wall of shelves held assorted beauty products, many of which featured a familiar daisy logo. I recognized it from the French bath soaps I'd found in the guest room at Bellman Manor. At the very moment I was studying the daisy image, I detected the buzz of my phone inside my purse. *Calvin.* Without looking, I knew it was him. My lips curved into a smile. I'd get back to him as soon as my nails were dry.

When our manicurists released us to a seating area, with strict instructions not to touch anything, I took the opportunity to wander around. Pausing at the threshold between the nail studio and the hair salon, I peeked into the brightly lit multi-mirrored parlor and counted eight salon chairs in two rows of four. About half the chairs were occupied. The woman who'd had aluminum foil in her hair now sported newly-dyed tresses in vivid shades of maroon and red— tresses that at that moment were being snipped and combed by none other than Anton, the wedding stylist. I ducked behind a large potted plant to observe him unseen.

As before, his long brown hair was twisted in a knot on the back of his head, á la the man bun. He wore colorful Lycra pants and a cropped gray sweatshirt—an outfit that managed to look simultaneously chic and comfortable. He wasn't unattractive, though his eyes were rather close-set and his lips seemed artificially plump. But there was something about him, in his manner and affectations, that gave him an air of phoniness.

As I watched, Anton set down the scissors and comb and walked over to a wall of metal shelving. He returned shortly with a cylindrical white bottle, balanced on the palm of one hand. He held it before his client, as if he were presenting a rare bottle of fine wine. While I couldn't make out his words, I gathered the tenor—he was in salesman mode. *Ah. Of course.* That explained the phony vibes. I wondered if he worked on commission.

He must have felt my gaze. Through the mirror, his eyes locked on mine and his eyebrows quirked up in an expression of pleasant surprise. Swinging around, he waved me over with an exaggerated gesture of welcome. I had no choice but to step out from behind the plant and give him an answering wave.

"Hello there!" I called. "Fancy meeting you here."

Deena sidled up and nudged me with her elbow. "'Fancy meeting you here'?" She mocked my words under her breath.

"I panicked," I whispered back.

Anton patted his client's shoulders and removed her cape. As she gushed at him, he simpered and sent her on her way. Then he turned and beckoned to me again. Holding my fingers apart to protect the wet nails, I approached him with a friendly smile. Deena followed close behind.

"Well, well," he drawled, "if it isn't the flower girl of Aerieville. You're a long way from home."

"Oh, not too long," I said lightly. "My friend Deena surprised me with a spa day for my birthday."

I introduced Deena to Anton. She fluttered her fingers at him, showing off her shiny nails. "This place had the best reviews," she said.

"Of course," he said. "That's because it *is* the best." He waited a beat, eyeing us with an inscrutable squint. "What a coincidence, though."

I decided to come clean—at least partially. I figured it might serve to open him up. "Also," I said, lowering my voice to a somber degree, "I heard Taz used to work here. I've been curious about him. I thought I might offer my condolences to his family and friends, but it seems as if not many people here knew him."

Anton retrieved a broom from a nearby closet and swept the hair trimmings around his chair, pushing them into a big pile of plum-colored fluff. "Taz wasn't here long. And, when he was, he mostly worked at night."

"Maeve remembered him," offered Deena.

"She seemed fond of him and his 'flashy' suits and jewelry," I added.

Anton smirked. "Taz did make an impression, that's for sure."

"Maeve mentioned he was still in school when he started event planning," I said. "It sounds like he found success really fast."

"It always seems that way, doesn't it? Everyone famous was unknown at first. Toiling away, year after year, until one day—boom. An overnight sensation." He flashed a coy smile, before bending to scoop up the dustpan.

I recalled the note Taz had made in his datebook, about Anton riding his coattails. "You're right," I said. "Along with the myth of the overnight sensation is the idea that successful people make it on their own. They usually have help along the way."

"Ain't that the truth," said Anton.

"Who helped Taz?" I did my best to maintain an innocent, just-curious, expression on my face.

Anton pinched his full lips and shot me a sly look. "Remember Regina Ervin?"

"Yeah, sure."

"The caterer?" asked Deena.

"Caterer, chef, event planner. She's about as ambitious as Taz was. They went to school together, you know."

I didn't know, but I wanted to hear more. "Hospitality school?"

He nodded. "They were friends, tight friends. They were going to be partners and open a wedding planning business together."

"What happened?" asked Deena.

"He ditched her. As soon as he started getting all the attention, he decided to reap all the glory and profit. Solo." Anton lifted one shoulder, baring a tank top beneath his boxy sweatshirt. "Can't say I blame him."

That explained the coldness I'd observed in Regina's reaction to Taz at Bellman Manor. It was a wonder she'd agreed to work with him at all.

"They must've stayed on good terms," I said. "Or else she decided to forgive him."

Anton placed his hands on the back of the salon chair and swiveled it slowly from side to side. "It was hard to say no to Taz. The bigger he got, the more influential he was. No matter your personal feelings about the guy, most folks in the business couldn't afford not to work with him."

I nodded. This was consistent with what Nick had told me. From a financial standpoint, it was worth it to put up with Taz's domineering ways.

"There's another stereotype," I mused. "The bigger and more powerful a person becomes, the more they can get away with." I was thinking of corrupt politicians and Hollywood bigwigs who'd been exposed as tyrants or abusers after years of avoiding any repercussions for their actions. I hoped it didn't really happen as often as the media made it seem.

To my surprise, Anton started laughing. It was a low

snicker at first, then grew into a belly-shaking chortle. He sat down in his salon chair and wiped his watering eyes.

"You," he said, wagging a finger at me. "You're a sly one."

I glanced at Deena, who looked as baffled as I felt. "What do you mean?"

"You're asking all these questions, but you clearly already have the scoop. Lord knows any one of a dozen people could have told you."

"Told me what?" I wracked my brain, trying to figure out what it was I was missing.

Anton fixed me with an amused stare. "About the kickbacks, of course. Taz commanded a hefty referral fee from every vendor who worked with him. He got his cut out of everyone else's earnings."

I scrunched my brow in confusion. "I wasn't asked to pay a fee like that."

"Of course not, honey. It wasn't exactly an ethical arrangement. And you weren't hired by Taz, right?"

"Right."

"Ah, well," said Anton, pushing himself to his feet. "No more finder's fees for Taz now. Someone put an end to *that* little scheme."

Chapter 18

First they took away the use of my hands, then they covered my face and took away my ability to see and speak. Was this a spa or a prison?

Lying on a chaise lounge chair with hardening mud on my face and sliced cucumbers over my eyes, I tried to relax. It wasn't easy. I could barely part my lips, and I had a million thoughts chasing through my head. Breathing slowly in and out through my nostrils, I reminded myself that this was good for me. This was self-care for the body, mind, and spirit. I should just let go and enjoy it.

Anton sure was candid—and quite generous with his knowledge. It was too bad he had a customer waiting for him. Who knows what else he might have revealed?

Then again, we'd had to move on too. Maeve had shown us to the facial area, through a doorway that was hidden behind a set of folding rattan screens on one end of the hair salon. The lighting was dimmer in here, and soft nature sounds played in the background. Even so, I was too keyed up to relax. As soon as the aesthetician removed the clay from my face, applied a thick moisturizer, and left once more, I tested my voice.

"Psst. Deena. Are you awake?"

"Of course," she replied from somewhere nearby. "What's up?"

"I can't stop thinking about what Anton told us."

"Same here," she admitted. "I would have asked if you'd want to skip the facials, but I think I was too stunned to form words."

"Me too. Anton basically just identified a motive for every one of the vendors, including himself. I'm sure no one liked paying those kickbacks."

Deena was silent for a moment, then said, "Do you think it was illegal? I don't think finder's fees are necessarily illegal."

I removed the cucumbers from my eyes and held onto them, blinking into the orangey dim light. "I don't know. But it sounds like Taz was enriching himself instead of prioritizing his clients' interests. You know? Instead of getting the best deals or the best services for Marissa's wedding, what if he was choosing vendors based on who would pay him the most?"

"Mm-hmm. It almost sounds like fraud. Maybe extortion too, if he was shaking down the other vendors." She paused for a second. "Is that the right term? *Shaking down*?"

I laughed quietly. "Sure." Thinking back to Taz's datebook, I said, "Maybe that's what he meant when he wrote that all the vendors were 'on board.' He meant they were on board with his fee arrangement."

"Didn't he also write that someone 'knew what was good for him'?" asked Deena.

"That's right. It was Gordon, I think. Takes on a whole new meaning now."

Deena shifted on her lounge chair. "Maybe *that's* why Tammy quit!"

"Could be. Though she must have agreed to pay Taz at first. She didn't quit until two weeks before the wedding."

"Do you still want to catch her at the concert tonight?"

"Yeah, as long as we're here, I'd like to try." Before we'd left Shelby, I'd asked her to describe Tammy's appearance. She'd done one better, and directed us to her boss's social media pages. Lucky for us, the florist had a penchant for selfies. She seemed to favor bold makeup, and she kept natural silver strands in her wavy dark hair. I guessed her to be in her fifties. I was reasonably confident I'd be able to recognize her in person.

The esthetician returned to cleanse our faces and apply toner. "Last step," she promised, no doubt sensing our impatience. "Youthful-glow serum. It just needs to set for a couple of minutes."

"Bring on the glow," said Deena.

"You know," I said, when we were alone again, "I was thinking about Kendall and how Taz thought she was up to something. What if she was sick of his bribery scheme, or whatever you want to call it, and she wanted to expose it? Maybe she was looking for evidence and planned to snitch on Taz to the Lakelys."

"And Taz found out and confronted her? So she killed him?"

"It's possible."

We both fell silent, each absorbed in our own thoughts. I was trying to imagine a scenario in which the stabbing could have been accidental. It wasn't working.

"How long is Kendall staying in Aerieville?" asked Deena.

"I have no idea. I think she just had the one photo shoot

on Thursday. For all I know, she could be back in Nashville
by now."

I almost suggested that we look her up to see if she had
a photography studio we could stop by. It might be worth
trying to talk to her again. On the other hand, it wasn't like
we had all the time in the world. We'd only booked the hotel
room for one night and planned to drive back to Aerieville
this evening. Besides, there was another vendor who'd captured my curiosity even more.

"It was interesting, what Anton said about Regina," I
said softly. "And the fact that she and Taz had been friends,
back in hospitality school."

"What was it Taz wrote about her in his datebook?"
asked Deena. "That she'd promised to 'behave'? Maybe he
was referring to some competitiveness between them."

I imagined how I might feel in Regina's shoes. "She must
have had some strong feelings about Taz," I murmured. "Not
only did he break off their partnership, but then he made her
pay to work with him. What a slap in the face."

Strong enough feelings to commit murder? Regina had
seemed like a nice, respectable woman, but I couldn't deny
she had a compelling motive. Two motives, really: revenge
and money. Besides the anger and betrayal she must have felt
toward Taz, she apparently had a lot to gain by his death—
the end of the kickbacks *and* a convenient break for her own
fledgling wedding business. Powerful motives indeed.

"I wonder if the police know all this," said Deena.

"If they don't now, they soon will. I'll tell them."

Dewy, flushed, and feeling as pampered as celebrities,
Deena and I sipped mineral water in the lobby while the
receptionist tallied our bill. I was about to check my phone

when Anton breezed in carrying a tray of assorted beauty products.

"I couldn't let you ladies leave without telling you about our special promotion. If you liked the products you experienced today, you should take advantage of the ten-percent discount on the Marguerite line of products. Today only."

Once again, I recognized the small flower logo on the bottles Anton held up. "Marguerite," I said, as a fuzzy memory surfaced from a long-ago French class. "That means *daisy*, doesn't it?"

"Oui. These are the most popular scents." He tilted two bottles in turn. "Le Cynique Fleur and Le Soleil Noir."

"The 'black sun'?" asked Deena.

Where's the "beautiful dog"? I wondered, snickering to myself. I lifted one of the bottles, caught a glimpse of the three-figure price sticker on the bottom, and promptly replaced it on Anton's tray. No wonder he kept pushing these products. He must make a pretty penny in commissions. This must be the "side hustle" Taz had mentioned in his planner.

"Sorry," I said. "They smell great, but I can't afford these."

Deena looked for herself and laughed. "Me either, unfortunately."

Unbothered, Anton shrugged and tossed his head. "Where there's a will there's a way. You know where to find me if you change your mind."

While Deena took care of the bill, I finally checked my phone. I had several missed text messages—most from my mom, asking questions and sharing gossip. And one from Calvin, which simply said, *Call me if you get a chance.*

I stepped outside to call him.

"Sierra!" he said upon answering. "How's it going?" He sounded pleased to hear from me and slightly harried.

"It's going well. We've picked up some interesting information." Admiring my pretty nails in the bright sunlight, I decided not to mention our stopover at the spa. I could tell him later. "Tammy wasn't at her shop, so we're going to try to find her at a concert she's supposed to attend tonight."

"Tonight?"

"Yes, so it will probably be late when we get back to Aerieville. How are things there?"

"Uh, fine. Not bad. Except Allie keeps dropping things. So far, she's broken two vases and a teacup."

"Yikes. Sounds like you're making her nervous." I couldn't help grinning a little in spite of the loss.

"What do you mean? Why—oh." He'd finally caught on. "You think?"

"Give her a wide berth," I advised, "and see if she doesn't become less clumsy."

"Roger that."

"Everything else cool? How's Gus?"

"He's a rascal, but good." Calvin chuckled. "Everything else is . . . pretty cool. We were busy in the café this morning. Luckily, Granny Mae came by and stayed to help."

"Granny's there?"

"Yeah, she said she'd gotten a sign, or something, and knew she was needed."

That sounded like Granny. "Did you tell her where I'd gone?"

"I told her you and Deena went to Nashville as a birthday treat. I didn't think I should tell her the real reason. I figured you wouldn't want to worry her."

"Good call." Knowing Granny, she'd probably already guessed something was up. I'd have some explaining to do when I got back.

"One more thing," said Calvin. "I have two messages for you. One's from that guy, Nick. He's called a couple of times."

"What does he want?"

"He wouldn't tell me. He just left his number and asked for you to call him."

I couldn't imagine why the DJ would want to talk to me so badly. "Go ahead and text me his number. What's the other message?"

"It's from Richard Wales. He said you weren't answering your cell phone, and this was too important to wait. He said to tell you his guest made an interesting comment last night. Evidently, he was showing off his bartending skills and, quote, 'loosened her tongue.'"

Good ol' Richard, mining for info. "He's talking about Kendall. What did she say?"

"Let's see," said Calvin. "I wrote this down to make sure I get it right. She said, 'Taz's past came back to bite him, but it doesn't end here. There will be more to pay.'"

Chapter 19

The frosted cakes in the window were dazzling. Four-tiered wedding cakes, flower-topped anniversary cakes, decorated birthday confections with thick swirls and colorful sprinkles—all displayed to mouthwatering effect. Deena and I stood transfixed, until a warning growl from my belly told me I'd better turn my attention to lunch instead.

"I heard that," said Deena. "And raise it with a rumble of my own."

"Who knew relaxation could work up such an appetite?" I joked.

I opened the door for Deena, and we entered Cakes and Eats. I'd been pensive on the drive over. Kendall's sinister statement was a puzzler. Her use of the word "bite" called to mind snakebites—which had to be a coincidence. She hadn't heard Taz's last words—which I knew since she'd asked me not once, but twice, what he'd said in the end. Mulling this over, I'd glanced in my rearview mirror and glimpsed a black scooter, swerving in and out of view. The sight gave me a jolt, but it was gone before I knew it. Had to be another coincidence.

Now all that was forgotten. I had only two main worries on my mind: that we wouldn't be able to get a table, or that we *would* get a table but the prices would break the bank.

Fortunately, I worried for nothing. An efficient hostess ushered us directly to a just-cleared table and handed us menus with reasonable prices.

Cakes and Eats was a bustling little bistro, open for breakfast and lunch only. The front of the place was dedicated to the cake business, with a row of bakery cases beneath a long pickup counter. The dining area in back offered occasional peeks into the kitchen through swinging doors off a short hallway. Across from the kitchen was a sign pointing to the restrooms, and at the end of the hall was a door marked Manager. A back exit in the dining room led to a courtyard with outdoor seating.

Our waitress, a college-aged girl with cornrows and a tiny nose ring, took our orders—hearty soup and salad combos for both of us. Before she could leave, I asked her if Regina was around. She answered without hesitation. "She just got in. I think she's in her office."

"Would you tell her Sierra from Aerieville is here? I'd love to say hello if she can spare a minute."

"You got it." She left, returned quickly with our beverages and a basket of warm rolls, then left again.

We immediately tucked into the rolls, slathering them with butter and reveling in their crusty, chewy, steamy deliciousness.

"Mmm," I said, around a mouthful of bread. "Kudos to Regina."

Deena took a sip of water and nodded. "At least you have a good conversation opener—compliments to the chef. But then what? Have you thought about what you want to ask her?"

I set down the roll. "I don't know. I guess I could tell her what we know and gauge her reaction."

Deena's eyes flickered around the room. I knew what she was thinking, because I was thinking the same. It seemed tacky to confront the woman in her own restaurant. To patronize her business, enjoy her food, and then put her on the spot with veiled accusations? I wasn't sure I could stomach it.

"What would Sherlock do?" I asked lamely. "Or Nancy Drew?" I was starting to doubt my abilities as a pretend detective. I'd thought I could just talk to the suspects, and I'd be able to catch someone in a lie . . . or something like that. I sighed. "I guess I'll do what Sierra Ravenswood would do. Wing it."

The waitress brought our food, deftly placing multiple bowls, plates, and silverware in front of us. After thanking her, I said, "Did you find out if Regina is available?"

"Uh, sorry. She's kind of busy, but I'll try again."

While we ate, I kept one eye on the hallway to the kitchen and office. The kitchen door swung several times, giving way to waitresses and busboys, but never Regina. I was beginning to wonder if she was really back there, when I caught a glimpse from the corner of my eye, a blur of motion from the office to the kitchen. As I finished my salad, I kept my gaze fixed on the kitchen door. A moment later, Regina emerged. She went straight back to her office, shutting the door behind her. She never even spared a glance our way.

A busboy brought our check and cleared our plates. Our waitress had disappeared.

"All those cakes and not even an offer of dessert?" said Deena, with a note of indignation.

"I have a feeling our waitress didn't want to be the bearer of disappointing news. Regina probably told her she doesn't want to see us." I started to push back my chair. "I think I'll just go knock on her door."

Before I could stand, Regina came out of her office again and made a beeline to the front of the restaurant, again pointedly avoiding the dining area. Twisting in my seat, I saw her approach a young couple at the bakery counter. The girl, cute as a Disney princess in a fluttery skirt and high ponytail, clasped a clipboard and pen. Her clean-cut escort was taking pictures of the cakes on display. Based on Regina's solicitous smile—the first I'd seen her with any kind of a smile—I gathered they were potential wedding customers. I made a snap decision.

"Come with me to the ladies' room." I leaned toward Deena and spoke with urgency.

"What? Why?" She'd been reaching for her purse and looked startled.

I slapped down my credit card on the bill and grabbed her arm. "Come on! We don't have much time."

I figured Regina would be occupied for at least a few minutes. I had to take advantage of the opportunity. It was too providential to waste.

In the hallway, outside the restroom doors, I told Deena my plan. "Stand here, as if you're waiting for me to come out of the ladies' room. But keep a lookout for Regina. As soon as she heads this way, knock on the office door twice, one long rap, one short. Okay?"

Her forehead creased with worry, but she nodded. "What are you looking for?"

"Evidence."

Before she could talk me out of it—or I could chicken out—I slipped into Regina's office and shut the door behind me. It was a small room, surprisingly cluttered for someone who'd seemed so organized. I assumed she never met with customers in here. There were no guest chairs, only a bench next to the door, covered with a pile of aprons and smocks. I approached the desk and looked at the top of it in dismay. Every inch was layered with papers and folders: handwritten

menus, shopping lists, budget spreadsheets. And I had no
idea what I was looking for.

With my heart rattling in my chest, I moved behind the
desk and gazed around. The computer screen was in sleep
mode. Using my elbow, I nudged the wireless mouse a frac-
tion of an inch to wake it up. The screen brightened, and a
log-in window appeared. Password protected, of course.

Biting my lip, I tried to decide where to focus my attention. The desk had nine drawers: four on each side, plus a pen-
cil drawer in the center, the latter jutting open and overloaded
with office supplies. Behind the desk chair, a pair of lateral
filing cabinets stood against the wall. One file drawer was
ajar, also too stuffed to close, with crumpled manila folders
visible through the opening. On top of the cabinets, assorted
knickknacks and a stack of business books collected dust.

I shook my head. This was ridiculous. I'd hoped to find
some proof of Regina's intention to take over Taz's wedding planner business. If she'd felt cheated by him, enough
so to resort to murder, the deed might have been premed-
itated. Among all these papers and files, could there be
any evidence that she'd planned to step into Taz's shoes?
Maybe. But I didn't have time to go through everything.
And if the smoking gun was in the computer, it might as
well have been in a bank vault. I had no way of guessing
Regina's password.

With a final visual sweep of the room, I started back
toward the door. My eyes landed on a corkboard on the wall
perpendicular to the desk. It was partially obscured by a
hat stand, holding a hoody, a rain jacket, and an umbrella.
Scooting around the wobbly stand, I took a second to peek
at the bulletin board. Pinned haphazardly in the center was
a wall calendar featuring an image of a covered bridge. It
was still opened to August and evidently not used to mark

appointments. Surrounding the calendar were thumbtacked photographs, curling at the corners.

It always interested me to see what pictures a person chose to display. Snapshots were usually personal. If someone takes the time to print a photo and pin it up, that had to mean something. Photo displays reveal what a person holds dear, where their priorities lie.

Regina's pictures mostly showed people I didn't recognize. I didn't know if she was married or had children, and it still wasn't clear. There were some large group photos, possibly featuring Regina with her parents and extended family. And there were some wallet-sized school photos of children who could have been nieces, nephews, or friends. There were none with Taz—or were there? A cluster of older-looking pictures showed Regina when she was a few years younger: one of her in a chef's hat, one in front of her restaurant, and a couple of her in outdoor settings, smiling into the sunlight. One showed her sitting astride a motorcycle.

Squinting, I leaned forward for a closer look. Yes, it was definitely a motorcycle and not a motor scooter. Regina appeared quite comfortable on it, holding a helmet beneath her arm. I wondered if she still rode.

Careful not to dislodge the tacks, I used my index finger to adjust some of the crooked, overlapping photos. A few candid group shots had been arranged in a haphazard collage. Based on the giddy, amused expressions, I gathered these were photos from a party. Or maybe they were classmates goofing off. Regina seemed to have a diverse circle of friends—including a slender, dark-haired white boy, with his arm slung casually around her shoulders. *Taz.* He was younger and plainer—no kitschy clothes or outrageous hairdo—but his smirk was unmistakable. Regina was making a face at him, as if he'd just told a tasteless joke.

The knock jarred me like a hammer to my heart. It was a single bang—not the signal I'd asked Deena to use. I rushed to the door and opened it a crack. A manicured hand reached in and clutched at my shirt.

"She's coming!" hissed Deena.

I ejected myself from the room, bumped into Deena, and barely had time to compose myself before Regina appeared at the end of the hall. Her office door was still open behind me.

A storm cloud descended over her features. In two long strides she was standing before us.

"What are you doing?" she demanded.

I swallowed my embarrassment. "Looking for you." Straightening my spine, I poured out my highly reasonable explanations. "I know you're busy. I won't take too much of your time. We happened to be in town, so we looked you up. I heard you're taking over coordination of Marissa Lakely's wedding, and I wanted to confirm the flower order. Do you have a list of the requirements and final numbers?"

Her face was impassive, except for a slight tightening of her lips. "I'm sorry. I didn't know you thought you were still on this job. The original florist is available again, so your services are no longer needed."

The overcast sky was appropriate to my mood. As I drove us around, pointing out some of my former haunts, Deena tried to cheer me up. But there were too many reminders here of old heartaches and broken dreams. How ironic that I'd return to Nashville, only to be fired from a job in Aerieville.

Passing a bakery, Deena reopened the sore topic. "At least we didn't buy Regina's cake."

"Ha. Yeah." *It did look good, though.*

"You know, the wedding probably won't even go forward," she pointed out.

"Probably not," I agreed. *At least not on the original date. It could happen later.*

"Anyway," said Deena. "Vendor selection is not really Regina's decision to make, is it? Who's paying for the wedding? Ultimately, it should be Annaliese's decision. Or Marissa's, since she hired you in the first place."

"Right—Annaliese who won't return my calls, and Marissa who's gone AWOL." I was in an uncommonly contrary frame of mind.

Rounding a corner, I caught a view of the Parthenon rising in the distance. It was a full-scale replica of the original, built for the 1897 exposition. Like the temple in Greece, this version boasted a giant statue of Athena—the goddess of wisdom and war. I had a sudden urge to visit the attraction, situated at the top of a grassy hill in Centennial Park.

"Feel like getting out of the car?" I asked Deena.

"If it'll perk you up, I'm all for it."

We left the Fiat along the street and strolled through the park and around the lake, where a family of ducks paddled the placid water, occasionally dipping their heads below the surface. Though the sky was cloudy, the temperature was warm and the air was sweet. My spirits lifted almost immediately.

Passing the sunken gardens, I paused and turned to Deena. "You know what? You're right."

"I often am. About what?"

"About what Regina said. It's not her decision to let me go. If the Lakelys don't want to use Flower House, then fine. We never signed a contract. But I want to hear it from Annaliese."

"Hear, hear."

A light breeze ruffled the lush garden plants. A pair of

butterflies flitted among the violet blue mistflowers and vibrant goldenrods. I laughed softly.

"What's funny?" asked Deena.

"I just realized why Tammy never returned my calls. She probably knew Regina was going to dump me and bring her back into the fold. Imagine her surprise when we show up at the concert tonight."

"You've got a devilish side, Miss Sierra," Deena quipped. "Who knew?"

We continued on to the Parthenon and paid the admission fee. There was a nice art gallery in the building, but the main draw was the 42-foot-tall gilded statue. We stood at the base and craned our necks to take in the glorious goddess. In her right palm, she held a life-sized statue of Nike, the winged goddess of victory. Athena's left hand rested on a giant shield, which seemed to protect her 20-foot-high golden serpent. Crossing my arms, I looked from the shiny scales of its coiled body to its flinty red eyes.

"What's the deal with Athena's snake?" I asked. Deena had more degrees than I had years in college. I figured she must know a thing or two about Greek mythology.

She didn't disappoint. "It's one of her symbols. In ancient times, snakes represented fertility. I think Athena was a fertility goddess, among other things. It might also indicate protection."

"So, I guess it's not the devil in disguise?" I said, half-joking.

"Hardly. That association came much later."

"Why fertility?" I wondered.

"Probably because they shed their skins. It symbolizes rebirth and transformation too."

"Ah. Of course." Somewhere along the line, snakes had lost their positive connotations. I'd always thought they were something to fear and revile. "Mean as a striped snake" was a phrase I'd heard to describe more than one lowdown, no-good rotter. Then there was the "sneaky snake" and the "snake in the grass." These cold-blooded, fork-tongued slitherers weren't to be trusted.

A group of other tourists gathered around us, so we moved on, allowing them to take our place. As we left the Parthenon, I pondered again why Taz had uttered "snake" in his dying breath. If he was trying to tell me the person who'd pushed him was a snake, that had to mean it was someone he'd thought he could trust. Someone who'd stabbed him in the back . . . figuratively *and* literally.

Deena and I walked back to the car, still discussing snakes and suspects. I remembered that I hadn't returned Nick's call, so I paused on the sidewalk to shoot him a text. With my attention on my phone, I wasn't paying any notice to the street. It wasn't until the sharp buzz of a motor pricked my ears that I jerked my head up.

"What's the matter?" said Deena. She'd been occupied with her phone too.

The street was empty, until the stoplight changed, releasing a line of cars.

"Nothing," I muttered. "I thought I heard something."

We hopped in the Fiat and merged into the traffic, making our way to the concert hall. A museum-like, neoclassical structure, it wasn't as large as the Parthenon, but it was still impressive, with a sweeping concrete staircase leading to a broad, columned portico. Our plan was to hang out near the entrance, each of us on opposite sides, and wait for Tammy. We arrived early to be sure we wouldn't miss her.

As we'd learned from the posters, the doors would open at six thirty, and the concert would start at eight. Until that time, wine and light refreshments were available in the lobby. Since Shelby had said Tammy needed to be here at six, we assumed she would be meeting someone, and then going inside as soon as the doors opened. My task was to stop her—politely and with sugar. To persuade her to talk, I'd have to swallow my pride and appeal to her humanity and our mutual love of flowers.

A few people arrived prior to six thirty, including some elderly patrons who wanted to beat the crowds. Once the doors opened, more guests trickled in. Soon the trickle became a stream, then grew into a small river, steadily rushing past us. I began to feel like I was in some kind of video game, where I had to stay on my toes and keep my eyes peeled, so I could tag every single face that came my way. After an hour of this, I'd had enough. I'd also had an epiphany.

I maneuvered my way to Deena and met her inquiring look with a grimace. "I've been a dummy."

"What do you mean?"

"The one piece of information we had should have clued me in. Tammy had to be here at six."

"So? We were here at six. You don't think we missed her? Maybe she changed her mind."

I shook my head. "Who else do we know with a symphony connection here in Nashville?"

Deena's confusion turned to understanding. "Gordon."

I nodded. "I remembered something. When Taz wrote about the vendors in his planner, he kind of lumped Gordon and Tammy together. He said something like 'Gordon and Tammy are on board.' I bet they're a couple, or at least friends. In that case, she probably met him here early at a back door."

"Ugh," said Deena, leaning on a pillar. "I bet you're right. Now what?"

I glanced around at the eager concertgoers. Some were dressed to the nines, while others were more touristy casual.

Every time the door opened, I could hear a murmur of buoy-ant chatter and felt a sort of charged anticipation in the air. It had been a long time since I'd been to the symphony.

"We could buy tickets," I said. "And look for Tammy inside. Maybe speak to her during the intermission?"

"A glass of wine and a soft seat sound wonderful right about now," said Deena. "I'm sure the music would be nice too."

It turned out to be a lovely choice. We never found Tammy, but we enjoyed the heart-stirring strains of Beethoven—from distant back-row seats. And we did spot Gordon, straight-backed and intense, on second violin. I was in awe of all the talent on the stage and let myself become immersed in the experience.

At intermission, there was still no sign of Tammy. We figured she must have been watching from the wings, or else waiting for Gordon in the green room backstage. Mill-ing among the throngs in the lobby, I checked my watch. It was nine o'clock. I motioned Deena to a relatively quiet spot along the gilded lobby wall.

"Should we cut our losses and go home?"

Deena gave me a searching look, as if trying to figure out what I wanted to do. "I'm not tired anymore," she ven-tured. "If you want to stay for the second set, it's fine by me. I can help with the driving on our way home. Plus, the later we leave, the less traffic there will be."

I smiled at how game she was. "What's that saying: in for a penny, in for a pound? We might as well see this thing through. Maybe we can catch up with Gordon after the con-cert."

Having made the decision, we visited the concession stand again, this time for coffee. I thought about texting Calvin. I'd already told him we would be in late, so he wouldn't be expecting me to pick up Gus until tomorrow.

I didn't need to inform him of our plans. But I still kind of wanted to.

Pulling out my phone, I saw that the battery was dangerously low. Luckily, I had a portable charger in the car. I told Deena I wanted to run out and get it.

"I'll come with you," she said. "I'd like to grab my sweater."

We had five minutes until the end of intermission, so we hurried to the exit and outside into the cool evening. Skirting plumes of tobacco smoke, courtesy of a smattering of outdoor smokers, we trotted down the steps, coffee sloshing in our paper cups.

Thanks to our early arrival, we'd found a nearby spot in the parking lot across the street, not too far away. At least, I thought we had. We slowed our steps, looking around in confusion.

"Where's my car?"

"This is the right lot, isn't it?" said Deena.

For a moment, I felt disoriented, like when you leave from the wrong exit in a building with identical sides. But that wasn't the case here. This was the right parking lot, and the right row, closest to the street. In a twinge of desperation, I scanned the lot for no-parking signs. If I'd accidentally taken a reserved space, my car might have been towed. No dice. There was only another car, a white sedan, where the orange Fiat should have been.

My heart sank as the truth set in. Someone had stolen my car.

Chapter 20

I'd been in jams before, but this one took the cake. I'd never felt such a confusing mixture of anger, loss, and helplessness, like a small child who's had her first bicycle stolen. I felt violated.

At least I had Deena. It was an immense comfort to have a friend at my side—and one with a fully charged cell phone to boot. We quickly ascertained that there were no visible security cameras and no one around to question. It was an unattended lot, and all the vehicle owners were likely at the concert. Deena snapped a picture of the license plate on the white car. If we could track down the owner, we could ask if they happened to see anything, or at least learn what time they'd pulled into the spot. We hurried back to the concert hall to speak to the manager and call the police.

The concert hall manager, Lloyd Watson, was a trim, balding man in a tailored navy blue suit. When we explained our predicament, he responded with kindness and deep concern. In contrast, the responding police officer, a stocky man with gray hair, was on the stony side and rather blunt. After a cursory look around the parking lot, he walked with us back to the concert hall to complete his report. He declined Lloyd's offer of coffee.

Sitting in the manager's office, I gave the officer my contact information and Deena's phone number. He handed me a copy of the report, dutifully saying he'd call me if my car should turn up. He also said it was unlikely it would.

"Don't wait around, and don't put off filing your insurance claim," he advised. "That way if the car turns up in one piece, you can be pleasantly surprised."

Great. After the cop left, we remained in the manager's office. He plied us with more coffee and gave us souvenir orchestra T-shirts, as if the gifts could make up for the loss of my car. I clutched my coffee cup with both hands. It was all I could do to squelch the hot tears that threatened to spring from my eyes.

It's just a car, I told myself. *Just a lifeless, replaceable object.* But I knew that wasn't entirely true. It was also a symbol. I'd bought the sporty "tangerine machine" in Nashville, back when my optimism and persistence had finally started to pay off. It was a time when anything had seemed possible, when it was as obvious to me as the stars in my eyes that dreams *do* come true for those who believe.

Of course, dreams unravel too. I'd ended up in a relationship with a cheater who'd stolen from me. Then I'd had a fall and lost both my starring role and my apartment. It was a discouraging setback when I'd been forced to return home and borrow money from my parents. But at least I'd still had my cute orange car.

Deena looked at me now with sympathy and worry. Twice in the span of one day, she'd seen my usual good nature slip into darker territory. Seeing her concern only made me feel worse. It was my fault she was here, and now we were both stranded.

Lloyd glanced at his watch. The concert would let out soon, and Deena and I would have to leave.

"Can I help you find a hotel room?" he offered.

"Already on it," said Deena, half-heartedly lifting her phone. With her free hand, she rubbed her opposite arm. Her sweater, along with all our overnight gear, was gone with the car. I dropped my head to my hand.

"You know," said Lloyd, "you might get your car back sooner than you think. The police prepared you for the worst, but it's possible the thief just decided to take a joyride. It could've been kids acting on a dare, or someone who needed quick transportation. I'd wager the car will be found abandoned before the night is over."

Deena looked up, brightening. "That's true. I've heard of that happening. Plus, Sierra's car is so conspicuous, no thief would want to keep it for long."

I nodded slowly. All those scenarios were possible. But I didn't believe any of them. I remembered the motor scooter I'd seen that morning, and the one I'd thought I heard before we drove to the concert hall. Another scenario was taking shape in my mind. What if we'd been followed? What if someone was trying to slow me down or put me out of commission . . . to keep me from investigating Taz's death?

Remarkably, that thought was more cheering to me than any of the more innocent possibilities Lloyd had suggested.

I set down the coffee cup and stood up, thoughtfully rubbing my hand over my face. I wasn't a random crime victim. I was targeted. And this realization inspired me with a new resolve. I knew what I had to do: carry on.

Taking a deep breath, I turned to Lloyd and mustered up a smile. "You've been so kind. Could I ask you for one more favor?"

"Of course," he said at once. I didn't know if his top concern was the concert hall's reputation or if he was a genuine gentleman, but it didn't matter. Deena shot me a curious look.

"We're acquainted with a member of the orchestra, Gordon Winslow. He doesn't know we're here. We were going to surprise him. Do you think you could help us find him after the concert?"

"Absolutely," said Lloyd, opening the door. "We can go to the green room now. I'll send word to the conductor and ask Gordon to meet us there."

In my short run with musical theater, I'd had occasion to hang out in a green room or two. Performers' waiting areas varied widely from venue to venue in their amenities and comforts. The room Lloyd unlocked was on the nicer end of the scale with several sofas and a long table laden with platters of sandwiches and crudités, canned sodas, and bottles of water. Lloyd left us alone to help ourselves, saying he'd return shortly. Resounding applause filtered in from the auditorium.

I crunched into a carrot, as Deena unscrewed a bottle of water. We didn't have time to discuss strategies or formulate game plans. Almost immediately, chattering musicians filed into the room, their onstage formality replaced with afterparty merriment. We stepped to the side as they stowed their instruments and made for the food table.

It was just as well. I didn't even have an inkling of a plan to share with Deena. I'd decided to surrender to the moment. *Go with the flow* was my new mantra.

Lloyd appeared at our sides, with a severe-looking Gordon in tow.

"Here they are," said Lloyd, presenting us like prizes. I detected a note of relief in his voice, as if he was glad to hand over the responsibility for us. To me, he said, "I told Gordon about your, ah, predicament."

"Surprise!" I batted my eyelashes at Gordon and dimpled my cheeks in what I hoped was an endearingly cute way.

Before he could utter a response, we were joined by a short woman with bright purple lipstick and gray-frosted, dark brown hair pulled back in a satin scarf. She wore a zipped-up windbreaker and a crossbody purse, as if she'd just come in from outside. I recognized Tammy from her social media photos. She stopped short when she saw me. For a split second, a flicker of stunned recognition crossed her face. Although we'd never met, I had the distinct impression she knew who I was.

Her features instantly softened into an uncertain smile. "Hello," she said pleasantly.

I stuck out my hand and spoke rapidly. "Hi there! I'm Sierra Ravenswood. I think we have mutual acquaintances in Aerieville. After meeting Gordon at Bellman Manor earlier this week, I was eager to hear him play." I placed a familiar hand on the violinist's arm, resolutely ignoring the curl of his lip. "The concert was *wonderful*. We were having such a nice time, until"—I bit my lower lip, hoping to convey bravery in the face of adversity—"someone stole my car from the parking lot across the street."

"That's terrible!" said Tammy.

I nodded, and for a moment the dampness I blinked back was genuine. It *was* terrible.

"The authorities are investigating," Lloyd put in quickly. "And I've been trying to assist in any way I can."

I smiled my thanks at the manager. "We were supposed to go home tonight, but now we're stuck."

"We really are," Deena added. "I've been looking online for a hotel, but everything nearby seems to be booked."

Someone called Lloyd's name. He clapped a hand on Gordon's shoulder. "It's lucky these young ladies have friends in Nashville." Handing me his business card, he made me promise to let him know as soon as I learned anything about my car. With a gallant bow, he turned and left.

"You poor things," said Tammy. Glancing at Gordon, she touched a finger to her lips. "We have a spare bedroom. You're welcome to it, as long as you don't mind cat hair."

I raised my eyebrows, surprised, yet somehow not. "Oh, wow! Really? That's so kind of you."

Deena looked shell-shocked. "Amazingly kind," she murmured.

Before we knew it, Gordon had packed up his violin and we were shuffled outside to Tammy's waiting SUV. It was a short drive to their home east of downtown across the river. Classical music thrummed through the vehicle's sound system, foreclosing any possibility of conversation. Now and then Gordon and Tammy exchanged a word or two, which Deena and I couldn't hear from the back seat.

It was late when we arrived, almost eleven o'clock. But when Gordon offered us a nightcap, I didn't even think of refusing. This was the first nice gesture from the aloof musician.

Tammy excused herself to straighten up the guest room. Gordon invited us to have seats in the living room, where he poured a finger of whiskey in a tumbler for each of us and passed them around.

"It's a tradition," he said. "One small drink after every performance."

"To tradition," I said, raising my glass.

He tipped his head in acknowledgment and took a long sip, draining his glass. I took a much smaller sip. I was a lightweight, and I knew it.

Deena cleared her throat and smiled at Gordon. "I don't think we actually met the other day. I'm Deena Lee. I work with Sierra at Flower House."

"Oh, jeez, I'm sorry!" I tapped my forehead. "I totally

forgot. This evening—this whole day—has knocked me for a loop."

Gordon wrinkled his forehead in an expression of wry commiseration. "I'd say this whole week has knocked many of us for a loop—starting with the murder of Taz Banyan." He reached for the bottle and poured himself another splash of liquor. "It must have been traumatic for you, finding him like you did. What was it he said, or tried to say?"

Nice try. "Nothing sensible. Just, sort of, groaning sounds."

For a moment Gordon gave me a calculating look. Then he sipped his drink. "I still have a hard time believing it happened."

"It was shocking for sure." I chose my words carefully. "On the other hand, Taz did seem to inspire strong feelings in a lot of people."

Gordon snorted and sat back in his chair. "For better and for worse."

Tammy came into the living room cradling a white Persian cat with a pink and blue collar.

"What a beauty!" said Deena.

"Aw," I said. "She sure is."

"This is Elsa, our little snow queen," said Tammy, taking a seat next to Gordon. "She thinks this house is her palace, so don't be surprised if she finds her way into your room tonight."

"That's okay," I said. "We're in her territory."

"I love cats," said Deena.

Gordon handed Tammy a glass of whiskey. "We were just discussing Taz."

Tammy pursed her lips in a look of distaste. Then she took a quick sip of whiskey, effectively hiding her expression. When she lowered her glass, her face was neutral. "Any news about the murder investigation?"

"You've probably heard the state is on the case," I said. "They're administering polygraph tests on Monday."

It occurred to me that Gordon might offer Deena and me a ride back to Aerieville. As practical as that might be, I couldn't imagine spending three and a half hours in a car with the stodgy violinist—not to mention a murder suspect. I'd rather rent a car.

"I don't know who they think is going to take one of those tests," said Gordon. "They haven't made any arrests, have they?"

"I don't think so," I said. "But they asked me to come into the station to answer more questions. I was under the impression they have a number of interviews set up."

Gordon's left eyebrow twitched up, and Tammy made a sound that resembled a suppressed laugh. I got the sense they thought I was being naïve. Maybe I was.

"I-I suppose I don't have to go," I said, hating how tentative I sounded.

"You can be sure *I'm* not," said Gordon. "My lawyer advised me not to volunteer anything. The police are fishing for evidence. Anything you say to them could be misconstrued or twisted."

Or "held against you," I thought. *Just like the cops say when reciting a person's Miranda rights.* I recalled my fingerprints all over Bellman Manor and realized Gordon was right.

On the other hand, I wanted to help the police. I liked to think we were on the same side. If Gordon and the others wouldn't talk, how else could the murder be solved?

Stroking her cat, Tammy gave me a "sorry not sorry" look. "You've been trying to call me, I believe. I've been busy with a number of weddings."

"Yes," I said. *Lucky lady.* "I wanted to talk with you about the Lakely wedding."

"The Lakely-Princely wedding," said Tammy, tacking on the groom's name. Why did I keep forgetting about the groom?

"Right. I was wondering . . ." My question died in my throat. How could I ask her why she'd quit without sounding like a police interrogator? *Was it Taz's rudeness and demands, or was it the kickbacks he forced you to pay?* Now that I knew Gordon and Tammy were a couple, anything that sounded like a motive for Tammy could translate into one for Gordon.

"You were wondering?" she prompted.

"Um. About the flowers you had planned. I was calling to consult with you about the wedding flowers. But I realize there's some uncertainty now about whether the wedding will even proceed."

She smiled, looking remarkably like her cat. "There's also uncertainty about who the florist will be. I'm not sure if you're aware. There's a new wedding planner now."

I nodded. "I heard. But I thought—didn't you quit?" *There.* I'd managed to ask my question after all. Sort of.

She raised her darkened eyebrows in a look of amusement. "Is that what Taz told you?"

"It's what everyone said."

"She didn't quit," said Gordon. He leaned forward with a fiery glint in his eyes. "Tammy's a professional. She puts up with a lot and has never walked out on a job."

She reached over to give Gordon an affectionate pat on his hand. Looking directly at me, she said, "I didn't quit. Taz fired me."

I frowned. This didn't make sense. Taz had told me himself that Tammy had bailed. Marissa had said something similar, that it was Tammy who had backed out. "Are you sure? Could you have misunderstood?"

She laughed shortly. "There's no mistaking the words

'You're off the job.' I even have it in writing. Or in text anyway."

Well, that explains Gordon's animosity toward me. They believed Tammy was dismissed, and I was her replacement.

In the ensuing silence, Elsa purred and Deena covered a yawn. I swirled the last of my whiskey, before raising the glass to my lips.

Gordon turned to Tammy. "Is Johnny staying here tonight?"

"He didn't say. He has a key, so we can lock up." To Deena and me, she said, "Don't be afraid if you hear someone coming in tonight. My son is a night owl, and he splits his time between his girlfriend's place and here."

"Did he get his scooter fixed?" asked Gordon. "That motor will wake up the neighborhood."

I choked on my whiskey. Through watering eyes, I sensed everyone staring at me in alarm, including the cat.

"Are you okay?" asked Deena.

Nodding, I patted my chest. "Wrong pipe," I wheezed.

"Can I get you some water?" asked Tammy.

"No, no. I'm fine." With one more cough, I was able to speak more or less normally again. "Your son drives a scooter? Is it a Vespa, or—?"

"It's an old Suzuki. He just drives it around town."

Gordon rolled his eyes. "It was a fad a few years ago. Popular with younger crowds."

"They get good gas mileage," said Tammy, in defense of her son.

I nodded slowly. "I'm thinking of getting one. If your son does come over, I'd like to take a look at his."

"I'm sure he wouldn't mind showing it off," she said.

Elsa jumped to the floor and stalked out of the room, tail held high. We all took her cue and stood up. Gordon gathered the glasses, and Tammy showed us to the guest room, pointing out a well-stocked hall bathroom on the way.

"Sleep in as late as you'd like," she said. "I have some errands to run in the morning, but Gordon will be here if you need help finding transportation."

We thanked her, then took turns using the bathroom to wash up and change into our orchestra T-shirts. There wasn't much to look at in the guest room. It was a small, neat space, dominated by a full-sized day bed with matching trundle. I claimed the smaller trundle, pointing Deena to the larger bed, and shut off the light. We were both exhausted.

"Tammy and Gordon seem nice," Deena said softly.

"Yeah," I agreed. "Above and beyond." I suspected the real reason Tammy invited us to their home was to get information from me, but I was still grateful.

Deena lowered her voice to a whisper. "You don't think Tammy's son was the person who knocked you over in Aerieville, do you? I thought scooters were for local roads and not highways. Unless he transported it on a truck or something." She sounded doubtful.

"I don't know. I think some scooters have big enough motors to go highway speeds. Also, I thought I saw a scooter following us today."

"*What?* Why didn't you say anything?"

"I thought I was being paranoid. I might've been mistaken." In truth, I still wasn't sure.

Lying in the dark, I replayed the events of the day. It was interesting to see some of the vendors on their own turf. Anton at the salon, Regina in her restaurant, Gordon in the orchestra. And I'd finally met the elusive Tammy. Speaking of which . . . where had she been coming from when she showed up backstage after the concert? She had her jacket on, as if she'd been outside. Could she have been involved in stealing my car?

I shook my head, doubting my own conjectures. She probably just had personal business to take care of. After spending some time with her, as a guest in her home, I had a hard time seeing her as a criminal.

I sighed. "It's probably all just a coincidence."

When Deena didn't respond, I thought she'd fallen asleep. A minute later, in a sleepy voice, she said, "What's the plan for tomorrow?"

"First off, I want to buy a phone charger and check in with the police. Then I guess we'll have to figure out how we're gonna get back home."

"Somebody could pick us up," she murmured. "My parents, or Rocky . . ." She trailed off, and her breathing became even.

I rolled to my side and faced the dark wall. Somebody had effectively put me out of commission. It had to be related to my inquiries about Taz, but why? Was the thief trying to stop me from digging around Nashville? I hadn't had a chance to visit Kendall or Nick, if they were even back in town. And I'd never found Taz's home or any of his other friends or acquaintances. Was there more to be found here?

Or was the culprit trying to keep me from getting back to Aerieville?

One thing I did know: I *would* get back home, one way or another. And then the cops would have easy access to question me—unlike all the other vendors. They'd all gone back to their daily lives. As Gordon said, without making an arrest, the cops couldn't force anyone to return for more questioning. It seemed that the only way any of them might come back would be for Marissa's wedding.

Which reminded me—where was Marissa?

Chapter 21

I slept horribly. It wasn't only the thin mattress and strange surroundings. It was also, and mostly, my nerves. All night long I kept expecting to be pounced on by a cat, or jarred by the growl of a motor scooter. Neither of which happened, thank goodness. I awoke with a slant of sunlight hitting my eyes from an opening in the bedroom curtain.

Rolling over, I stretched my stiff muscles and collected my bearings. Deena was already up and dressed, quietly putting on her shoes. She was the kind of poised and prepared woman who carried a hairbrush and makeup kit wherever she went. Consequently, she looked as refreshed and elegant as she always did. I ran my fingers through my short mop and called it good enough. At least my fingernails still looked nice.

The house was quiet. A quick peek out the front window revealed no parked vehicles, two-wheeled or four. We followed the aroma of strong coffee to the kitchen, where we found sliced grapefruit, bagels, and a note from Gordon, informing us he'd gone out and would return shortly. It was a relief to find ourselves alone. I needed to think.

Sitting on stools at the kitchen island, we helped ourselves to the coffee and food. Elsa sauntered in, sniffed at us, and decided I was worth a leg rub with her silky back. I tried to pet her, but she moved out of my reach.

"I miss Gus," I said.

Deena reached down, and Elsa went straight to her beckoning fingers. "Should I get a cat?"

"Yes." I nodded sagely. "If you're asking, I think the answer is definitely *yes*."

Savoring a tart bite of grapefruit, I gazed around the kitchen. I was itching to snoop, but I was also afraid of getting caught. Then my eyes landed on a cell phone charging station on the counter. I jumped up to try it out on my phone. To my delight, it worked.

"This is a good sign!" I proclaimed. "This is going to be a good day."

While my phone charged, I wandered to the living room, where we'd sat sipping whiskey the night before. Deena remained in the kitchen cooing at Elsa. Casually, I browsed the books on the shelves and thumbed through magazines on the coffee table. The longer I idled in the quiet room, the bolder I became, peeking inside the liquor cabinet and opening the end-table drawers. Finding nothing of interest, I headed toward the hallway leading to the bedrooms. I was passing the front door, when the click of the lock made me freeze. A second later, the door opened and Gordon stepped inside, followed by a young man wearing a checkered shirt, skinny jeans, and a loose beanie.

"Good morning!" I said innocently. *Nothing to see here.*

Gordon nodded in greeting, then waved toward his companion. "This is Johnny. I had to play chauffeur and pick him up."

With an affable grin, Johnny stuck out his hand. "How do you do?"

"Hi," I said. "I'm Sierra."

We all went into the kitchen, where Gordon poured himself a cup of coffee and Johnny grabbed a bagel. After introducing Deena and Johnny, I wasted no time in questioning the young man. "I hear you drive a scooter."

"Yes! Poor Ruby. She's in the shop. That's why I needed a ride."

Gordon grunted behind us and took a seat at the kitchen table, where he unfolded a newspaper.

"Ruby?" I said. "Your scooter has a name?"

"Of course. Want to see a picture?" With a few swipes on his phone, he brought up a gallery of photos, which he proudly showed to Deena and me. They all featured a small zippy-looking scooter with a shiny frame—in apple red. Definitely not the black scooter I'd seen in Aerieville, and possibly on the streets of Nashville yesterday.

With a sigh of relief, I smiled at Johnny. "She's real pretty. I don't think I've ever seen one quite like her."

"Yeah, she's a vintage Suzuki Smash, with custom details. And usually she's super reliable. Some of my friends have motorcycles, but I prefer scooters. They're cleaner and have more personality, if you ask me."

"They're mostly for city driving, aren't they?" asked Deena.

"Oh, mine can handle highway speeds just fine."

"I suppose there's not much room for any cargo, though," I said, thinking of all the wedding vendors. Then again, didn't they all have cars or vans anyway? Where did the black scooter fit in?

"I usually wear a backpack if I need to bring anything with me," said Johnny. He pocketed his phone, then excused himself and left the room.

As soon as my phone had enough juice to power on, I

checked for messages and shot off texts to Cal and Rocky. When I explained our predicament, they both offered to come and get us. I told them to hold off. I still held out hope that the police would come through. Unfortunately, I had no missed calls or messages about my car.

Gordon chuckled from the table. Glancing over, I saw that he was reading the comics. For some reason, this made me grin. It was refreshing to see that the stuffy violinist had a sense of humor. I studied him for a moment. *He doesn't look like a killer.* Could I remove him from the suspect list?

As if sensing my gaze, Gordon looked up suddenly. His expression of amusement dropped away. "Are you going to need a ride someplace?"

"Oh, no," I said quickly. "Thank you, but we'll call a cab."

He folded his paper and finished off his coffee. I caught Deena's eye. She cocked her head in a questioning manner, as if to ask what I was waiting for. Were we going to leave, or what?

Swallowing my nerves, I inched toward the table. Gracious host or not, Gordon was still a suspect. And this was probably my last chance to interrogate him.

"So, Gordon, can I ask you a question?"

He gave me a slight nod. "What would you like to know?"

Here goes nothing. "The, uh, vendor fee Taz was charging—was that typical? I mean, it was kind of high, right?"

He stared at me for a moment, as if trying to gauge my sincerity. "He made you pay too, did he?" When I didn't answer, Gordon curled his lip in an expression of resigned distaste. "Yes, it was high. Some might even say it was against the law. But sometimes you have to spend money to make money."

"Oh," I said, unsure what to make of this.

"None of us were happy about it," he continued. "But if you think Taz was killed over that fee, you must be even more naïve than you appear."

My mouth dropped open at the dig. *Really, Gordon? Was that necessary?*

He pushed back from the table and stood up. "Taz got away with charging kickbacks, because his jobs were so lucrative. Whatever the motive was for killing the poor bastard, it wasn't that. Now, if you'll excuse me, I need to make some phone calls."

As soon as he left the kitchen, Deena hopped to her feet. "What a pompous little—"

"Dee," I interrupted, laughing. "Forget about it. It's okay." By now, I was getting used to Gordon's gruff personality. He may not have liked Taz, and he was obviously unhappy about Tammy being fired, but I didn't think he'd committed murder over it. He seemed too mature, somehow, to do something so rash. "I'm going to call the police station now."

Crossing my fingers, I made the phone call. Alas, after being transferred twice and placed on hold for several minutes, I was finally told the police had no news.

Well, shoot. At least, the day is still young. I was trying to decide what to do next, when my phone rang. The display showed that it was Granny.

I hesitated for half a second, then picked up. "Hi, Granny!"

"So, you *are* alive," she said. "That's a relief."

"Why wouldn't I be?"

"I saw the Johnsons yesterday. Both of the older kids, Allie and Toby, acted kind of odd when your name came up. They said you'd left town, real sudden. When I pressed 'em, they said it must have something to do with the federal agent that paid you a visit at Flower House."

"Federal? No, it was a state agent." Which, of course, was beside the point. I'd have to start being more discreet around my employees.

"Calvin was acting strange too," said Granny. "Anxious. He said you and Dee took a trip for your birthday, which should be a nice thing to do. Except he had worry in his eyes."

Granny was sharp. I had to give her that.

"Then," she continued, "I had a dream about you last night. You were lost in a hedge maze. When I woke up, I knew it was a portent."

"I'm not lost, Granny Mae. But . . . I am kind of stuck."

"I knew it," she said matter-of-factly. "You went stirring up trouble, didn't you? If you poke a hornet's nest, what do you think's going to fly out? Butterflies?"

I sighed. I had no choice but to come clean. "I haven't been trying to stir up trouble. I've been visiting some people who knew Taz—the wedding planner who was killed. It was meant to be a quick trip, but, unfortunately, somebody stole my car."

There was silence on the other end of the line.

"Granny?"

"I'm thinking. You said you lost your car? That zippy orange thing?"

"I didn't lose it. Somebody took it."

"So, you're not lost, but your car is."

"Well, I guess so. In a manner of speaking."

"You just need to find it."

"Ideally, the police will find it. Though, they didn't seem very confident about their prospects."

"Hmph. You don't need them. You can find it. Here's what you got to do. Find yourself a granddaddy long legs."

Did she just say what I think she said? "Granny, where am I going to find a daddy long legs?"

Deena had been watching me expectantly. Now her eyebrows shot up.

"Under a rock or a log," said Granny. "Or in a pile of
leaves. Any place damp." She was serious.

"Um."

"Put it in a jar and take it to the last place you had your
car. Then take it out and say 'Granddaddy, Granddaddy,
where is my car?' Whichever way it points one foot is the
way to go."

I shook my head. I didn't know whether to laugh or write
down her instructions.

"One more thing," said Granny.

"There's more?"

"You need to protect yourself. Can you find any acorns
or buckeyes?"

Closing my eyes, I took in a slow inhale through my nostrils. "I don't know. I'll keep a lookout."

"Alrighty, then. I'm comin' to town this evening. I'll see
you at your folks for supper."

I hung up, chuckling. *Granny and her superstitions.* She
had given me an idea, though. It couldn't hurt to return to
the scene of the crime and ask around. The police officer
hadn't done much yesterday. He didn't look for witnesses or
show any interest in tracking down the owner of the car that
had taken my spot. I couldn't leave Nashville without at least
making an effort.

It was midmorning when a taxi dropped us off at the
parking lot across from the concert hall. The lot was half-
empty now. Being a Sunday morning, the nearby office
buildings and restaurants were closed. And the matinee concert wasn't scheduled for several hours yet.

We strolled around the block. On the far side, I spotted a

small city park. Out of respect for Granny, I decided to take a minute to see if I could find an acorn on the ground. At least it was a pleasant morning. Soft sunlight filtered through the tree branches, casting dappled shadows on the patchy grass. Deena sat on a bench while I examined the ground for acorns.

Some of the trees showed their first hints of changing leaves. A few had begun to drop nuts and seeds. It didn't take long to find a handful of acorns beneath an old oak tree. It wasn't surprising Granny considered acorns lucky, I mused. Such a small thing contained such immense potential. To think, all the giant oaks, with their miles of twisty roots and sprawling branches, sprouted from little nuts no wider than my thumbnail.

A line from a play popped into my mind: *Luck is believing you're lucky.* As I recalled, it was a character in Tennessee Williams' *A Streetcar Named Desire* who'd said it. For years, the idea had stuck with me. Everything about superstitions, good and bad, came down to one's belief. It was the belief itself that held all the power.

Reaching for one more acorn, I imagined seeing a long-legged spiderlike creature picking its way among the sticks and leaves. Then I did see it. Without thinking, I dropped the acorns in my pocket, grabbed a stick, and placed it in the creature's path. The moment it crawled onto my trap, I picked up the stick and ran over to Deena.

"Quick! Quick! Come on, before this thing falls off."

Deena hopped up from the bench. "What is it? What do you have?"

"What else? A daddy long legs! Or 'granddaddy long legs,' as Granny would say."

Holding the stick in front of me like a dowsing rod, I scurried back to the parking lot. Deena trotted along at my side.

"I don't understand," she said. "Why did Granny want you to find a daddy long legs?"

"To lead us to the car," I answered. No explanation necessary. With my eyes fixed on the critter, nearly camouflaged on the stick, I returned to the spot where I'd last seen my Fiat.

"Okay. Let's see," I muttered. "Granddaddy, Granddaddy, where is my car?"

"Have you lost your mind?" demanded Deena.

"Just humor me," I said. "There's no harm in trying. Help me watch its feet."

"Does it *have* feet?" Somehow Deena managed to lean forward and hold back at the same time.

"Granny said it should point one foot in the direction of my car."

"It has eight legs," said Deena. "How is it going to point just one?"

"Hmm. Maybe we should try following it." I set the stick down on the pavement. The daddy long legs didn't move.

"You probably scared it to death," said Deena.

"It's not dead. But it probably is scared. Freezing up is its defense mechanism."

Deena nudged the end of the stick with her toe. "You know, if it does start moving, it won't go very fast. We'll be here all day—all week—trying to follow it."

She sounded so earnest, I started to laugh. This was absurd. I picked up the stick again and carried it to a strip of grass between the parking lot and the street. Deena kept a speculative eye on the critter, but I transferred my attention to the street. Instead of trying to get into the mind of an arachnid, I ought to be thinking like a thief. Or thieves.

There had to be more than one. Did somebody play the lookout while the other broke into my car? And how did they get here in the first place? Somebody else must have dropped them off.

I looked back at the empty parking space. *Once inside my car, they must have hotwired it. Then they simply drove away.* I glanced at the lot exit—there was only one. It opened to a one-way street, so the thieves had no choice but to turn left. Presumably, they didn't want to draw attention to themselves by breaking traffic laws.

I started up the sidewalk. Abandoning the daddy long legs, Deena followed me.

"They had to go this way," I said. The next street, which ran past the north side of the concert hall, was also one way and ended at a T, so we continued to the next corner. "They probably went right here. If they'd gone left, they would have risked us seeing them. We were standing outside the concert hall for more than an hour." I felt sure my car was taken shortly after we'd left it. I may have given up on the daddy long legs, but I was still enough like Granny to follow my intuition.

We proceeded in the direction I indicated and paused at the next intersection.

"Now what?" said Deena. "Left, right, or straight?"

Turning in place, I looked all around. I was afraid I'd reached the limits of my deductive reasoning, when I spotted something catty-corner across the street. "Look!"

"At what?" Deena followed my gaze. "Oh! No way."

It was a restaurant called Granddaddy's Bar-B-Que. We crossed the street, waited for the light to change, and crossed again. The restaurant appeared to be closed.

"It opens at eleven," said Deena, reading the sign on the door. Then she glanced at her phone. "It's only a quarter to ten now."

Once again, I stood gazing around. *I believe, I believe.* This new mantra felt right to me. Opening myself up to whatever I might see, I let my eyes wander to a nearby wedge-shaped plaza. A smattering of people rested on benches facing a circular, three-tiered fountain. A pair of squealing children chased each other around the plaza. An older lady was showing a toddler how to toss a coin in the fountain. On the edge of the sidewalk, a ruddy-faced newspaper vendor smiled at passersby. I nudged Deena and pointed.

As we approached the newspaperman, I realized he was selling *The Contributor*, a well-known street paper that provided work for the homeless. I reached into my purse for some cash to buy a paper and included a generous tip.

"Thank ya kindly," he said, with a dip of his chin. An ID on a lanyard around his neck stated his name was Chester.

I smiled in return. "By chance, were you here yesterday evening?"

"Yes, ma'am. I'm here every weekend."

"I wonder if you happened to notice a bright orange car go by, sometime after six o'clock. A Fiat, a little two-door hatchback. It was stolen last night."

He sucked on his teeth. "Stolen, eh? Sorry to hear that. I don't remember seeing a car like that last night."

My heart sank. It was a long shot anyway. "Oh, well. Just thought I'd ask. Thanks any—"

"I can guess where they took it, though," he said.

That got my attention. "You can?"

"You didn't hear it from me, mind ya."

"Of course. We won't breathe a word." I used my fingers to cross my heart.

He crinkled his eyes. "I believe ya. I don't know if I should tell ya, though. It's not exactly a safe place, especially for nice ladies such as yerselves. Of course, nobody'll be there before noon. Most of their work takes place at night."

"Please tell us," I begged. "We'll be careful."

Deena pulled out her wallet. "I think I have a twenty."

"Put your money away," said Chester. "I'm not tryin' to take advantage of you. Listen, this place is down by the river, past the docks. There's some old junkyards and bulk storage facilities. Beyond that is an overgrown lot with a barbed-wire fence and a sign that says Private Property. Back in there are some warehouses and, farther back, is a big garage. There's a chop shop in there."

I blanched. A chop shop? Was my poor Fiat even now lying in pieces, stripped for her more valuable parts?

"Let's call the police," said Deena. "We won't tell them where we got the info."

Chester chuckled. "The cops can't go in without a search warrant. And I didn't actually see your little car in there. This is only conjecture. Pretty good conjecture. It's not that far away, and the crooks would want to get off the road fast."

"The property is surrounded by a chain-link fence?" I asked.

"With barbed wire. I know a way in, though."

Deena and I exchanged a glance. *What are we getting ourselves into?*

"Like I said, if you get in and out before noon, you should be okay. Probably."

I gave him a grim smile. "We'd better hurry then. Now tell us about that way in."

It was eleven thirty by the time we made it to the river and found Chester's secret entrance. We'd had to tramp down a dusty service road, duck under a graffiti-covered railroad overpass, and sidestep broken glass on a weedy, earth-packed trail. When we finally reached the garage, a large, corrugated metal structure, I was sweaty, scratched, and scared. Deena looked like she'd been on a walk in the park.

"Chester would have told us if there were guard dogs, wouldn't he?" she said, giving the building a wary look.

"I'm sure he would have." If he knew about them.

My heart tap-danced in my chest as we circled the building. The garage doors were down, and the side entrance was locked. On the back wall, we found a grimy window. It appeared to be our only way in.

Of one mind, we dragged over a couple of cinder blocks and climbed up to peek inside. The interior was dark and dingy. As my eyes adjusted to the darkness, I made out evidence of a working garage. In the center was a freshly painted muscle car on a hydraulic lift. Worktables held hand tools and jugs of fluid. Used tires and other auto parts were strewn about on the floor, while mysterious metal drums and stacked cardboard boxes lurked in shadowy corners. Several tarp-covered vehicles hulked in two rows against a wall. Any one of them could be mine.

I tried to open the window, but it wouldn't budge.

"It's twenty 'til twelve," Deena whispered.

I bit my lip. I had to know. "Okay. Stand back."

She complied. I picked up a cinder block with both hands and tried to swing it.

"Oh, jeez," said Deena. "Let me help you."

She took one end of the cement block, and together we heaved it through the window. The sound of shattering glass pierced the silence like a gunshot. We jumped back.

"I can't believe we just did that," said Deena, with a slight tremble in her voice.

"Believe it." I climbed onto the remaining blocks and carefully removed the jagged pieces of glass still attached to the window frame. Then I crawled inside and dropped to the floor.

Deena poked her head in the window. "Give a girl a hand?"

I helped her climb through. For a second, we stood wide eyed, looking around. Then I shook myself. "Alright, let's check all the cars. There's no need to cover our trail. It will be obvious someone broke in."

"Righto."

Like game-show contestants in a grocery store, we raced around the garage, pulling tarps off covered vehicles. On my third try, I caught a glimpse of orange.

"I found it!"

Deena rushed over. "Is it in one piece?" She helped me pull the tarp all the way off.

"It seems to be." I opened the driver's side door and peered inside. The dome light came on, proving that the battery still worked. Popping the trunk, I confirmed our luggage was intact, apparently untouched.

Deena pulled out her phone and snapped some pictures, then checked the time. "It's almost noon. What do we do now? It's not like we can drive out of here. Even if we can get the garage door open, the gate outside is padlocked."

"I know." In the movies, the heroes would drive right through the locked chain-link fence. In real life, I was afraid I'd destroy my car and damage our bodies. "I'll call the cops."

Deena returned to the window, where glass now littered the floor. She squinted doubtfully at the high dusty opening.

"We can leave through the door," I pointed out.

"Right. I knew that." She headed to the door and unlocked it.

I lingered beside my car. "I hate to leave it."

"Sierra, we don't have a choice."

"I know. How about—let me just call the police now. Keep an eye outside."

Deena opened the door, as I dialed 9-1-1. I tried to explain the situation in general terms, but it took a few attempts to get the dispatcher to understand. While I told her who I was and described where we were, I roamed around the garage. It definitely had a sketchy vibe. I could easily envision it as the base of operations for other crimes besides grand theft auto. Drug running, maybe, or counterfeiting. Who knew what else took place in this well-hidden den?

More importantly, who was behind it?

I promised the operator I'd meet the police at the gate, then ended the call. In my wanderings, I'd come to a small glass-walled office. I tried the knob and found it unlocked.

"Sierra!" hissed Deena. "It's after twelve o'clock. Are you coming?"

"Yeah. Just a sec."

The office appeared to be little-used. There was a metal desk but no computer. The only papers in sight were an old phone book and some car magazines. Opening the center desk drawer, I found some small tools and screws. Another drawer contained a mishmash of crumpled business cards. *Those might provide some leads for the cops.*

I started to close the drawer when something caught my eye. I took a second look. *I know that card.* I had a copy of my own.

"Sierra!" Deena sounded frantic. "I hear a car coming! We have to go *now.*"

"Coming!" I left the office and dashed across the garage, casting a brief look of regret at the Fiat—and wondering how the business card of Taz Banyan, Wedding Planner, had wound up in a desk at a chop shop.

Chapter 22

We ran like the hounds of hell were barking at our heels. I didn't know if we'd been seen, because I didn't look back. We retraced our steps to Chester's secret entrance and jogged to the front gate in time to hear sirens shrilling in the distance. It was that sound that made Deena and me look at each other, panting, with a new fear in our eyes.

"Are we going to get in trouble?" she asked. "For trespassing, or breaking and entering?"

The sirens grew louder. I pushed my bangs off my damp forehead. "Listen, admit nothing, okay? The less we say, the better. Just the bare facts: Someone told us where to find my car. We found it. We don't have to tell the cops how we got in." I hoped they'd be more interested in arresting a gang of car thieves than bothering with us.

Deena nodded, then took out her brush and ran it through her hair, instantly making it neat and shiny once more.

As it happened, I was partly right. The police team was very interested in what we'd found and impressed with Deena's photos. Together, our statements and the pictures provided the "probable cause" the authorities needed to enter the property without a warrant. As one officer cut the chains on the gate, another one offered us a ride to police head-quarters in the back of a squad car.

That's where the easy part ended. Deena and I were separated and taken into different interrogation rooms. The officer who questioned me was polite enough, but kept cir-cling around to ask how we'd found the place. At one point, she even suggested I was in on the scheme. It was harder to keep my promise to Chester than I'd expected, but I did it. I only fibbed a little, in saying I didn't know my informant's name. When I mentioned my connection with the murder of a Nashvillian in Aerieville, I was subjected to a whole slew of new questions from another investigator.

Besides all the questioning, I also hadn't anticipated not getting my car back right away. After all, it was my prop-erty. Unfortunately, it was also evidence. The police confis-cated the Fiat, along with some of the other cars, and had them towed to the impound lot. We had no choice but to wait while the police investigated the chop shop and exam-ined my car.

The long afternoon turned into a longer evening. Finally released from interrogation, we hung out for a while in the lobby at the station. My mind kept mulling over everything that had happened, trying to make sense of it all. I also kept my ears pricked for any snippet of information. Fortunately, the second shift were prone to chatter. When one cop told another about the discovery of the chop shop, the other made a strange comment that caught my attention.

"That'll be one of the last of the Fleece shops," said an older cop.

"Oh, right," said the younger one. "I heard about that. What was it called? Operation Fleece Monkey? You're an older-timer, you must've been around for that."

The two officers laughed and moved out of our hearing.

Deena and I looked at each other, and she raised an eyebrow. "What did they say? 'Fleece Monkey'?"

"As in *grease monkey*?" I guessed. I picked up my phone and typed a quick search of *Operation Fleece Monkey.* "Ohh," I said, as the results appeared on the screen. "*Fleece* as a verb. It was a government operation to take down this big gang of professional car thieves back in the nineties."

"The nineties? That's a long time ago," said Deena.

"Yeah, it says here the gang was part of an organized criminal network led by a dude who went by the name of Philo."

"Interesting nickname," said Deena. "Was it meant to be ironic? 'Philo' means *loving.*"

I chuckled. "I don't know. But when Philo was arrested, the gang apparently unraveled. Car thefts dropped off dramatically after that."

According to the articles I read, chop shops used to be more prevalent back before the 1980s and '90s when vehicle manufacturers began marking auto parts. But that didn't mean they weren't still around. I also learned that Philo's criminal enterprise encompassed more than car theft. They were involved in all kinds of racketeering operations, from the sale of counterfeit consumer goods to music piracy.

"Well, it's always good to branch out," Deena said wryly. "Diversify."

"Right. And that also means there were a lot of people involved. Philo wasn't the only one arrested, but I wonder if some of the gang got away."

In another bit of overheard conversation, we also learned that we weren't the only ones questioned tonight. Evidently, the police found the person who had driven up to the garage, sending us running. He was a mechanic who claimed he was only paid to do bodywork. Naturally, he swore he didn't know the vehicles were stolen. Whether he was telling the truth or not, the fact remained that I still didn't know who was behind the theft of my car.

We killed the rest of the time by finding something to eat and making phone calls. Deena informed Lloyd Watson my car had been found, much to the manager's great relief. I called Granny to let her know her advice had helped, but that I wouldn't make it back to Aerieville in time for dinner. In fact, I began to think we were going to have to stay another night in Nashville. Neither Deena nor I wanted to do that. No matter how late it was, we wanted to go home.

Finally, shortly after nine o'clock, I was told I could have my car. Driving home in the quiet Tennessee night, I felt like I was traveling in a dream. It had been such a strange and emotionally draining forty-eight hours.

Deena and I kept each other awake by singing old songs and swapping stories of our most embarrassing moments. I had quite a few. By the time I dropped her off at her apartment near the Aerieville town square, I felt my friend was no longer just a friend. She was my sister.

I could have gone home then, and picked Gus up in the morning. But I didn't want to wait. Calvin had assured me he'd still be awake. I parked by the back door of Flower House and found Cal and Gus waiting for me in the kitchen. Gus's ecstatic welcome was a good distraction from the sudden shyness I felt around Calvin. Would we ever get past these constant separations and awkward reunions?

"Do you want to come upstairs?" he asked. "Have something to eat or drink?"

It was nearly one thirty in the morning, and I was more than beat. I nodded anyway. After what I'd been through, I didn't feel like being alone. "A glass of water would be great."

I sat on Calvin's couch with Gus's head on my lap. Calvin sat on the pup's other side, with his attention fixed on me. He didn't say much, but he was a good listener. I told him everything. The whole chaotic, twisty-turny saga. Of course, he had a chuckle when I told him about "Operation Fleece Monkey." Calvin always loved a good pun.

When I finished the tale, he shook his head in disbelief. "That's a lot." He quirked his lips into a slight smile at the understatement.

"I know. It makes me think . . . multiple things are going on. Right? With Taz's murder, and people following me. Setting fires and stealing cars. It has to be more than one person."

By this time, I realized my voice was fading and my eyelids felt heavy. Calvin brought me a pillow and blanket and coaxed Gus to the floor. I stretched out on the couch and dropped instantly to sleep.

A melodic ringing sound penetrated my dreams. I ignored it. There was no way it could be time to get up. My body protested.

The ringing stopped, and I drifted off again, vaguely wondering where I was. My left arm dangled toward the floor. Something wet touched my fingers. Opening one eye, I saw Gus sniffing my hand. I stretched my fingers to scratch the top of his head.

The ringing started up again. Groaning, I pushed myself to my elbows. Now I remembered. I was in Calvin's apartment. The gray light filtering through the living room windows indicated it was early morning.

I fumbled for my purse and found my phone. I figured it was my mom calling, but the display said it was Richard.

"Hello?" My voice sounded thick with grogginess.

"Tell me you're back from Nashville," he said.

"I'm back."

"Thank goodness. You need to stop digging around into the wedding planner's murder."

Something in his voice made me sit up, suddenly more alert. "Why? Has something happened?"

"It's Kendall. She was found about an hour ago at the bottom of a ravine."

I clapped my hand over my mouth. "Is she—"

"In the ICU," he supplied. "In critical condition."

"Richard! You could have led with that. I thought she was dead."

"She may well be yet. She hasn't regained consciousness, and she got pretty banged up. Her car is totaled."

Calvin came into the living room, wearing rumpled plaid pajama bottoms and a white T-shirt. His hair stuck up in a kind of adorable way. My eyes flickered to him and then away. I needed to focus on what Richard was saying.

"That's terrible, Richard. I hope she pulls through."

"Me too. But I'm more worried about you."

"Me? Why?"

"Davy says it's possible Kendall was run off the road. From the things she'd said to me, I could tell she was scared. She knew she might be in danger. She'd been poking around, making somebody nervous. Just like you are."

Calvin moved to the kitchen, which was separated from the living room by a breakfast bar in a wall cutout. I could hear him opening and shutting cabinets and running the water. A minute later, I heard the gurgle of the coffee pot. Richard was still going on about how Kendall must have been targeted—and probably by the same person who had murdered Taz.

"I'll be careful," I promised.

"You gotta be more than careful, Sierra. You really should stop playing detective. Taz was mixed up in something, some bad business. Whoever killed him won't hesitate to kill again."

"Relax, Richard. I don't have the energy for sleuthing right now anyway. Today I'll be focusing on flowers."

"Good. I'll check in with you later. We should do lunch. And seriously, take care of yourself."

I told him goodbye and joined Calvin in the kitchen. He was scrambling eggs and making toast. As I set the table and poured myself a cup of coffee, I shared what Richard had said.

He put eggs on a plate and handed it to me, then helped himself. We sat across from each other at his small kitchen table, with Gus at our feet.

"When did Kendall's accident happen?" he asked.

"Richard didn't say. I think it must have been last night."

"And your car was stolen the day before, on Saturday night. If Kendall really was forced off the road, it could have been the same person responsible for both incidents."

"Yeah. They sure get around, huh?" I tried to picture this person, the faceless, helmeted scooter driver. Who was this brazen individual zipping back and forth between Aerieville and Nashville? It *had* to be one of the wedding vendors, right? They'd killed Taz, then shoved me in the street the next day. They'd followed me to Nashville, arranged for my car to be stolen, stranding me for hours, while they hunted down Kendall.

I stared into my coffee cup. Did this same person break into the mayor's office and set the wedding programs on fire? Or could it be that all the mischief at Bellman Manor was caused by someone else?

Calvin cleared his throat. "Did I hear you tell Richard you're going to stop looking into Taz's murder?"

Ha. Fat chance. "I told him I won't be doing that today.

I'm not going to quit altogether, but I don't want him to worry."

Calvin didn't respond. He took a bite of toast and tossed a crumb to Gus.

I regarded him over my coffee cup. He looked like he had something to say and was holding back.

Finally, he glanced at me with a half grin. "Have you given any thought to the Arwin Treasure? It's an excellent excuse to skip town for a while."

I stared at him for a moment. "Seriously? You know I can't just up and leave the flower shop like Felix did. I'm trying to run a business here."

His smile faltered and he stood up, taking his plate to the sink. "You can do anything you want," he said. "In the grand scheme, I mean. You do have a choice. We all do."

I pushed back from the table and stood as well. He was being weird, and I didn't have time for it.

"Right now, I need to go home and take a shower." I called Gus with a kissing sound. "Thanks for letting me sleep on your couch. And for breakfast. And for watching Gus."

"Of course." Calvin took the plate from my hand.

I grabbed Gus's leash from a chair beside the door and attached it to his collar. He was always excited to go outside. I let him pull me out the door and down the steps, suddenly in a hurry to get home.

Chapter 23

My house felt stale and neglected. It had only been a week-end, yet my plants were droopy and the leftovers in the fridge needed to be tossed. Maybe the neglect had started before I'd left. My mind had been elsewhere.

I threw open all the windows and gave Gus a puzzle toy. As I showered (using my non-luxury but perfectly functional all-natural drugstore soap), I tried to process everything that had happened. It was a lot. A lot of food for thought, any-way. Nothing much definitive. In fact, I was finding it dif-ficult to draw any clear conclusions—especially since my mind kept wandering back to Calvin.

I felt bad about leaving him so abruptly. He was worried about me, that much was obvious. I could also tell he was try-ing not to overstep his bounds, especially since it wasn't his place to tell me what to do. After all, he was the one who'd gone off and left me over the summer, without bothering to try to define our relationship. If we even had a relationship.

I couldn't blame him for worrying, though. As soon as my family found out about my escapades retrieving my stolen car, they'd probably all gang up on me to drop this case too.

Then there was Kendall's car accident. I had to admit that was concerning. As I pulled on a pair of faded jeans and a long-sleeved baby blue T-shirt, I tried to work out what might have happened. Had she discovered something related to Taz's murder? Or was she getting too close? Was she forced off the road by another vehicle—such as a scooter? Was that even possible? Maybe she'd been driving while impaired. Or maybe someone had tampered with her brakes. There was so much I didn't know.

Applying a dab of makeup, I noticed my fair skin was pinker than usual. In all my traipsing around outside I'd picked up a little sun. *What else did I pick up?* Enough to make someone nervous?

I couldn't deny the parallels between Kendall and me. We'd both been sneaking around—as Taz had written, she was definitely "up to something"—and somebody had tried to put us both out of commission. Considering the timing, it very well could have been the same "somebody." Of course, if multiple people were involved, the timing didn't even matter.

Something else was bothering me. Something my tired brain finally comprehended. Kendall could end this thing in an instant, if she woke up and could talk. If someone felt threatened by her before, they'd surely feel ten times more so now. Kendall could be in danger.

I washed my hands and reached for my phone. Deena's parents worked at the hospital, her mother as an administrator and her father as a surgeon. I rang her up and filled her in on Kendall's "accident." Then I locked up the dollhouse and hustled Gus back to the car. *No rest for the weary.*

By the time we met up at Flower House to open the shop, Deena had the inside scoop.

"The doctors have Kendall drugged up on sedatives and painkillers," said Deena, prepping a vase at the kitchen sink.

"She'll probably pull through—she's relatively young and in good health otherwise. But it's still serious."

I stood at the worktable, looking at a flower order but not seeing it. "Is she under guard? Can she receive visitors?"

"No visitors except family, who apparently are flying in from New York later today or tomorrow." Deena set the vase down in front of me and picked up the order to read which flowers we needed.

"So, no one can, like, sneak in and pull the plug or anything, right?" I said it in a half-kidding way, but I really wanted to know.

Deena smiled. "It's not like in the movies. No one is going to steal a lab coat and a stethoscope and sneak into her room. There's a nurse's station right across the hall and all kinds of activity around there, at all hours."

"That's good." So, Kendall was safe. For now. But if she'd been on to something—even if she didn't realize it— and someone had tried to silence her . . . who was to say they wouldn't try to finish the job?

For the next hour, I filled orders and ruminated. I couldn't shake the feeling that time was running short. I had to do something. I couldn't just back off and wait for something else to happen.

An image of Bellman Manor wavered in my mind, and the elegant great hall, fit for a royal family. Perusing our flower selection in the pails and refrigerated cases, I selected white phalaenopsis (aka moth orchid), white lilies, and blush pink roses. I arranged them in a pedestal vase with abundant greenery. Then I told my team I was stepping out to make a delivery. I wanted to see Annaliese.

Since she didn't expect me, I parked in the circle driveway and rang the front doorbell. The housekeeper, Gretchen, must have been in the foyer. She answered the door at once.

"Oh. Hello," she said, looking behind me. Evidently, she was expecting someone else.

"Good morning. Is Mrs. Lakely in? I brought her flowers." I held up the arrangement as proof.

Gretchen took the vase. "I'll see that she gets it."

To my dismay, she started to shut me out. I grabbed the edge of the door, hoping I wouldn't get my fingers slammed.

"Could you please tell her Sierra is here? I have some information for her."

She hesitated a moment, then nodded and told me to wait. A few minutes later, she returned and invited me in to the sitting room.

Annaliese was reclining in an armchair, her bronze-shadowed eyelids closed. Though dressed in a designer outfit (I assumed) and sporting a fully made-up face, she'd lost her luster. She reminded me of a wilted flower, once bold and beautiful, now faded and dying.

She opened her eyes at my approach. "Ah, Sierra. Thank you for the flowers." She waved one listless hand toward the arrangement, which Gretchen had placed on a console table.

"Are you okay, Mrs. Lakely?" Without waiting for an invitation, I perched on the sofa across from her. "I haven't heard from you in a few days."

"I've been better." She touched her right temple with the tips of her golden-ringed fingers. "I'm plagued with headaches."

"I'm sorry to hear that."

She smiled without humor. "Also husband aches. Frank found out about the affair with Taz. The *non*-affair, I should say. Not that it matters. He's quite cross with me."

"Have you heard from Marissa?" I asked.

"Not a word." She winced, and I gathered her daughter's disappearing act was more painful than her headache. "Naturally, the wedding is off."

"I'm sorry," I repeated. It was sad to see Annaliese like this, so defeated and deflated. Especially when she'd displayed such determined optimism before. Where was her spark?

She sighed. "I have a lot of calls to make. Cancellations. Maybe Regina will do it for me."

"Did you hear about Kendall?"

"The photographer? Yes. I know she was in a bad accident. Yet another reason to call off the wedding, I suppose."

I frowned. "Mrs. Lakely, a few days ago you wanted to hire me to solve Taz's murder. I take it you don't want that anymore?"

She gave me a startled look. "Why? Have you found out something?"

"I've found out a few things. I just returned from Nashville late last night."

She sat up straighter, finally looking more like her old self. "You've been investigating? You said this was a police matter."

So I had. "That's true. It is. And I've been asking questions anyway." I couldn't seem to help myself.

"Well, what have you learned?"

I was happy to see the light in her eyes again. "I learned Taz may have made a few enemies in his climb to the top." I told her about his rejection of Regina as a business partner and about the kickbacks he'd demanded from everyone who'd worked with him. He'd enriched himself at their expense, and without regard to his clients' wishes.

Annaliese sprang from her chair. "Why, that little devil. Did he really? But he was so charming."

"Who said the devil wasn't charming?" I said. "In fact, I think he was two-faced." I remembered how Taz had pivoted from berating Anton to flattering Annaliese in the blink of an eye.

She paced to the window and looked outside. "Is that why he was killed? Because someone had had enough? It seems so extreme."

"It *is* extreme. But I also suspect there was more to it." I recalled where I'd discovered Taz's card. Thinking out loud, I said, "He might have been mixed up in other illegal activities besides extortion . . . and maybe Kendall was onto him. Remember how he'd written that she was up to something?"

"That's right! We should talk to her."

"Unfortunately, she can't talk right now. She's still unconscious in the hospital."

"Oh. Of course." Annaliese returned to her chair and stood behind it. "You don't suppose her accident . . . wasn't an accident?"

I gave her a level gaze. "I think the sooner the killer is caught the safer everyone will be."

Two little lines appeared between her eyebrows. "So, what now? What can we do?"

I bit my lip, vaguely aware it was becoming a bad habit. "I've been thinking. The only way to catch the killer is to lay a trap."

"That sounds dangerous. What do you have in mind?"

Standing up, I moved toward the console table and centered the vase of flowers. "We need to get all the vendors to come back here." I looked up at Annaliese. "The wedding must go on."

She raised one thin eyebrow. "That's a little difficult without a bride. Marissa isn't here."

"We have to find her."

The doorbell rang, but Annaliese didn't acknowledge it. She was staring at the fireplace, lost in thought. "I've asked everyone. I just can't figure out who it is."

"Who it is?" Now I was lost.

She turned to face me. "Who it is that she's staying with. I spoke with Michael-William. *He* heard from Marissa."

"That's great!" I'd begun to worry something might have happened to her. "What did she say to him?"

"She told him she's staying with an old friend for a little while. Evidently, she wouldn't say who, and he doesn't know. I've contacted all her school friends—and their mothers—and no one has heard from Marissa." Annaliese sighed. "That girl can be as stubborn as a goat sometimes. Michael-William, bless his heart, still plans to fly in on Wednesday. As soon as we clear Marissa's name, we hope she'll come out of hiding. But who knows when that will be."

Gretchen appeared in the doorway. "Mr. Peters is here."

"Thank you, Gretchen. Show him in, please." Annaliese patted her hair and moved toward the door. "My lawyer. The state police are pressuring Frank and me to come in and answer questions. This is such a mess, Sierra."

I picked up my purse from the sofa. It was clear she wanted me to leave, but first I needed to extract a promise from her. "Will you hold off on canceling the wedding? Call Regina and tell her to set up another vendor meeting. Tell her she can choose a new photographer and florist."

"A new florist? What about you?"

"I found out Tammy wants to come back on, and I think it's a good idea to let her." It pained me to give up the job, but there were bigger matters at stake. Matters of life and death.

She nodded. "Alright. If you say so. What about Marissa?"

"I'll find her."

When I returned to the shop, I found Calvin outside repairing the wooden fence marking the boundary between the Morrisons' property and the Flower House lot. Gus was running circles in the grass. The corgi trotted up to greet me as I walked to the back door. Calvin barely looked up. With a twinge of guilt, I promised myself we'd sit down for a heart-to-heart sometime soon. At the moment, I had more pressing concerns.

Deena was at the register ringing up a customer, a young man purchasing a dozen dark pink roses.

"Nice choice," I said, smiling at him as Deena handed him the wrapped flowers.

His face turned a shade of pink to match the rose petals. "I hope she likes them," he said.

"She'll love them," I assured him. I didn't know who they were for, but I couldn't think of a single person who wouldn't appreciate receiving roses. I held the door open for him and wished him luck.

Returning to Deena, I rested an elbow on the checkout counter. We spoke at the same time. "Any news?"

She shook her head. "None from me. Allie is in the café. I thought it might be nice to rotate her job duties, so she doesn't get bored."

"Good idea. Say, I have a question. You mentioned meeting Marissa at a birthday party when you were kids. Whose party was it?"

"Janie Meadows. Why?"

I told Deena about Marissa supposedly hiding out with an old friend. Since neither her mother nor her fiancé could identify the friend, I figured it might be someone she knew from before her boarding school days.

"Do you remember Janie?" asked Deena. Something about the tone of her voice gave me pause.

"A little. Wasn't she on scholastic bowl with you? Then she transferred to some special school for smart kids, didn't she?"

"The Math and Science Academy," Deena affirmed. "She

went on to study engineering and got a patent for a new technology she invented. I don't know the details, but it was a pretty big deal. She became quite rich."

I scrunched my eyes, trying to remember if I knew this. "Sounds familiar. That must have been around the time I was hitting my stride in Nashville. So, where is she now?"

Deena shrugged. "That's the thing. For a while, she was in Silicon Valley. Then she moved back east and became a recluse. I heard she built some kind of a fortress-of-a-house deep in the mountains, where she can work on her inventions out of the spotlight. I guess she got tired of all the attention she was getting simply for being a woman in STEM."

I made a wry face. I couldn't blame her there. But a fortress? *What a perfect place for Marissa to hide out.*

"Does Janie have any family around here anymore?" I asked.

"I don't know." Deena appeared doubtful. "Her parents moved to Europe, I think. The house where we used to have the parties was sold a long time ago. When we had our class reunion last year, Janie was one of the few people the reunion committee couldn't locate. Even though she didn't graduate with us, she would have been invited."

I drummed my fingers on the counter. Surely someone must have a way of contacting Janie.

My phone rang, and Deena snapped her fingers. "That's probably Richard. I forgot to tell you. He wants to have lunch with us."

She was right. Richard asked if we could meet at the Bluebird Café. To his surprise—and mine—I suggested Nell's Diner instead. A couple of ideas were percolating in the back of my mind. For more than one reason, it was high time to pay a visit to Nell Cusley, Aerieville's own gossip queen.

Chapter 24

We arrived at the diner, a classic greasy spoon in a narrow, vintage-looking building, at the tail end of the lunch rush. Richard was already there, in one of the red vinyl booths next to the windows. He waved at us when we entered. We caught up with small talk before placing our orders. The menu was standard diner fare, not the healthiest but always satisfying. Recently, Nell had added grilled veggie burgers as a Meatless Monday option. I opted for that, rationalizing the fact that I planned on a slice of pie for dessert.

Nell could usually be found behind the counter taking orders and serving the folks at the bar. Today, she gave the waitress a break and brought us our orders herself. I'd had a feeling she might.

"Hello, hello," she said. "Good to see the Flower House crew. Shame about what happened at the mayor's mansion." She never was one to waste any time when it came to juicy topics. She'd missed her calling as a news reporter—or a gossip columnist.

"Yes," we all agreed.

"A shame," Richard echoed.

"I guess the focus is on the family now," she prodded. "The mayor, and his wife and daughter."

"Why do you say that?" I asked, wondering what she'd heard. With the police station so near, staff and officers often stopped in for a bite to eat. And Nell always had her ear to the ground.

"I heard there's a *personal* angle to the investigations. A love-triangle situation? Poor Marissa was so distraught, she ran away. And now the wedding's off." She tsked like a mother hen.

I decided to spread some rumors—er, information—myself. "Marissa didn't run away."

Nell cocked her head with interest. I continued in a voice of authority. "I just came from Bellman Manor. The wedding isn't off. Marissa is taking a brief R and R, considering what happened, but she'll be back." I'd see to that.

"You don't say," said Nell. "Seems like an ominous way to start a marriage."

Richard lifted his glass of Coke. "Cheers to the bride and groom. May nothing stand in the way of love."

Deena clinked his glass with her own, and Nell left us to our lunch. As soon as she was out of earshot, Richard fixed me with a stern glare.

I stopped mid-bite into a French fry and widened my eyes innocently. "What?"

"You just came from Bellman Manor, did you? And the wedding is proceeding? Did you not heed my warning?"

Deena gave Richard a "get real" look. "You ought to know by now," she said. "Sierra doesn't heed anything but her own heart."

I put down the French fry. "I'm taking your warning *very* seriously. That's why I'm trying to uncover the truth as quickly as possible." Dropping my voice, I leaned forward. "At this point, I don't care if the wedding proceeds or not.

I want to find Marissa, so I can ask her some questions and, hopefully, convince her to come back. I want all the vendors to *think* the wedding is happening. It seems to be the only way they'll return to Aerieville."

Richard looked from me to Deena, and she lifted one shoulder in a slight shrug. Then she grinned. "You should have seen us in Nashville, Richard. We tracked down suspects and got people to talk to us better than the cops could have. Sierra is really good at this sort of thing."

"You're a regular Cagney and Lacey, huh?" His voice was mocking, but I knew it came from a place of affectionate concern.

"Something like that," said Deena.

I resumed eating my fries, chewing around a smile. Now that we were home safely, it was easier to remember the fun parts of our trip.

But Richard wasn't ready to let us off the hook. "Don't forget, Cagney and Lacey had something you two don't."

"What?" we said in unison.

"Guns."

Nell returned to refill my water glass and remove Deena's salad plate. "Guns? Who has guns?"

Richard flexed his biceps. "These kind of guns. Deena and Sierra don't have them. They need to get to Dumbbells and work on that."

Deena looked thoughtful. "That's not a bad idea. Maybe we should."

I tried not to roll my eyes. There was only one reason she'd want to go to Dumbbells, and it wasn't to tone muscles. The only biceps she cared about were my brother's.

Nell still hovered, so I decided to test her knowledge of famous local residents. "Nell, do you remember Janie Meadows, the inventor? Or her family?"

"Janie Meadows? Sure I do. She was supposed to be the

female Elon Musk of Tennessee—until she dropped off the face of the planet. Why do you ask?"

"Mrs. Lakely wanted to invite her to the wedding, but she couldn't find her address." It was a fib, but I didn't think Annaliese would mind.

Nell gazed out the window toward the parking lot. I could almost hear the Rolodex spinning in her brain.

"Her parents moved away. Their people weren't from these parts. I believe Janie moved back, though. She came in here, oh, about three years ago. She was looking at land in Sevier County, as I recall." Nell redirected her gaze to me. "Anyone else famous on the guest list? The groom must know some bigwigs from Washington."

"Uh, I couldn't say." Of course, I had no idea.

Richard sucked air noisily through his straw. When he had Nell's attention, he smiled cheekily. "May I trouble you for a refill?"

She took his empty glass. "Certainly."

"Sevier County," I muttered. "If Janie bought land, shouldn't there be documentation of the land transfer?"

Richard tilted his head. "Not necessarily in her name. Some people set up land trusts so they can purchase property anonymously." He used to work at a bank, so he'd know.

"Dang. That's sneaky."

"What about building permits?" asked Deena. "If she built a big house, wouldn't there be a permit under her name?"

"Maybe," said Richard.

I pulled out my phone and looked up the county records office in Sevierville. After a moment, I made a face. "This isn't going to be easy. We can submit a request for copies of public records, but it will take a few days to get a response. Also, we have to know exactly what to ask for."

"Sevierville," said Deena. "Now that you mention it, I think I know someone who works in a government office there.

Remember Eric Chamberlain? We were on the debate team together."

"Vaguely," I said. "Do you have his number?"

She was already scrolling through the contacts in her phone. "Here he is. Let's see what he knows."

While she typed a rapid text message, Richard pulled out his own phone to check his messages. "Oh!" he said, sounding pleasantly surprised.

"Something good?" I asked.

"Davy is on his way here. He wants me to order him a sandwich."

Deena looked up and smiled. "Nice."

"That's great," I said. "Does that mean . . ." I trailed off, not wanting to be presumptuous. Richard's boyfriend hadn't been as open about their relationship as Richard was.

Richard smirked. "Let's just say the door is open, and Davy has one foot out of the closet."

I was about to ask him if Davy had shared any news about the murder investigation, but Nell returned with Richard's refill. After taking the order for Davy, Nell started to ask me something, but my phone buzzed in my purse.

"Excuse me," I said, taking it out.

Seeing that we were all three bowed in contemplation over our phones, Nell scowled and left us again.

My message was from Calvin. *Hey—Your mom is here. Will you be back soon?*

Oops. I hadn't called my mom since returning to town last night. I should have figured she'd come looking for me.

"Whoop!" exclaimed Deena, causing Richard and me to stare at her. "Eric got back to me! He knows someone in the permitting office, and he thinks they should be able to help us. If it was a new residential construction as big as we think, he said someone ought to remember it."

"It pays to know people," said Richard.

The diner door opened, and a stocky, dark-haired police officer came in. Davy Wills was Rocky's age and one of the nicest guys I knew. He slid into the seat next to Richard.

"How's it going at the station?" I asked, after exchanging pleasantries. "Has Agent What's-his-name taken up shop?"

"Agent Collins? Chief gave him a cubicle." Davy's eyes sparkled, but he made no comment.

"So," I said casually, "are they using the polygraph today?"

Davy pursed his lips, not fooled for a minute. "The polygraph examiner has been waiting all morning, and no one has come in yet. If not for the accident investigation, somebody might have come looking for you."

"I've been busy," I said.

"You and everybody else," said Davy. "The mayor and Mrs. Lakely are supposed to come in this afternoon."

"With their lawyer," I said, since I was in the know.

"Mayor doesn't have much of a choice," said Nell, suddenly at our table again. It was as if she'd never left. "No one believes he wasn't at home when the murder happened." She set a plate of food in front of Davy and remained standing there, waiting for someone to respond. Davy took a bite of his sandwich.

My phone buzzed again. Before I could check it, Davy wiped his mouth and nodded at me. "By the way, Renee mentioned she'd be popping over here for a late lunch pretty soon. Just so you know."

Ugh. I really didn't want to run into Captain Bradley. Between that possibility and Calvin's pleas to rescue him from my mom, I needed to get back to Flower House. I placed my napkin on my plate and took a final sip of water.

"Ready for some pie?" asked Nell. "We have lemon meringue, coconut, and chocolate silk."

"Yum," said Deena.

I glanced over at the pie case with regret. "Unfortunately, I have to pass today." Touching Deena's arm, I said, "My mom is waiting for me at Flower House, but you don't have to leave. Maybe Richard can give you a ride back." I looked at him, and he nodded his ascent. Davy gave me a friendly wave.

Nell took my plate and followed me to the door. "By the way," she said to my back, "I've been meaning to look in on you."

I turned around. "Oh?"

"Since you were almost hit by a car out there in the intersection last week."

"You heard about that?" It seemed so long ago now.

"I saw it myself," she said. "It was that demon on the racing bike. Going too fast and driving on the sidewalk. It was an accident waiting to happen."

"Racing bike? You mean a motorcycle?" I couldn't believe what I was hearing. Why hadn't I come in here sooner? Of course Nell would know something about the incident.

"It was a motor scooter," she said. "One of them racing types. I saw it again late last night, speeding down Main Street." She shook her head in disapproval.

Late last night? "Any idea who it was?"

"No, or else I'd report them for sure. They wore a big black helmet and a full-body riding suit."

"What kind of scooter was it? Did you see the make or model, or the license plate?"

Noticing my intense interest, she softened her stance. "No, hon. It was going way too fast. All I know is, whoever it was, they weren't from around here."

Mom's car was parked along the street in front of Flower House. I entered through the back, as usual, and found her in the café with Calvin and Allie. It was the sound of salsa music that led me to them. To my amazement, they were in the center of the room, the tables having been pushed to the side. Mom was teaching them a line dance.

I stood back for a moment, my hand covering my mouth. Mom was so enthusiastic, as she always was when she led her aerobics classes. Allie's face was scrunched in concentration, her forehead moist with perspiration, as she swayed her hips and kicked her leg under Mom's instruction. Calvin was a sport, stepping right along—though, as I watched, I saw that he seemed to be making up his own moves. I laughed in spite of myself.

Mom looked up and beckoned me over. "Come join us, Sierra! It's a great workout. Super fun."

"This isn't the gym, Mom."

She waved her hands dismissively. "No one is here anyway."

Calvin grinned at me before moving over to turn off the music. Allie looked mortified.

"I'm sorry, Sierra," she said quickly. "I'll get back to the register."

"It's okay, Allie," I assured her. "I'm not mad."

She hurried out anyway as Calvin pushed the tables back to where they belonged. Mom grabbed me by the elbow and guided me to the velvet sofa near the front window.

"What have you been up to?" she demanded. "I want to hear all about this impromptu trip you took to Nashville."

I showed her my pink glittery fingernails. "Deena treated me to a spa day." I showed her the pictures I'd taken at Centennial Park and other spots around the city. Luckily, it was Deena, and not me, who had taken photos at the chop shop. I didn't have the heart—or the guts—to share that bit of our adventure.

After a while, Mom checked her watch and said she

needed to get back to the gym. "You're coming for dinner on Wednesday, I assume. Will you be bringing Calvin again?" He'd left the café, thank goodness, and didn't hear her question.

"I'm not sure, Mom. I'll let you know."

I walked with her to the front door. She faced me before she left. "You should go visit Granny Mae, whenever you have a chance. She's been worried about you. You know how she is with her dreams and portents." Mom gave me a piercing look, as if waiting for me to confirm whether or not Granny was right to worry.

Impulsively, I leaned in and gave my mom a hug. "I'll visit Granny the first chance I get."

A short while later, Toby came in from the greenhouse and asked if I had any deliveries for him to make. After checking the computer, I told him we had a couple for the next morning. Then I handed him a bag of leftover cookies and sent him and his sister home.

I locked the front door and headed toward the register as Calvin walked up the hallway. We were alone again for the first time since early this morning. Gus trotted out of the office and cocked his head, looking from one of us to the other. He probably wondered which one of us would feed him tonight.

"Do you have dinner plans?" asked Calvin. "Feel like going out?"

What's this? Is he asking me on a date? With all we'd been through together, we'd never been on a proper date. I searched his blue eyes for a clue to his intentions.

Misreading my silence, he bit the inside of his cheek. "Or are you still mad at me?"

"I'm not mad at you. I'm just . . . confused." I decided to lay it on the line. "I don't know what we're doing here."

He opened his mouth to respond, when Gus gave a bark

and the front doorknob jiggled, then turned. Deena let herself in with her shop key.

"He-ey," she called. "I got it!"

Calvin and I turned to her in surprise.

"You got—" I began.

"The address! Janie's address, GPS coordinates, and everything. And you were right. Her place is so deeply off the beaten track, it has to be where Marissa is hiding out." Deena seemed exceptionally pleased with herself—as well she should be. I was impressed too.

"That's great! I'll get my purse."

Deena faltered, quirking her eyebrows in consternation. "Wait. Do you mean to go now?"

"Of course. This can't wait. Kendall could wake up any minute. And the wedding is supposed to happen in five days." I dashed into the office and grabbed my purse. Sensing my excitement, Gus ran after me, yipping at my heels. Deena and Calvin followed too.

"It's a long drive," Deena said. "And it's starting to cloud up outside."

"It's not that late," I countered. "We can grab some food on our way."

"Oh, well." Deena shifted her feet, her enthusiasm all but gone. "I thought we might go tomorrow."

Gus barked again. Calvin called him into the kitchen and shook the dog-food bag. That was enough to distract the pup. *Food before friends.* He darted into the kitchen as the sound of kibbles rattled into his metal bowl.

I studied Deena's face. *Ah. She has plans.* "You don't have to come," I said. "Text me the address, okay?"

"You can't go by yourself," she said. "Can't you wait 'til morning? This place is going to be hard enough to find in broad daylight, let alone after the sun goes down."

I set my jaw. "I told you, this can't wait. I'm going now."

"Sierra." Deena's voice was pleading. "Let me call Rocky, then. We'll ask him to go too."

Calvin came up behind Deena and placed a hand on her shoulder. "It's okay, Dee. I'll go with Sierra."

"You will?" I asked. I'd been afraid to ask for his opinion on this venture. I'd assumed he wouldn't approve.

"Yeah. I'll drive. You can navigate. Deena, can you text Sierra the address?"

Gus had gobbled his food and was now underfoot again. He knew we were talking about going someplace, and he didn't want to miss the fun.

Deena nodded, looking brighter. "Okay."

Calvin found Gus's leash. "Let's bring the pooch along for the ride."

"Sounds good. Thanks." I cast a warm look to Calvin, suddenly feeling as excited about this outing as Gus was.

Chapter 25

Here we were again, side by side, driving off into the night. This time, instead of Mom's home-cooked meal, we'd eaten peanut butter and jelly sandwiches whipped together by Calvin before we left. Now I crunched into an apple, as he negotiated the twists and turns of the mountain road. Gus was curled on the back seat, content to be along for the ride.

Deena had been right about the thickening clouds. It was a moonless night, and the charcoal sky, made darker by the leafy tree canopy stretching overhead, felt like the domed roof of a secret cave. And Cal and I were the intrepid explorers.

For the first part of the drive, we discussed the route we should travel and figured how long it should take—probably about thirty-five or forty minutes. That settled, we fell into a pocket of silence. Then Calvin gave me a sidelong glance.

"So, you're confused, huh?"

I looked over at him, startled at the sudden return to our earlier interrupted conversation.

"A little bit." I wasn't sure if this was the best time to have this discussion. Having each other as a captive audience could cut either way.

"Can I ask you something?" he asked.

"Yes."

"Are you confused about your feelings about me?"

"No." I spoke without hesitation. I didn't have to think about it. I knew how I felt about him. "Not that. What I'm unclear on is our relationship—and what it is you want."

He glanced at me again, looking conflicted. "You know I care about you, right? I came back because I missed you, and I want . . . I want to get to know you better."

Something told me that wasn't what he'd been about to say. I smiled briefly. "I like you Calvin," I said simply. "And I'd like to get to know you better too."

"Good." He chuckled quietly. "Now that that's cleared up . . ."

"So, then, we're dating? Is that what you'd call this?"

"Sure. If you want to label it, that works."

I frowned out the window. Why was this so difficult? I wanted to know if he wanted to be exclusive, or if he believed in dating around. I wanted to know how invested he was in our fledgling relationship. Was he here to stay, or was this going to be temporary?

He reached out his right hand and set it on my thigh, palm up, fingers loose. It felt like an overture. Or possibly an invitation, a question awaiting my answer. I placed my hand in his, and our fingers entwined, like two matched pieces in a puzzle. I felt my lips curl upward.

Maybe labels didn't matter after all. *All that matters is the present moment.* Whatever might happen in the future, this moment was pretty nice.

As we rose in elevation, and the wilderness crowded in, our GPS signal became spotty at best. I studied a map I'd pulled up on my phone. After we'd been driving for more than half an hour, I was afraid we'd missed our turnoff. Calvin found a place to turn around, and we headed back in the other direction, our eyes straining for the private road I'd found on the map. We almost passed it a second time, until I spied the flash of a reflector set back from the road. Calvin slowed the car and pulled onto the blacktop lane. We disregarded the sign marked Private Property.

Before long, we came to a tall metal gate. There was nothing much else to see, just trees on either side and a solid barrier in front of us. In vain, I peered through the windshield, hoping to find an intercom.

"I guess they weren't kidding when they said she'd built a fortress," I said.

Calvin shifted into Park. "Oh, I don't know about that. It's not like we're facing a crocodile-infested moat. If we continue on foot, I bet we can find a way in."

I raised my eyebrows, impressed with his fearlessness. He probably *would* make a good treasure-hunting partner for Felix.

Gus sat up in the back seat and rested his paws on the lower edge of the closed window. Unlike every other time we visited a new place, he showed no inclination to get out of the car. I didn't blame him. The woods might not hide alligators, but there were surely other creatures I, or Gus, wouldn't want to run into.

Scanning the gnarled trees, I caught sight of a tiny circle of light. For a second, I thought it might be the shining eye of a nocturnal beast, lying in wait as we entered its lair. Then I remembered the security cameras at Flower House.

"Aha. Of course."

"What do you see?" asked Calvin.

"A camera, I think. Which gives me an idea. Could you flash the headlights a few times? I want to get their attention."

Calvin did as I asked. Nothing happened. It occurred

to me that the video feed was probably not watched at all times. Still, considering Janie's wealth and access to high-tech gadgets, I felt sure she'd be alerted to a vehicle sitting at her gate.

"Okay. Plan B." I opened the car door, got out, and stood in front of the headlights. Facing the camera, I waved my arms like I was trying to flag down a rescue plane over a desert island.

A clanking sound made me jump. Then the gate slowly swung inward. Maybe Marissa really was there, and had seen it was me, or maybe I just looked like someone in need of help—whatever the reason, I was grateful. I ran around the car and hopped back in.

"Amazing," said Calvin, shifting into Drive.

"Well, I didn't come all this way not to get in. Sometimes you just gotta believe things will work out, and they do."

"Good advice," he said softly.

We moved slowly up the winding lane. A minute later, a glow of light appeared ahead of us, like a beacon in a murky sea. At last, we rounded a bend, and a house came into view, with the front porch and first-floor windows lit up.

Even in the partial darkness, the building was a striking sight. From what I could tell, it seemed to be both modern and timeless, with large windows and flat rooflines, like a sprawling Frank Lloyd Wright home built into the side of a hill.

Calvin parked in the middle of the driveway, and we climbed out of the car. I let Gus out, and held onto his leash as he sniffed the landscaped grounds. The front door opened, sending out another shaft of white light.

"Sierra Ravenswood," said a female voice. "I heard you were a detective now."

We approached the front door. "Hi, Janie," I said.

I probably wouldn't have recognized her, if I hadn't

known this was her house. With a short, boyish haircut and
red, angular glasses, she was a far cry from the stringy-
haired shy kid I vaguely remembered from middle school.

She ushered us into her home, offering a hand for Gus
to inspect. If she was surprised to see us, she didn't show it.
She led us through a minimalist front room, down a short
hall, and into a spacious den. In the center of the room, a
slender, low-backed curved sofa faced a white wall, where a
large abstract painting took center stage, with bold splotches
and streaks in vivid primary colors. Scattered ottoman cubes
matched the colors in the painting. I was so distracted by the
decor, I didn't notice Marissa at first, until she stirred from a
wicker swing chair, hanging in a corner next to a curtained
window and a potted palm tree. She appeared relaxed, in a
pale lavender velour tracksuit. Her golden hair was pulled
back in a low ponytail.

"Have a seat," said Janie, waving us toward the sofa. She
perched on a red leather cube and removed a pack of ciga-
rettes from the breast pocket of her loose cotton shirt.

Marissa extracted herself from the swing and strolled
to a sideboard, where she poured margaritas from a crystal pitcher. Without a word, she handed a glass to each of
us, then sat on a blue cube across from the sofa. *I see she's
made herself at home.*

Calvin eyed the drink with a skeptical glint, then set it
quietly on the glass coffee table. Feeling nervous, I took a
sip of mine and licked my lips. Strong, but not bad.

Marissa sipped from her glass and regarded me with a
tinge of bemusement.

"Your mom is worried about you," I began.

"Is she?" Her voice was languid, unconcerned.

"Yes. She's been worried ever since you left so suddenly.
She's been hoping to hear from you." I couldn't understand
why Marissa was being so blasé.

"You're mistaken," she said. "It's not me my mother cares about, so much as it's the wedding."

Frowning, I decided to be blunt. "She cares about the fact that you're a murder suspect. That's why she asked for my help."

Marissa's mouth fell open. "I'm a murder suspect? Since when am I a suspect?"

"Since you told the police you were upset over rumors about your mom and Taz. Your mom told me—"

"My mom told you," Marissa interrupted, scoffing. "And you believed her? My mom would say anything to get her way. If you haven't noticed, she tends toward exaggeration."

I wracked my brain, trying to remember. Was it only Annaliese who'd told me Marissa was a suspect? I didn't have the impression she was lying. Her concern for Marissa was real. Maybe she misinterpreted Captain Bradley's questions and jumped to her own conclusions. Or maybe Marissa really was a suspect and refused to believe it.

I kept my expression neutral. "Also, you were on the premises when Taz was killed."

"I never went into the house," she retorted. "I didn't know anything had happened until later, when my dad got a call from the police chief."

"Then why—if you don't think you're a suspect, why did you run away?"

Dropping her gaze, she took another sip of her drink and didn't answer.

I glanced at Calvin, who was scratching the top of Gus's head, keeping the pup docile. Meeting my eyes, he gave me a subtle twitch of his eyebrows. I took it to mean he didn't trust Marissa. She was definitely being cagey. I decided to try another tact.

"Marissa, what happened is terrible. Tragic. I know how

upsetting it must be for you. Everyone will understand if you want to postpone your wedding."

She nodded slowly. "Thank you."

"It just seems a little odd," I continued, "that you went into hiding and haven't been in contact with your parents."

She gave me a curious look. "Why do you care?" She didn't sound rude, only puzzled.

"I care about truth and justice." *And the American way?* I heard how cheesy I sounded, but I pressed on. "I don't like the idea of someone getting away with murder."

Marissa rubbed a finger along the salty rim of her glass. Janie struck a match and lit a cigarette. This was getting nowhere.

Something tickled at the back of my brain. As I watched Marissa, it occurred to me that there had always been something off about her behavior—from the moment I'd met her through the following week, and even before that, according to what Taz had recorded in his planner. He'd written something about how distraught she'd been when she thought her gown was ruined. Yet, when she came to me at Flower House looking for a new florist, she hadn't seemed overly upset. She didn't even care what flowers I used in her bouquet. It wasn't the demeanor of a woman invested in her wedding.

I sat up taller as the realization hit me. "You don't want to get married." I looked at Marissa dead-on. "You never did."

She slid her eyes to mine and smiled, a sad, rueful smile. "I wouldn't say 'never.' There was a time, when I first met Michael-William, that I wasn't opposed to the idea. Then my parents got involved." Her voice took on a hard edge. "You might think arranged marriages are a thing of the past. They're not. Not when money and politics are involved."

I frowned. This was so far outside my worldview, I had

trouble relating. As meddlesome as my family could be, they would never push me into a marriage I didn't want.

"The worst part," Marissa went on, "besides being forced to have a big, high-profile wedding, is being forced to move. Recently, I found out Michael-William intends to remain in DC." She shuddered. "It's so far removed from Appalachia; it might as well be another planet."

"She wanted out," said Janie, her voice gravelly.

"I wanted out," Marissa repeated.

"So, you decided to sabotage your own wedding," I said. "It was you who changed the date on the invitations, wasn't it? And gave the tailor the wrong measurements for your gown?"

A wicked grin appeared on her lips. "I had a little fun, I admit. I couldn't simply tell Mother and Daddy I wanted to defy their wishes. I couldn't risk them cutting off my allowance or canceling my inheritance."

"I keep telling you," said Janie, "you need to make your own money. It's the only way to true freedom."

Calvin eyed Marissa warily. "You must have wanted out pretty bad. Did you arrange for the first florist to quit too?"

She grinned again—way too amused at the havoc she'd caused. "Taz set his phone down one day. I used it to fire Tammy. Then I told Taz she'd quit. It was an easy sale. They didn't seem to like each other much anyway."

"I suppose you called the building inspector too," I said.

"Yes. Again, too easy. I don't know what happened with the smoke alarms, though. Call it a bonus."

"Did you burn the wedding programs?" I asked.

"Burn?" Her face was blank. "I don't know anything about that."

That was odd. She was eager to take credit for all the other mischief. Why would she deny setting the programs on fire, unless she really didn't have anything to do with it?

"You must have been getting pretty desperate," said Calvin. "All that trouble you caused . . . yet the wedding was still going to happen."

Marissa sighed. "I know how childish this sounds. And passive-aggressive. Part of me knew I couldn't really stop the wedding. I was resigned to my life as a trophy wife. But as the day drew nearer, it got harder to accept."

She stared into her glass. "I thought about leaving. The evening of the vendor meeting, last Monday, I almost did it. That's why I didn't meet my parents for dinner. I came back to the house instead, planning to pack some things and take off."

I felt Calvin tense beside me. Were we about to hear a confession? Was Marissa so desperate to get out of her wedding that she'd killed her wedding planner?

I didn't think so. I placed a hand on Calvin's leg to keep him from saying anything accusatory.

"Marissa," I said gently, "do you have any idea who murdered Taz? Did you see or hear anything that might indicate who did it?"

She looked up, and I detected a flash of defiance. "No. I liked Taz. I'm sorry he's dead, but I have no idea who did it. All I know is that the murder gave me an opening. A legitimate reason for calling off the wedding."

Janie took a puff on her cigarette. "Out of death springs new life."

Calvin shot Janie a look of disapproval. I had to agree. It was in poor taste to speak of a murder in that way, no matter how eloquent the sentiment.

Marissa glanced at Janie and smiled. "Jane has been such a good friend. I don't know what I'd do without her."

This was going to be tricky. With Marissa determined to see Taz's demise as her way out, how was I going to convince her to come back?

A high-pitched beeping noise cut into my thoughts. Janie grabbed a cell phone from the coffee table and silenced the alarm.

"Another vehicle turned into my private drive," she said, looking at a screen on the phone.

Marissa furrowed her smooth forehead and turned to me. "Did you tell anyone else where I am?"

I shook my head and exchanged a glance with Calvin. The only person who knew where we'd come was Deena. Could she and Rocky have decided to join us? Or had we been followed?

"What kind of vehicle?" asked Calvin.

"Some sort of van," said Janie. "They're at the gate now."

Fear flickered in Marissa's eyes. Perhaps she was only afraid of facing her parents, but this gave me an idea. There were more valid reasons to be scared.

"Marissa." I spoke with urgency. "Taz's killer is still at large—and dangerous. I think Taz was murdered because he knew something. Now the killer is going after anyone else who might know the same thing."

I had everyone's full attention now. Calvin regarded me with a mixture of surprise and pride. The truth was, I was only guessing. But the more I thought about it, the more it made sense.

"Someone has been following me around," I said. "Probably because they think I know something."

Marissa gasped. "And you led them here!"

"The van is backing up now," said Janie, evidently watching the security camera feed on her phone.

"I don't know," I responded. "But I'm not the only one. Did you hear about Kendall Waite? She was trying to figure out what it was Taz knew, and someone ran her off the side of the mountain." At this point, I was going to assume that was what had happened. "She's lucky to be alive, but she's in even more danger now."

"And Mother is still pushing for the wedding to go forward? You can see how irrational she is." Marissa stood up and walked over to look at Janie's phone. "Are they still out there?" Her voice betrayed a slight tremble.

Calvin stood too, clutching his phone in his hand. "Maybe we should call the cops."

"It's gone now," said Janie.

Marissa pinched her lip. "You're sure?"

Nodding, Janie reached over to tap her cigarette on the edge of a glass ashtray. "I saw it drive it away."

I exhaled in relief. *Thank goodness.* I took another sip of the margarita, then puckered my lips. It tasted too sour now. Setting it on the coffee table, I leaned forward. "Marissa, I'm not here to talk you into getting married. I'm here because the police need our help. Your help. You can help catch the creep and end this thing once and for all. Wouldn't you like to do that?"

"You can't hide out forever," Calvin pointed out.

"I don't understand what you want," she said. "What can I do?"

"I want you to pretend the wedding is going forward. You don't really have to go through with it. You can disappear again at the eleventh hour. Or you can be honest with everyone and say this isn't what you want. But for the next few days, we need to reset the stage as it was before. Same characters, same everything."

"Like a spider," said Janie, "weaving a sticky web to catch an icky fly?"

"Uh, yeah. Exactly," I said.

Marissa drifted toward the sideboard, where she refilled her margarita glass. I crossed my fingers and waited as she

appeared to wrestle with her inner demons. Finally, she
turned around and nodded. "Alright. It would be the de-
cent thing, I suppose. After everything I did to thwart the
wedding. . . . I do feel kind of bad for causing so much
trouble for Taz, considering what ended up happening to
him. This will be my amends. I'll do it."

I hopped up and handed her my phone. "Call your
mom?"

She rolled her eyes and took my phone. "Fine."

Chapter 26

When we left Janie's house, we were greeted by a howling wind. It stirred up leaves and grit that pelted our skin and stung our eyes. For an instant, we stood in the yard, squinting into the darkness. Was the van really gone? Or was it lying in wait at the end of the drive, out of sight of Janie's cameras?

A streak of lightning flashed above the dancing trees. Gus let out a spirited bark, making me jump. Calvin said something I couldn't quite make out, but I got the gist. We needed to get out of there.

With my hair whipping around my face, we bolted for the car. Calvin made it first and held open the door for Gus and me.

"Whew!" I exclaimed, rubbing my arms.

"Where did *that* come from?" Calvin turned the wipers on high speed and cranked the heat. Inside Janie's cloistered den, we'd had no idea the weather was turning on us. By the time we reached the end of the private lane, large splats of rain blurred the windshield.

"You okay?" he asked, slowing the car to turn onto the main road.

I looked warily out all of the windows. "Yeah," I murmured. It was hard to see anything, but it seemed we were the only people out braving the storm. After a moment, I relaxed.

"Actually, I'm great. Tonight was a success!" I'd found Marissa, convinced her to come home, and solved the mystery of the wedding sabotage. At least, most of the sabotage. It did trouble me that there were a few incidents Marissa claimed not to have caused.

I was pondering this problem, and fingering through the tangles in my hair, when I noticed Calvin pressing down on the accelerator, picking up speed in spite of the heavy rain.

"We've got company," he muttered.

I twisted in my seat to look out the rear window. Two bright headlights bore down on us.

"Yikes! What are they doing?" Part of me felt I ought to be relieved it was two headlights instead of one, but somehow that provided little comfort. I squinted through the streaming raindrops. "Do you think it's the van from Janie's?"

"It could be a van," said Calvin. "Hard to tell. Whoever it is, they're following too closely."

"What if you slow down and let them pass?" I suggested.

"I don't think they want to pass." Calvin let up on the gas anyway. We slowed down, but our follower didn't. The interior of our car was soon flooded with a blinding white light. Calvin sped up again. He had to, in order to avoid being hit.

My heart thudded and my throat tightened with fear. This was not good. The driver behind us was trying to run us off the road—just like what happened to Kendall. I was sure of it. Even if they didn't succeed, we were liable to have an accident anyway. The highway was wet, and visibility was terrible.

We came to a curve, and I clenched every muscle in my body. Calvin gripped the steering wheel like a race car driver. Swerving around the bend, the old car started to hydroplane. I let out a squeal as Calvin struggled to keep us on the road. After a horrifying zigzag, he managed to set us straight again.

"Jeez," he breathed. "Is that maniac still back there?"

His question was answered by another flash of bright light in our cabin.

"We can't keep doing this," I said, teeth chattering now. "We have to lose them."

"I'd love to. Got any suggestions?"

I peered frantically out the window, trying to determine where we were. My cell phone was no help. There was no GPS signal. *On second thought.* I took another look at the phone, pulling up the saved map. Then I looked out the window again.

"Have we passed Raptor Ridge Lane?" I asked.

"I have no idea."

Up ahead, a veiled light shone beneath a sign on the side of the road. As we whizzed by, I caught the words Sunny Crest Lodge. I looked at the map again and found our location.

"Okay! Raptor Ridge is coming up. It's a right turn."

"Tell me when," said Calvin. He sounded grim.

"I see it! There's a barn or something. See it? Slow down now."

Calvin continued barreling ahead. At the last moment, he hit the brakes and turned sharply, causing Gus to slide across the back seat.

"Sorry, buddy!" he called.

Bracing myself on the seat back, I made sure Gus was okay then looked behind us. To my chagrin, our pursuer turned too. From the shape, I could now confirm that it was a van, though I still couldn't make out any details.

"Take the next left," I commanded. "Take every turn you can. We're going to lose this son of a gun."

Calvin did as I asked, taking first one turn and then another. I was sure we'd become hopelessly lost. Then I glimpsed a road marker with the words Hidden Hollow Creek.

"I think I know where we are!" I said excitedly. "We're going to come to a bridge soon."

"Terrific," said Calvin. "With our luck, it'll be washed out."

Biting my fingers, I strained to see through the rainy blackness ahead. When we came to the bridge, I was relieved to see it still intact. The creek beneath rushed and roiled, but stayed within its banks.

"Take the next left," I said. "Then follow the road up up up."

I twisted around again and reached back to give Gus a reassuring pat. "I think we're safe. I don't see the headlights anymore."

Calvin let out an audible breath. "Thank God. I didn't want to mention it, but we're getting pretty low on gas."

I laughed in relief. "I don't know how far back we lost them, but I'm pretty sure we did."

"And lost us too, huh?"

"No. I know exactly where we are. See that clump of trees beyond the fence on the right? Turn into that lane."

"Where are we going?" asked Calvin, coasting to a near stop.

"Over the river and through the woods," I said. "To Granny Mae's house we go."

Granny Mae's farmhouse had never looked more welcoming. Nearly all the windows were lit up, showing the outlines of ruffled curtains and, in one window, her cat Tiger. The front porch light illuminated a barrel of mums and a willow wreath on the door. The door was ajar, as if we were expected. In fact, I had no doubt we were.

Although Granny's home was set pretty far back from the road, we still hid the car. Leaving it behind a tall, sprawling pine tree, we ran up to the porch, where Granny immediately pulled the door open wide. She handed each of us a towel and took Gus's leash from me.

"I knew it," she said, stating the obvious. "I knew I'd have visitors, come to seek shelter from the storm. Come on in. Take off your shoes."

We obeyed without question. Calvin looked at Granny as if she might be a witch, but I was used to her sixth sense. Whether she'd seen an omen or merely had a feeling, she often knew when she was needed.

"Soup's on," she said, drying off Gus with another towel. "Come on in to the kitchen and tell me what you're doin' up in the mountain on a night like this."

"It wasn't like this when we started out," I said. Then I gave her a hug. "But I'm not sure that would have stopped us. We had an important mission."

Calvin and I sat at Granny's small wooden table, eating potato soup and soda crackers and feeling better by the second. Gus was nearby, happily gnawing on a bone. Between the two of us, Calvin and I told Granny all about finding Marissa at Janie's house, and Marissa's admission about trying to disrupt her own wedding. I also mentioned that someone seemed to be following us for a while, though I downplayed the danger.

"Land sakes," said Granny, cradling a cup of herbal tea. "If that don't beat all."

"Yeah," I agreed. "It's hard to believe Marissa did all those things. It was so devious. And all because she felt she couldn't just say no to the marriage."

Granny gave us a wise look. "Folks have married for reasons besides love forever. For security, for somebody to help raise youngins after a spouse dies, for honor or duty." She saw me stick out my lower lip and chuckled. "Of course, love is always better."

"Love is *always* better," I echoed.

Calvin grinned, but didn't comment. He reached down to ruffle Gus's fur—another kind of love, to be sure.

"It helps to have good role models," Granny continued. "It's not a requirement, mind you. But it helps. Grandpap and I had a loving marriage, and your mom and dad do. So, there's a real good chance you will too."

I felt a blush rising and gave Granny a quick smile. I didn't intend for the conversation to be about me. At least Granny wasn't as obvious as her daughter. If Mom were here, she'd probably ask Calvin about his parents' marriage.

"I reckon Marissa Lakely might be lacking a bit in that department," Granny said. "It's just a guess."

I tended to agree. I had yet to meet her father, but from what Annaliese had shared, it seemed there were a few issues in her relationship with Frank. Not that it was any of my business.

"I could mix up a happy-heart love tonic," Granny offered. "It might help the girl make up her mind."

"That would be nice, Granny." Maybe I'd try it myself.

She started to take our empty bowls to the sink, but Calvin intercepted. He washed and I dried, while Granny finished her tea and told us about the projects she'd been working on to get ready for fall. It was understood that we'd stay the night. That is, Granny and I were on the same page. Calvin seemed a little surprised when Granny said she was going to bed, and that I should show him where the "boys' room" was. Ever since my grandparents had raised their own eight kids in this house, there had been the boys' bedroom and the girls' bedroom, and it had remained that way over the years.

After Granny went upstairs, Calvin and I moved to the living room and sat down on Granny's well-worn sofa. I called Deena and filled her in. She said she'd open the shop in the morning and urged me to stay away as long as possible. If I was really being followed, it was best to remain out of sight. I couldn't argue with that, but I did wonder what next steps I could take while keeping a low profile. At the least, I'd check in with Annaliese tomorrow and find out if the vendor meeting was a go.

Calvin was watching me as I finished up the call with Deena. He rubbed a hand over his jawline, shadowed with a hint of late-day whiskers. "I wonder who it was," he said pensively. "My guess is they could have had a scooter in the back of the van. It's got to be the same person who followed you before."

I bit my lip and nodded. "I was thinking the same thing." I thought about who I knew for sure drove a vehicle like that: Nick with his DJ mobile, and Regina with her bakery van. Of course, they were both marked, and Nick's snake decal was hard to miss, but it *was* exceptionally dark outside. I didn't recall seeing any other vans the day of the vendor meeting, and I knew Tammy drove an SUV. For all I knew, she could also have a van for her florist business. So could anyone else I didn't know about.

Shivering, I pulled Granny's afghan over my lap. I was happy to be inside, out of the storm—and safe from any crazy stalkers.

Calvin stood up and wandered over to the window. "The rain is letting up," he commented.

"Hey," I said, causing him to turn and look at me. "That was some fantastic driving tonight. You'd make a good getaway driver."

He raised his eyebrows and laughed. "That's not really a job I aspire to. It was quite exciting, though."

"A little too exciting," I said. "I'm glad you were with me. At Janie's too. I'm glad I didn't have to do that alone."

He rejoined me on the sofa. "We make a pretty good team." His eyes twinkled, and I fully expected him to mention the treasure hunt again. But he didn't say anything. Instead, he reached out and lightly brushed my hair from the side of my face. My eyes flickered to his lips. We'd *almost* kissed so many times, I was starting to overthink the whole thing and become self-conscious. Too many *what-if*s muddled my mind.

Then he leaned in, and, just like that, we were kissing. I melted into him, all my thoughts flying out the window, like birds to the wind.

That night I dreamed of weddings. Lovely weddings in beautiful locations: on a beach, in a rose garden, in a grand cathedral and a tiny chapel. They were fairy-tale weddings, with all the participants dressed for a ball.

But something wasn't right. Someone was trying to stop the weddings. The officiant was about to ask the question that never seems to come up in real life: "Does anyone object to this union?"

I was torn. I didn't know if I should stop the objector, or if I should be the one stopping the wedding. All I knew was that time was running out.

Speak now or forever hold your peace.

Chapter 27

After the storm the night before, Granny's big yard was a minefield of fallen branches and sticks. Calvin and I assigned ourselves pick-up duty, making trip after trip to the burn pile in the clearing behind her house. Gus chased birds and dug holes. When we finished, we joined Granny in her vegetable garden, where she was harvesting tomatoes, zucchini, and beans.

I picked up an empty basket and headed to the end of a row of green beans. Going for a long ripe bean nestled in a bushy plant, I thrust in my hands to part the leaves—then jumped back and screamed.

"Snake!"

Calvin was at my side in two seconds. "Where?"

"Probably just a garter snake," Granny said mildly.

I pointed, and Calvin squinted at the ground. I gasped when he reached down and picked up a limp, green snaky object—until I recognized it as a garden hose.

"It doesn't bite," Calvin said with a grin.

I laughed sheepishly. "False alarm!" I called to Granny. "I guess I'm jumpy."

Granny walked over, chuckling. "I shouldn't have left that out here. Been too busy, I guess. Every year, I think I ought to plant less, and every year it ends up being more."

Calvin coiled the hose for Granny, and I went back to the beans, quickly filling my basket. Naturally, the thought of a snake took me back to Taz's final words.

"Who is the snake?" I muttered.

I hadn't expected an answer, but Granny heard me. "If you're talkin' about a person, it would be somebody mean, most likely. Or somebody who lies and cheats. Maybe a counterfeit friend or a backstabber."

Nodding, I stood up and stretched my back. "I imagine all those attributes might apply to a murderer." I gazed out toward the tree line on the edge of Granny's property. *Then again, like with the garden hose, things are not always what they seem.*

Before we left her house, Granny gave Calvin a gallon of gasoline she had safely stored away for her lawnmower. While he added it to his gas tank, she called me back into the house.

"I didn't forget about the tonic I promised you." She handed me a clear glass bottle containing a dark pink liquid. "This is a special blend for attracting happiness. I sometimes use it when a customer asks for a love potion. The truth is, it's more about loving yourself and your life."

"Aw, that's real sweet, Granny."

"Mm-hmm. It's useful for a number of problems. If you're stuck on a decision, it can help you see your true heart's desire. If you're lonely for company, it puts you in a good mood so *you* become good company."

"Ah. Sounds like the Law of Attraction to me. Like attracts like."

"It's common sense, really. And tasty too."

"What's in it?"

"Mainly rose petal water and cherry wine, with honey and a sprinkle of cinnamon. It's good chilled, but a little goes a long way. You can get several servings out of this one bottle."

"I wouldn't mind trying it," I said. "For the taste, I mean."

Granny gave Gus a treat from her pocket. "I don't think you need it, but it can't hurt."

I thanked her, and she put the bottle in a brown bag and walked with me out to Calvin's car.

"What do you have planned for the rest of the day?" As independent as she was, I still hated leaving her alone.

"Wanda is coming over. She's going to help with the canning. And the eating too. She always takes home a couple jars for herself."

"That's good. Tell her hello for me!"

I hugged Granny goodbye and piled into the car with Gus. Once we got going, Calvin asked me what I had in the brown bag.

"A gift from Granny. It's something she thought Marissa could use."

"Oh, yes. Happiness in a bottle, huh?"

I grinned. "If only it were that simple. Actually, I've found Granny's charms and tricks often do end up working, just in unexpected ways."

"If you say so," he said, skeptical but good-natured.

On the drive down the mountain, I kept looking out the back window. Every now and then, I saw another car or truck, but never a van or scooter. Thank goodness.

At my request, we stopped at the dollhouse first, so I could change and bring in the mail. When I came out of my bedroom, I found Calvin at my kitchen table repotting a spider plant.

"This fella wanted a little more breathing room. Hope you don't mind."

I had to laugh. He truly was a plant lover. "Not at all, professor. Have at it."

As I restocked Gus's travel bag, I thought about that phrase—"breathing room." Anytime I had people over, the dollhouse seemed even smaller than its compact four hundred square feet. And Calvin's presence now felt somehow even bigger than before. Or maybe it was his masculine energy, which I seemed to be hyperaware of.

My mind tried to jump to the future. Where would I live next? Where did I *want* to live? I used to have such big dreams. They seemed to be shifting lately, almost without me even noticing.

My phone rang, bringing me back to the present. As Calvin cleared off the table, I stepped away to answer the call. It was from Deena.

"Hey," I said. "I'll be in soon. I—"

"You might want to make another stop first," she said.

"Why? What's up?"

"Kendall is awake."

Other than making flower deliveries, I hadn't been to the county hospital in a long while—knock on wood. I had to rely on Deena to lead the way to the ICU. As it happened, I'd decided to stop at Flower House first, where Calvin offered to stay with Gus. Deena was ready with a cheerful bouquet for Kendall. We'd hopped into my car and taken off again.

Knowing how strict the hospital visiting policy was, I didn't expect to be able to stay for long. I was hoping for at least five minutes. We met Kendall's sister in the hallway. She was glad we were there, because she needed to leave to pick up their parents from the airport.

Kendall, however, seemed confused to see us. She cocked her head at Deena. "Who are you?"

"I'm a florist from Flower House." Deena set the bouquet on a table against the wall and took a chair near the foot of the bed. "My name's Deena Lee."

I sat in the chair next to Kendall. She looked small and frail, lying there in a white hospital gown and connected to tubes. Purple bruises shone starkly on her pale face, and one arm rested in a sling. Her pink hair was flat and faded, and her nose ring was gone.

"I'm Sierra," I said gently. "Remember me?"

Kendall scoffed quietly. "Of course. I don't have amnesia." Then she winced. "Ow. My ribs."

"I'm so sorry this happened to you," I said.

She didn't reply, and for a moment no one said anything. I began to wonder if it was a mistake to come. I glanced at Deena, who only gave me a helpless look.

"If there's anything I can do . . ." I began.

Kendall's eyelids fluttered and she turned her head, staring at me with a spark of her old intensity. "Tell me what Taz said before he died."

I swallowed. That, I could do. "I think he said something about a snake. 'It was . . .' something 'snake.' Does that mean anything to you?"

She screwed her eyebrows in bewilderment. "Snake? What snake?"

I shrugged. "I don't know. What were you expecting him to say?"

"I figured he'd say who murdered him. If not a person, maybe an organization."

"An organization?"

Kendall frowned. "He was involved in something illegal. He was up to no good."

Funny enough, Taz said something similar about you.

I decided to keep asking questions. "I know he required his hires to pay him a kickback. Is that what you're talking about?"

She narrowed her eyes. "That drove me crazy. He took advantage of his position. I was trying to get all the vendors to band together and revolt, but no one wanted to alienate him."

Ah. That made sense. It explained the significant glances I'd observed her give at the vendor meeting. *That must also be why she threw Tammy's business card in the trash*. Even though Tammy thought she'd been fired, she wasn't willing to jeopardize Gordon's standing with Taz. Which must have frustrated Kendall.

"That sounds like a worthy cause," said Deena. "Like union organizing. It takes guts to speak truth to power."

"Yeah, well, I had the guts. I just didn't have the proof. I would have exposed him by myself, but it would be my word against his—and he probably would have sued me for slander."

Now that she was talking freely, I felt free to keep probing. "Is that why you searched his suitcase? You were looking for some kind of proof?"

She opened her mouth, as if to deny it, then gave up the game. "I was. How did you know about that?"

"You left behind a pink hair." I hoped she wouldn't ask how I happened to find that hair. I didn't want to admit I'd been snooping too. Luckily, it didn't seem to occur to her.

"My hair could have gotten there any number of ways. I was close to Taz earlier that day." She paused, looking tired. "But, the truth is, that's where I was when Taz was killed."

Her face took on a troubled aspect. I could only imagine what she must be feeling. What would have happened if she'd walked in on Taz and the killer? Could she have stopped it? Or would she have been killed too?

"I take it you didn't hear anything?" I asked.

"Not then. I did earlier." She gave me a smug look. "Before the meeting, I overheard Taz arguing with someone in his room. Taz said he wanted out. He said the person was expecting too much of him, and it wasn't worth it anymore."

This was new. And it was striking how similar these statements were to what Marissa had said to me the night before.

"What did he want out of?" I asked. "Surely not the wedding?"

She shook her head, evidently at a loss. "I think he was involved in something bigger than vendor kickbacks. I told the police, of course, but they apparently haven't figured it out yet."

A nurse came into the room to take Kendall's vitals. Before he left, he informed us that visiting hours were almost up. Kendall laid back on her pillow, wincing slightly.

"Kendall," I said softly. "Do you remember how your accident happened?"

"I was being chased, and I lost control of my car." She said it in a resigned, emotionless voice. "Like I told the police, it was dark and the other vehicle had its high beams on. I don't know who it was."

"Could it have been a van?"

"Sure."

"Were you still investigating Taz after the murder?" asked Deena. "It seems like you must have made someone nervous."

"I was asking around, but I never learned anything. Not that I know of, anyway."

Her voice sounded strained now. I glanced at Deena, and she stood up nodding. It was time for us to leave.

I leaned forward and rested my hand on the bed rail. "I'm going to find out who did this. I think I'm getting closer."

Her mouth twitched, in a ghost of a smile. "You go, girl." Then she furrowed her brow. I thought she was experiencing pain, but it must have been something on her mind.

"Something has been bothering me," she murmured. "Something I couldn't tell the police."

"What is it?"

"After the meeting, I was supposed to go up to the ball-room with Nick. So, that's where I said I was. Only, I wasn't. I was really searching Taz's room."

"Yes," I said. "You told me that." I wondered if her mind was getting foggy. She seemed to be repeating herself.

"Nick never said anything." She locked on my eyes. "He didn't contradict me. I was afraid he'd say I wasn't up there, and then I'd be the top suspect in Taz's murder."

"You mean Nick covered for you?"

She shook her head. "I mean, maybe he wasn't up there either."

I was eager to talk things over with Deena. As we left Kendall's room, I turned to her, about to ask if she wanted to go grab some coffee. Then I saw her eyes widen. Following her gaze, I saw the reason: Chief Walden. He was striding up the hall, his cane thudding like a drumbeat. He appeared as surprised as we were—and none too happy to see us.

I made myself smile. "Good afternoon, Chief."

He didn't smile back. "What are you two doing here?"

"Visiting Kendall." I waved back toward her room.

"We brought her flowers," Deena added.

The chief looked down at us with a stern glower. "Just visiting? Or interfering with police work again?"

I willed myself not to turn red. "I don't think we're interfering. If anything, we're just trying to be helpful."

"Does your dad know you're here?"

Deena folded her arms in front of her chest. "Sierra is a grown woman. Why should she tell her dad everyplace she goes?"

"I was talking to you." He directed his narrowed eyes at Deena. "I doubt if Dr. Lee would approve of his daughter harassing patients in the ICU."

"Harassing!" Deena's voice rose to an indignant pitch. A passing orderly gave us a curious stare.

"Chief Walden, honestly—"

"That goes for both of you," he said, cutting me off. "You don't know what you're getting yourself into. I have enough to deal with, without having to worry about a couple of amateur busybodies."

Busybody? As if! I'd intended to inform the chief about everything I'd learned—and report the van incident in the mountains—the first moment I could, and here was a perfect opportunity. Now I wasn't inclined to tell him anything; I worried my temper would get the better of me.

"Come on, Deena," I said, clasping her arm. "Let's go."

She shot daggers at him as we stalked away. Before we reached the end of the hall, my phone buzzed in my purse. I pulled it out and saw that it was Annaliese. I showed the display to Deena, then answered. "Hello!"

"Sierra, darling! You are a wonder." She was so enthusiastic, I couldn't help feeling gratified. "When Marissa called last night, I have to admit I was skeptical. But she's here now, and everything is all set. The vendors will be here to-morrow afternoon to finalize all the arrangements."

Glancing down the hall toward Kendall's room, I saw that the chief had disappeared inside. "That's wonderful," I said. "I'll be there as a member of your household staff."

She chuckled lightly. "Brilliant, darling. However you want to proceed is fine with me."

"I'm glad to hear that, Annaliese. Because I'll be bring-ing a few friends."

Chapter 28

Somehow, in spite of my distracted state, I managed to get in a few hours of work at Flower House. I was plotting the whole time. Before I went home, I'd called Rocky and Richard and huddled with Deena and Calvin. By the end of the day, I'd laid the groundwork for my half-formulated plan. I went home feeling a smidge more confident than I had in the past several days.

It was weird sleeping at the dollhouse after so many nights away. I could have stayed at Deena's or Calvin's. They'd both offered. And I could have gone home to my folks' house. But I refused to let my life be dictated by fear. I made sure I wasn't followed home, locked all the doors and windows, and called it a night. My home reclaimed.

The next morning started out like a regular Wednesday, with a bulk flower delivery from our wholesaler and a smattering of customers in the café. After lunch, I told Toby and Allie that we were closing early, but that they'd be paid for their full shifts. They didn't ask any questions. By now, they were well used to my unconventional ways.

To limit the number of vehicles at Bellman Manor, Deena

rode with Rocky, and Calvin rode with me. At the last minute, we'd decided to bring Gus along. He always put up such a fuss when we left him, and he was *almost* always well behaved. Calvin promised to play corgi wrangler to make sure the pup stayed out of trouble.

As with my first visit to the manor, Gretchen let us in the back door. Richard and Davy had already arrived and were chatting with Annaliese in the kitchen—and charming her from the looks of it. She was back to her breezy, elegant self. Wearing a short floral-print skirt and sleeveless red top, she looked more like a sister to the bride than the mother.

My friends and I had opted for generic staff attire, with black pants and white shirts. Even Davy, off duty from his police job, wore a similar outfit—with the addition of a loose sport coat, the better to conceal his handgun.

It was heartening to have so many people on my side, but I was still a bundle of nerves. Clustered in the breakfast nook, everyone turned to me for direction. As they all knew, I'd decided to use Taz's planner as bait. Not the actual book, but a fake one. Annaliese had given the real one to the police, but the vendors didn't know that. We would spread the story that she'd found it behind the radiator, just as I'd found the real one, only we'd say the discovery had just happened this morning. We'd let it be known that a police officer would be coming by this evening to pick it up. In the meantime, it would be kept in Frank's home office.

I looked at each of the expectant faces watching me and took a deep breath.

"Okay. Davy, I think you should stay here in the kitchen, over on the side where you can watch the door to the study. If anyone enters that room, you'll alert everyone else via the group text I started this morning. You'll also know if anyone comes in or out through the back door."

He nodded soberly. Richard had told me he'd agreed to participate on two conditions: that none of us engage in anything illegal and that I come into the station first thing tomorrow morning to answer all the questions the authorities wanted to ask me. I'd agreed at once. If all went well, maybe we'd catch the culprit and that second condition would be moot.

"Calvin," I continued, "you should stay outside in the grassy area near the rear driveway. That will give you a view of the window to the study. You can also keep an eye on any vehicles coming or going."

"Gus will be my cover," he said, feeding the pup a bite-sized treat. "He's a perfect excuse for hanging outside."

"So true," I said with a grin. "He always is."

Rocky stepped forward, and he wasn't grinning. His white shirtsleeves were rolled up, cutting across sculpted biceps—which, I noticed, seemed to snag Deena's attention. In a fleeting moment, I wondered just how serious things were getting between the two of them. Not that it was any of my business.

I shook off the irrelevant thought to hear Rocky's blunt statement. "Don't worry about assigning me to a specific location. I'll be shadowing you."

Sometimes my little brother's protectiveness could be overbearing. Not this time.

"I'm good with that," I said. "I'll be moving around, talking to people and offering my help with wedding preparations. Dee and Richard will be doing the same, with Deena focusing on the vendors and Richard . . ." I trailed off, aware that Annaliese was still listening. Richard's focus was going to be Marissa. Considering all the mischief she'd caused to damage her own wedding, I still didn't fully trust her.

"Richard will be a floater," I continued, "as we discussed."

He winked at me, showing he understood.

Annaliese held up a shopping bag and partially removed the contents to give me a look. It was a leather day planner, just like Taz's—or close enough, anyway. "I'm ready for my part," she said. "Also, Dennis helped me install a hidden camera in the study."

"Good thinking," said Davy. "It's possible the target might take one look at the book and decide not to take it."

"Exactly," said Annaliese. "That's what Sierra said."

"Is Dennis around?" I asked, recalling he was the private security guard Annaliese had mentioned lived nearby. It couldn't hurt to have another body on our side.

"He's with Frank at the golf course." Annaliese checked her watch. "They should be back within the hour."

A door clicked open behind me. Looking over my shoulder, I saw Marissa emerge from the back staircase, followed closely by an older man wearing a striped golf shirt and white seersucker pants. Marissa appeared cool and placid, in a short white dress, with long sleeves cut out at the shoulders. She introduced herself to those who hadn't yet met her, and she presented the man as her fiancé, Michael-William Princely.

With one hand on Marissa's back, Michael-William shook hands with the guys and nodded politely at the ladies. In person, he looked a lot like his online pictures: attractive in a bland sort of way, with a stiff, plastic smile.

"I'd planned to go golfing with the mayor," he said, indicating his attire. "But I couldn't tear myself away from my bride." He gave Marissa a squeeze, which she endured with a closed-lip smile that didn't quite reach her eyes.

Deena and I exchanged a brief glance. I was sure she'd made the same observations as me: that Michael-William referred to his future father-in-law as 'the mayor,' and that Marissa was playing a part she really wasn't into.

I only hoped she could keep up the charade long enough to out the killer. I hoped we all could.

As the vendors arrived, Annaliese directed them all to the dining room. At my suggestion, Marissa made a brief statement to thank everyone for returning and to let them know that Taz would be honored at the wedding ceremony. Of course, that wasn't the main reason for gathering them in one place. It also ensured they would all hear about the datebook.

After Marissa's speech, Annaliese stepped into the room and called Marissa over. With the datebook in hand, she informed her daughter that she'd be leaving it on Frank's desk and that an officer would stop by later to pick it up. When they left, I turned to my buddy Nick and confirmed that the book was what it appeared to be and explained where it was found. I made sure my voice was loud enough for the others to hear.

That part of the plan went off without a hitch. And, fortunately, none of the vendors questioned my presence. When Annaliese had told Regina she could bring Tammy back as florist, she added a caveat. She said she wanted me to remain involved as an assistant. Annaliese was known to be a gracious lady, so it wasn't an entirely unusual request.

Although Tammy had brought her own assistant, Shelby, they were both happy to accept additional help. Deena took on the task of second assistant, hanging garland in the great room and marking the spots where fresh flowers would be placed the morning of the wedding.

Regina, for her part, was less enthusiastic. However, she begrudgingly accepted my help.

"Here," she said, handing me a stack of freshly printed programs. "You can fold these."

"Sure thing," I said, having little choice.

Rocky joined me at the dining room table, where we got to work on the monotonous task.

"I can't protect you from paper cuts," he muttered. "So, you be careful there."

"Ha ha," I said.

At least Anton and Nick were friendly to me. The stylist admired my fingernails with a knowing grin, and the DJ apologized for not returning my text the other day. I'd almost forgotten he'd been trying to reach me when I was in Nashville. He said it wasn't important and left the dining room before I could question him further.

Even Gordon was cordial, asking me if I'd heard anything about my car. When I told him it had been recovered, he said he was glad to hear it. Then he, too, left the room.

Now that we were alone, Rocky tapped a program with his index finger. "Do we really need to do this? The whole wedding is a sham anyway."

"Shh! Don't let anyone hear you say that."

He made a face and gestured at the empty room. "There's no one in here."

"Let's just finish quickly." I was feeling antsy. I hadn't expected to be stuck in a closed room with no suspects to observe. I hated not knowing what everyone else was up to.

A few minutes later, my phone buzzed. I grabbed it up so quickly, I knocked over my stack of folded programs.

"Who is it?" asked Rocky.

"It's Richard." I scanned the message and summarized for Rocky. "He's just giving me an update. Marissa and Michael-William are in the ballroom talking with Nick and Regina."

No sooner had I set my phone down when it buzzed again. This time it was Calvin.

"He says a car just pulled in. It sounds like the mayor is back from his golf outing. The neighbor, Dennis, is with him."

Before I'd finished reading the text to Rocky. My phone buzzed yet again. It was Deena, reporting that Tammy had left the great room. Evidently, she'd told Deena and Shelby that she was going to use the powder room, but she'd been gone a while. I tensed at this news. Was Tammy going to sneak into the mayor's study?

"Why is no one using the group text?" I lamented.

"Group texts are obnoxious," said Rocky.

"Maybe so, but we all need this information. Davy and Calvin most of all, since they're watching the study."

I was about to text everybody, when Deena sent a follow-up. "Tammy's back. Disregard last message."

"Ugh." I set down my phone and returned to the programs.

A minute later, Rocky stood up and bounced on the soles of his feet. He always found it difficult to sit in one place for very long. Sighing, I folded faster. Rocky bounced his way over to the hall door and opened it a crack. The sound of voices drifted in from the kitchen.

"Who's out there?" I asked.

"Two guys in plaid and polka-dots are talking to Davy. It's the mayor and his security detail."

"Is there a problem?"

"No, I don't think so. They seem to be shooting the breeze."

I frowned. "I hope they don't distract Davy from watching the study."

Just then my phone rang. I snatched it up and saw it was Richard again, calling this time. "What's up?" I said.

Richard rasped out a whisper I couldn't understand.

"What? Can you speak up?"

"Marissa is missing!" he hissed.

I slapped my forehead. *Not again.* "Are you sure?"

"Pretty sure. Michael-William can't find her. She was

supposed to meet her mother for a gown fitting, but Annaliese and the housekeeper are in the sewing room and haven't
seen her. And she's not in her room."

I bit my lip, trying to think. She couldn't have left the
house or driven away without Calvin seeing her. Where
could she be?

"Listen," I said. "Try to assure Michael-William as best as
you can. Tell him she probably went downstairs for a drink
or something. Whatever you do, don't tell anyone else she's
missing." I was afraid this would distract from the trap we'd
set. If everyone started searching for Marissa, we could
miss someone else sneaking into the study.

"I'll try," said Richard. "Um, there's something else.
Probably nothing."

"What is it?" Nothing was ever *nothing*.

"It's Nick. He was acting kind of weird around Marissa
and Michael-William. Real twitchy, like he was nervous or
something."

I suddenly remembered my first encounter with Nick—
sneaking out of Marissa's bedroom. "What's he doing
now?" I asked.

"That's just it. He's missing too."

Chapter 29

Rocky and I abandoned the wedding programs and split up. I dashed into the great room to tell Deena what was going on, and he cut through the kitchen to go outside and fill in Calvin. It was only after we'd parted that I remembered he was supposed to stick to me like glue. *Oh well.* So much for my shadow. I wasn't too worried. We'd meet up again shortly. When he came back inside, Rocky would go up the back staircase, and I'd go up the grand staircase. We planned to meet on the second floor to search for Marissa there. As long as Davy and Calvin didn't leave their posts, our mission shouldn't be in jeopardy.

In the great room, I found Deena and Shelby measuring garland. Tammy was on the other end of the room with Gordon. They were head-to-head, apparently deep in conversation. They didn't look up when I entered.

"Deena, can I borrow you for a minute? I want to show you something."

She hopped up immediately and followed me to the sitting room. I closed the door behind us and glanced around the room. "Have you seen Marissa or Nick?"

"Yeah, why?"

That stopped me cold. "You have? When? Where?"

"Ten minutes ago, maybe. They went out the front door."

I closed my eyes, praying for patience. If Richard had just sent out a group text instead of calling me, we might have avoided the fire drill.

"What's wrong?" asked Deena, looking concerned.

"Richard said Nick was acting weird, and Marissa disappeared without telling Michael-William where she was going." I walked over to the window and looked outside. The long front driveway and sweeping lawn were empty. "Did they say anything as they passed by?"

"Nothing," said Deena. "No, wait. He held the door open for her, and she thanked him. I assumed they were going to his van to get some music or something. I figured they were using the front door because she didn't want to run into her dad."

"How did you know her dad was back?" As far as I knew, Calvin had texted only me.

"Gordon mentioned it. He came in from the kitchen a little bit ago."

I shook my head. There were too many people to keep track of.

"Do me a favor, Dee. Will you send a group text bringing everyone up to speed? I'm going to step out the front door and look around. I'll meet up with Rocky outside." I'd just have to catch him before he came back in again.

"How about if I come with you?" said Deena.

I moved to the sitting room door, anxious about the ticking clock. "I think you should stay here. The great room is a central location. We need eyes in here."

She was right behind me. "Then maybe just wait for Rocky?"

"I can't wait. I have a funny feeling about Nick."

Seeing her uneasiness, I held up my phone. "We'll stay in communication. Don't worry. I won't do anything stupid." With that, I hurried to the foyer and out the front door.

It was still daylight, though the light was beginning to fade. I stood on the veranda for a moment, trying to decide which way to go. Maybe Deena was right, and the missing pair took a roundabout way to Nick's van. Heading in that direction, I walked along the side of the driveway toward the back of the house.

On the other side of the driveway, a grove of trees provided a natural buffer between Bellman Manor and the neighboring property. Scanning the area, I admired the picturesque view—and noticed a footpath winding among the trees. It was an inviting-looking trail of cut grass, bordered by wildflowers and shade trees. I jogged over to take a peek and, before I knew it, I was meandering into the woods.

They had to have come this way. How could they not?

A minute later, I came to a charming wooden footbridge spanning a trickling stream. Pausing here, I pulled out my phone to dash off a quick text. After a moment's hesitation, I decided to message Deena and Rocky alone, ignoring my own instructions about the group text. I didn't want to risk confusing or distracting the others.

I proceeded down the path, listening to the chatter of evening birdsong and rustling leaves. Then I halted, as the sound of murmured voices joined the quiet forest sounds.

Cautiously looking around, I spotted a small gazebo several yards off the path. I picked my way toward it, being careful to remain out of sight. The hilly terrain worked to my advantage. I was able to creep quite close to the structure and settle into a hiding spot beneath a crisscross of fallen trees. The distinct voices of Marissa and Nick floated through the brush.

"I've been looking for you all week," said Nick.

"I'm sorry," said Marissa, not sounding at all sorry. "I needed space to clear my head."

"You could have returned my calls." When she didn't respond, he pressed on. "I heard you'd run away. And your mom hired that florist, Sierra, to go looking for you?"

He sounded confused. I couldn't blame him there. But why had he been looking for Marissa? Did they know each other before?

"They wouldn't take my calls either," he said. "Neither your mom nor Sierra. I was really worried about you."

Okay, they definitely must have known each other before. And that explained why he'd been trying to reach me when I was in Nashville. He wanted to know if I knew where Marissa was.

Nick dropped his voice, so I could no longer make out his words. A moment later, Marissa replied in a careless, almost blasé way.

"You're sweet. I had no idea you felt that way."

"Come on, don't you remember?" Now his voice was plaintive. "Every weekend. I came to your school every weekend senior year. And that time you brought me here, when your parents were away?"

"Sure, I remember," said Marissa.

"And those letters we wrote in college . . . I still have every letter you sent me. I thought we had something special."

"You were a good friend," she said. "You listened to my adolescent complaints and always cheered me up. . . . It was a long time ago."

"It wasn't that long ago," Nick retorted. "I was there when you met Michael-William." He spat the name, clearly disgusted. "I know you don't love him. I know you've been trying to get the wedding called off. I've been trying to help you."

Ah, I thought. *The missing piece of the sabotage puzzle.*

The disruptions not caused by Marissa were caused by Nick. He must have snuck in and set fire to the wedding programs.

"You're a sweetheart." She might have been speaking to a little kid. Marissa and Nick were clearly not on the same page.

I heard someone stir. Was Nick getting agitated? Or was Marissa moving away from him?

"You don't understand," he said. "I would do anything for you."

There was a pause, then a quick intake of breath. When Marissa spoke again, there was a new note in her voice, as if she'd just come to a startling realization.

"Oh, my God. You didn't."

"Marissa," Nick began.

"How could you?"

"Now hold on a minute. Calm down."

Both their voices were raised now, Marissa sounding frightened and Nick sounding angry. I knew what Marissa was thinking. What I couldn't quite make out was the nature of Nick's reaction.

"You killed Taz!" she cried.

"What? How can you say that? I didn't kill anyone!" He sounded so affronted, I almost believed him.

Could he be telling the truth?

"Don't touch me!" shrieked Marissa. "Stay back!"

I had to do something. Thinking fast, I pulled out my phone and rapidly typed a text—to Nick.

"Hey," I wrote, keeping it casual. "Your van is standing wide open. You better come and take a look."

I pressed Send. Half a second later, a ping sounded from the gazebo. I was afraid Nick might be too worked up to heed it. Then I heard a muttered oath.

"This isn't over," he snarled.

I crouched farther into my hiding place as Nick stomped

off. Marissa let out a sob—of relief or sorrow, I couldn't tell. Before I could react, someone grabbed my arm. I yelped and wheeled around. Crouched behind me was Deena, trying not to lose her balance on the uneven ground.

"Who's there?" called Marissa.

I reached for Deena's hand, and we both stood up. "It's okay," I said to Marissa. "It's just us."

"Sorry," Deena whispered. "I tried to be quiet."

"It's okay," I repeated. "I need to talk to Marissa anyway." I helped Deena over the fallen tree. "Did you see Nick?"

"Sort of. I hid behind a bush as he ran by."

Marissa stood at the railing, looking down at us. "What are you doing back there in the dirt?"

"Looking for you." We joined her in the gazebo and dropped onto a bench. "You tend to raise alarm bells when you disappear," I said. "Michael-William is worried."

She rolled her eyes. "If Michael-William expects to be my husband, he better get used to not knowing where I am every second of the day."

As if on cue, my phone buzzed. It was Richard demanding to know what was going on. *M-W is freaking out!*

I sent a quick reply. *Found Marissa. She was just getting some air. Will be back soon.* Then I turned to Deena. "Where's Rocky?"

"I couldn't find him," she said. "I thought he'd be with you."

I cringed at that. If Rocky was tramping around in the woods looking for me, he must be so mad.

Marissa stood before us. "I don't know how much you heard, but shouldn't we be calling the police? Nick killed Taz!"

"I'm not so sure about that." I gave Marissa a speculative

look. "Did you really not know Nick was trying to help you stop the wedding?"

"I had no idea."

"Ah," said Deena, catching on. "Nick is in love with Marissa?"

"Big time," I said.

Marissa played with the ends of her hair, as a sheepish expression came over her face. "I have a lot of . . . admirers. I knew Nick liked me, but I didn't know the extent of it."

"Does he drive a scooter?" Deena asked.

Marissa wrinkled her nose. "How would I know?"

I stood up and paced to the other side of the gazebo. It didn't add up. I understood that Nick wanted to stop the wedding. That explained his behavior this whole time. But, besides the fact that stabbing the wedding planner wasn't exactly a logical move, it didn't explain the other pieces of the puzzle. Like the argument Kendall had overheard. She'd said Taz had been arguing with someone and saying he "wanted out." Kendall thought Taz was mixed up in something illegal, something more serious than taking kickbacks. Gretchen had also overheard Taz mention something about not wanting to go to jail.

I remembered the chop shop in Nashville, where I'd found Taz's business card. Come to think of it, I wasn't even sure Nick lived in Nashville at all. I'd assumed he did, but he also clearly had ties to Knoxville.

I turned and walked back over to Deena and Marissa. They were watching me, waiting for my direction.

"Deena, do you still have those pictures you took of the garage where we found my car?"

"Yes." She pulled out her phone and waved it. "Right here. Want me to pull them up?"

"Yeah. I just realized I never looked at them." There was

something about that place. From the moment I saw it, I'd felt certain it was used for more than breaking down stolen cars.

Deena opened her photo app and handed me the phone. I scrolled through the pictures, one by one, passing quickly over the ones that featured only the Fiat. I was more interested in the rest of the garage.

I came to a photo showing a heap of stacked boxes along the wall. The image was dark, so I played with the settings to lighten it, then I zoomed in.

"And there it is," I murmured.

"What?" asked Deena, leaning forward. "What do you see?"

I showed her the photo. "See that logo?"

She squinted. "What is it? A flower? It looks familiar."

"It should. It's a daisy. *Marguerite* in French. It's on all those expensive products Anton keeps pushing."

"Anton?" said Deena. "You mean he—"

"Is involved in something sketchy," I finished. Staring out into the darkening trees, I wondered, once again, what Taz had been trying to tell me.

Who is the snake? Things aren't always what they seem. What if Taz wasn't saying "snake" at all?

Now there was an idea. What else could he have been trying to say? *Sneak? Snitch? Essence?*

Cynique?

Like the pop of a flashbulb, I realized the truth. Taz wasn't naming his killer. Not directly, anyway. He was revealing the killer's secret. He was naming the motive. "Le Cynique Fleur."

It all came back to those high-end spa products. Taz had met Anton at that spa. And Taz had come into money before he'd made it big as a popular wedding planner. How did he make so much money so fast? The answer to that question, I had a feeling, would explain why boxes of Le Cynique Fleur were stashed at the base of a criminal operation.

"They're phony," I said. "Counterfeit products. Or watered down. Something illegal."

"Ohh," said Deena. "So, that's what Taz wanted out of? A scheme of selling fake beauty products?"

"I don't get it," said Marissa.

I looked from her to Deena, my brain suddenly jumping from the past to the present. "Where is Anton?" I asked. "Where did he go after the meeting?"

Deena widened her eyes. "I saw him go up the grand staircase, but I don't know where he went after that. Maybe he came down the back stairs?"

"He wasn't in the ballroom with Richard, I know that much." I pulled out my phone again and opened the group text. *SOS! Watch out for ANTON. I think he's the one.*

"He probably went to the guest house," said Marissa.

Deena and I stared at her. "What guest house?" I asked.

"There's a coach house at the rear of the property." She gestured toward the trail, where it continued deeper into the woods. "Mother told Taz he could have it, but Taz wanted to be in the main house. I think Taz let Anton have it."

Hmm. "I wonder why he didn't go for the day planner," I said.

"Maybe we have the room too well guarded," said Deena.

"Yeah. That's probably it." I pursed my lips in thought. "He's gotta know his time's about up. He's been following me around, probably afraid Taz had identified him in some way. And he suspected Kendall knew something. Now that she's awake, she's a threat to him again."

"Oh!" said Deena. "I just remembered. We were talking about Kendall at the spa. Anton must have overheard us. Maybe that's why he took your car. To keep you in Nashville, while he came back to Aerieville to-to harm her."

I nodded. "I bet you're right. But we found the garage, which he must know. And he knows we found Taz's day planner." I tried to get into Anton's mind. What would he see as his options at this point?

"You think he's going to do something desperate?" asked Deena.

"He might. At a minimum, I think he might run." This thought spurred me to action. "Marissa, will you call the police? Deena, run back to the house and tell the others."

Deena held up both hands. "Wait a minute, Sierra. If you think I'm going to leave you, you're crazy."

Marissa frowned at me. "What are you going to do?"

"Is there a road or driveway from the guest house?" I asked.

"Yes. There's a private lane."

That's what I thought. Why didn't I look for Anton's vehicle sooner? "I'm going to take the air out of his tires," I said. "If he's not gone already."

"At least wait for Davy," Deena pleaded.

"I can't wait, Dee. Like you said, Anton is probably feeling desperate. He might go after Kendall."

"Then I'm coming with you." Deena set her jaw, not allowing for argument.

"Me too," said Marissa, looking more determined than I'd ever seen her. "He killed my wedding planner. I'm not going to let him get away."

Chapter 30

Dusk fell like a curtain, shrouding the small cottage in murky shadows. Marissa led the way, following a shortcut through the trees. We approached from the back to avoid being seen. Deena, an expert multitasker, texted the group as we hiked down the trail. She let them know what we were doing and stressed that Davy should call for backup.

Of course, I had no intention of confronting Anton. I just wanted to confirm that he hadn't already left—and slow him down if he hadn't.

I spied the van right away, parked behind the cottage. It was plain white, with no markings on the side. I wanted to peek in the rear window to see if it held a scooter. Then I spotted the two-wheeled vehicle, under a tarp along the side of the house.

"What do we do?" whispered Deena at my shoulder. "Uncap the air valves?"

"We need to slash the tires," said Marissa. "Does anyone have a knife?"

"I have a nail file," Deena said. "But it's not very sharp."

We looked at one another helplessly. With a sinking

heart, I realized I hadn't thought this through. "I guess we should just wait for the cops," I said. "At least we know he hasn't left yet."

"Good idea," said Deena, backing toward the trees already.

"Wait!" Marissa said. "There's a toolshed on the other side of the cottage. If there's not something sharp enough, there ought to at least be a screwdriver. We can use it to release the air from the valves."

Leave it to Marissa the saboteur to know what to do.

"I don't know," I said. "I'm getting a nervous feeling about this."

"Wait here," she said, darting around the cottage.

I turned to Deena and shrugged. "Did anyone respond to your text?"

"I don't know." She pulled out her phone to check.

At the same time, it occurred to me that it might be easier to disable a scooter than a van. I could at least take a look. "Be right back," I said, touching Deena's arm.

I jogged up to the scooter and pulled off the cover. It was shiny and black, with a small lightning streak painted on the side. *Should have been a snake*, I joked to myself.

I'd barely begun to examine the two-wheeler, when I heard footsteps behind me. I assumed it was Marissa—until I caught a whiff of expensive cologne. Suddenly, the presence was at my back. A rough arm wrapped around my neck and jerked me backward.

It happened so quickly, I was more astonished than afraid. At first. Then I saw a shiny blade flash in front of my eyes and hover inches from my throat. If I wasn't mistaken, the blade belonged to a pair of styling shears.

"Don't make a sound." It was Anton's voice, low and fierce. Not a trace of friendliness.

I bit back a whimper and tried to nod. His chokehold on

my neck was so tight, I could have cried—if I wasn't petri-
fied with fear.

"You!" he yelled. "Open the van. The back door. Now!"

"Don't hurt her!" It was Deena, in a high-pitched, frantic
voice. "I'll do whatever you say." I heard the sound of a vehicle door clank open.

"Put your hands up high!" he yelled at her. "And stay
where I can see you."

Anton dragged me toward the van. Of all the feelings I
could have felt, the strongest one was anger—at myself. How
did I get myself into this predicament? I had to get out of it.

Bending my knees, I tried to make myself heavy. This
tripped him up for a second, causing him to stumble into
me. But that deadly blade was still so close to my neck.

"Hey!" he growled. "Don't get cute. I know how to use a
pair of scissors."

"I know you do," I squeaked. "You stabbed Taz."

"Very good," he said sarcastically. "I knew it was only a
matter of time before you'd figure it out. Whatever Taz said
to you, it had to be a reference to me."

"That's why you were following me around? To-to get
rid of me?" I swallowed hard. "And Kendall too?"

"You're both too nosy for your own good."

He gave me a shove, but I dragged my feet. I had to distract him.

"Taz was your friend! You'd known him for years. How
could you do that to your friend?"

Anton scoffed. "Some friend. He turned on me. And he
owed me! When he had nothing, I got him a job."

"A job selling counterfeit beauty products?"

"That too," said Anton. "He was in deep. He helped with
the rebottling, he found customers."

Rebottling. So that's what they did. They must have been
watering down the actual product, probably with a cheap

soap or filler, so they could sell more and pocket the difference. Considering the luxury price tags, it must have been a lucrative scheme.

"And Taz wanted out?" I ventured.

"Taz was a traitor." Anton seethed with righteousness. I felt it in the tremble of his wiry muscles. "He threatened to expose me. He claimed he was smart, that he covered his tracks and no one could prove he was involved. Does that sound like a friend to you?"

"If he tried to get you to go straight and stop being a criminal, then yes. That's what my friends would do."

"Yeah, right. He was always more concerned about his own neck than mine."

I remembered Taz's worry about going to jail—and the chop shop in Nashville. What was it I'd read in those old newspaper articles online?

"You were *both* in pretty deep, weren't you," I guessed. "Were you part of the—the Philo gang?"

For a split second, Anton froze. Then a humorless laugh burst from his lips. "Aren't you clever? My cousin was one of Philo's men. But he was smart and stayed under the radar when the old guard went to prison. Now he's building a new empire, more modern. And he put me in charge of . . . imports/exports."

There was a tinge of pride in Anton's voice—and something more. Fear? I had a feeling he was beginning to realize how much trouble he was in, and not just by the authorities. Perhaps the gang posed an even more serious threat.

"You don't have to do this, Anton," I reasoned. "If there's a bigger operation going on, you could agree to testify. You know, cut a plea deal." Of course, he'd still have to answer for Taz's murder, but I wasn't going to bring that up. I was already treading on thin ice.

He didn't reply. Instead, he forced me to shuffle forward.

We were at the back of the van now. Inside, I could see that it was stuffed to the ceiling with boxes of Marguerite beauty products, presumably adulterated. In the center was a narrow space just big enough for the scooter. I figured he kept both modes of transportation so that he could easily get around, while keeping his stash hidden away as much as possible. Regardless, I did *not* want to get into that van. I tried to calculate my chances. Should I fight now and risk getting cut? Or get in the van and try to escape later?

From out of the ether, my new mantra surfaced in my mind. *Go with the flow.*

I shouldn't fight. It was too dangerous. I took a deep inhale and consciously relaxed, from head to toe.

The sudden change in my posture caught Anton off guard. His grip loosened. At the same time, a rapid string of yelping barks pierced the night air. From the corner of my eye, I detected a blur of fur flying toward us along the ground. *Gus!* Anton was so startled, he dropped the shears. In the next moment, I jumped back.

My first thought was to protect Gus. I thought for sure he was going to clamp his teeth on Anton's ankle and get kicked or hit in the process. To my surprise, Gus came for me instead. He tackled my legs with unabashed delight, slathering me with puppy kisses. I fell to my rear and caught him up in my arms.

Anton *was* pounced on, but not by the corgi. Calvin got to him first, walloping him in the stomach. Then came Rocky, immobilizing the murderer by clamping both of his arms. It was Davy, with his gun drawn, who probably saved Anton from a beating. Everyone else backed away as Davy pulled out a pair of jingling handcuffs. Anton dropped his head to his chest, and Davy read him his rights.

Deena ran over to me then and pulled me to my feet. "Are you okay?" she asked, tears wetting her eyelashes.

"Yes," I breathed. "I'm so sorry I put you in danger."

"Stop," she said. "We're grown women. We both make our own decisions."

"True," I said, mustering a small smile.

A porch light flashed on, lighting up the yard around the guest house. I now noticed a small crowd had gathered. I saw Richard, with both hands over his mouth. He caught my eye and shook his head. I knew I'd get an earful from him later.

I also saw Marissa, wide eyed yet looking pleased. She stood next to Michael-William, who had a protective hand on the small of her back. Nick was off to the side, glaring at them. I watched him for a moment, trying to gauge his intent. At the time Taz was killed, he must have been sneaking around, probably in Marissa's room again. Talk about creepy. Then I noticed his shoulders slump, and he looked away. I sensed he was done pining for her, but if I were Marissa, I might still consider a restraining order—Nick had gone too far.

Rocky and Calvin walked up to me, with equally inscrutable expressions. I imagined they both felt a mixture of relief and annoyance. I smiled at them, hoping to defuse any tension.

Calvin reached down and grabbed the end of Gus's leash. "This little guy got away from me. He did *not* want to play lookout in the yard."

Rocky shook his head, allowing a half-hearted chuckle. "When I went outside, I saw Calvin running like mad toward the garage. I thought he was going after Nick or Marissa or the murderer. I went after him to help, only to find out he was chasing down Gus."

Calvin grinned at me. "I think Gus was looking for you all along."

"He has separation issues," I said, grinning back at him.

Annaliese approached us next, along with her husband, Mayor Frank Lakely. He was a burly man with short reddish-gray hair and a lined face. Either he smiled a lot or squinted a lot. At the moment, he was smiling. He stuck out his hand and gave me a politician's greeting.

"The famous Sierra Ravenswood! I knew we were right to bring you on the case."

"Frank," said Annaliese, in a tone of mild warning.

He tapped the side of his nose. "Right, right. Unofficial. As a, er—"

"Florist?" I suggested.

"Yes!" He snapped his fingers. "Flower House. Beautiful business."

Calvin had been inching toward me and was now at my side. I reached out my hand, and he clasped it tightly.

"Beautiful," I agreed.

Chapter 31

Three days later, Marissa married Michael-William. I'm sure it was a lovely ceremony. I wasn't there. Annaliese gave me a sizable check for my time and efforts, writing "florist consultant" on the memo line, and accepted my resignation from any further involvement with the Lakely-Princely wedding. I'd had more than my fill of Bellman Manor.

I was happy for Marissa, though. She'd given me a call the day after Anton's arrest to thank me personally—and to let me know about her change of heart. After everything she'd confessed at Janie's house, she felt she owed me an explanation.

"There's nothing like being close to a murderer to help you rethink your priorities," she'd said. "I'm sure you can relate."

"All too well," I said, matching her wry tone.

"Not to mention an obsessive stalker." She told me it was Nick's criticisms of Michael-William that made her realize how much she really did love her fiancé. And it was her mother's surprise apology that helped her wise up.

All along, it had been her parents she was upset with, not

Michael-William. All their pressure and high expectations had soured her on the wedding. Evidently, Annaliese finally came to this understanding herself. She even offered to pay the plane fare if the couple wished to elope. But Marissa decided the ceremony should proceed. Besides all the mischief she'd caused, she felt especially bad about informing the police of her mother's bogus affair.

I wished her well and turned my attention to my own life for once. The day after the wedding was my birthday. I was twenty-nine and feelin' fine. Or "twenty-nine and lookin' fine," as Calvin sweetly said. Deena and Richard planned a party for me at Flower House. I don't know how they did it, considering all that had happened in the last two weeks. That's talent for you.

It was a day full of surprises. Not only was the café decorated for a birthday bash, with streamers, balloons, tissue paper pompoms, and colorful flowers galore (vibrant zinnias, gerbera daisies, and full-blown roses among them), but there was also a gorgeous four-tier birthday cake, courtesy of Cakes & Eats in Nashville. As it happened, Regina was so grateful for my role in seeking justice for Taz, she forgave me for snooping in her office.

When I called to thank her, Regina admitted the reason she was interested in her old friend's last words was because of their history. She'd wondered if he'd expressed remorse or regret for shutting her out of his business. For a long time, she'd been waiting for an apology and expected she'd get it someday. Sadly, with his life cut short, someday would never come.

I told her what he'd actually said, which wasn't much. However, as I pointed out, at least he'd been trying to free himself from Anton's illegal activities. She agreed that perhaps that meant he'd wanted to turn over a new leaf. And now she had an opportunity to break into the business after all. In my opinion, I was sure she'd be good at it. To be sure, she was nicer than her predecessor, and a great chef to boot.

I was thrilled with the cake, and said as much to Deena. But it was so big, I was sure we'd have to freeze half of it. Then I found out the party was not to be the intimate affair I'd expected. My friends had arranged it as an open house.

"Of course, this shindig is all about celebrating you, dear Sierra," said Richard, giving me a one-armed hug, while balancing a glass of wine in his other hand.

"At the same time," said Deena, "it allows us to showcase the café as a great space for parties."

"Smart," I said, admiring the setup. With the tables moved aside and the furniture rearranged, the room appeared more spacious than usual.

Calvin came up to me and spoke softly near my ear. "You don't mind, do you? You're more admired in this town than you realize. I'm starting to feel a little jealous." He quirked his lips in a heart-melting half smile.

"You've got nothing to worry about," I said.

I still had a hard time believing many people would show up, but I guess I should have known better. There was a nonstop stream of well-wishers. Besides my family, including Granny's friend Wanda, and all the Flower House neighbors, several townsfolk stopped by. Deena's parents made an appearance, as well as Nell Cusley from the diner, Valerie from the dance studio, and the entire Johnson family from Allie and Toby's mom to all their siblings. Gus was beside himself. As a people-pleasing pup, he wanted to greet each and every single guest.

I was in the front room, chatting with Richard and Davy, when the shop door jingled open yet again. I glanced over, expecting to see another acquaintance or neighbor. It was a short, older man who came inside, with unruly white hair and sun-kissed cheeks. I stared for a long moment, fighting the urge to rub my eyes. Was I seeing a ghost?

He looked around, slightly befuddled, then spotted me and made his way over. With well-worn hands, he presented me with a cracked geode the size of a softball. The sparkling crystals inside matched the sparkle in his eyes. "Happy birthday!"

"Felix! What a surprise!"

For a split second, I believed my old boss had returned to reclaim his flower shop. This thought gave me an immediate punch of regret. I didn't *want* to give up the business. But I soon realized that wasn't the case.

He gazed around, peered into the café, and shook his head in wonder. "Incredible. You've done alright by the old place. It's never seen so many customers at one time."

"Well, it doesn't usually look like this," I explained. "It's set up for a party."

Richard appeared tickled at the sudden arrival of Felix. He gave me a wink, before pulling Davy back into the café. As they crossed the threshold, Gus skirted their ankles and came charging toward the newcomer.

Felix looked down in delighted surprise. "Augustus? Is that really you?" Glancing up at me, he said, "Can't believe he remembers me. I hadn't had him long, you know."

"Of course he remembers," I said. No need to tell him Gus greeted almost everyone with the same enthusiasm.

"Aw, shucks. Good boy." Felix patted the top of the corgi's head. "I'm glad he forgives me. Where I was going, it was no place for a puppy. I thank you, Sierra, for adopting him."

"My pleasure," I said sincerely. *And thank goodness he doesn't intend to reclaim the little guy either!*

Felix looked around again. "I can tell Flower House is flourishing. I was smart to sell it to you."

"I suppose so," I said, smiling. Though "give" was more accurate. He'd sold me the business at the price of one dollar. Either way, it was, of course, mine now.

"Alrighty then, where is the young professor?" he asked.

Before I could answer, Calvin emerged from the kitchen, carrying a bag of ice. He did a double take when he caught sight of Felix. Evidently, Cal hadn't been expecting him either.

"Flower man!" Calvin transferred the ice to his other hand and gave Felix a hearty handshake. "What brings you back to Aerieville?"

"All in due time," Felix said mysteriously. "All in due time. Right now what I need is the key to my cabin."

"Oh! Sure. I have it right here." Calvin removed a key ring from his pocket and took off a house key. Giving it to Felix, he said, "Come in for a bite to eat. There's a delicious fancy cake."

"Maybe later," said Felix, gesturing with the key. "I have some unpacking to do."

He turned to leave, just as the door opened again and Marissa Lakely walked in. The tall golden-haired beauty was a comical contrast to rumpled, travel-worn Felix. He tipped an imaginary hat to her and left the shop.

At that moment, Granny Mae came out of the café and looked around with a perplexed expression. "I could've sworn I heard Felix Maniford out here. I must be hearing things."

"No, Granny, he was here! He's back, and he just now left."

"And he didn't come in to say hello? I have a thing or two to say to that old coot." She hurried out the front door after him.

Calvin took the ice into the café, and I greeted Marissa.

"Hi, there! Shouldn't you be on your honeymoon?"

"We leave tonight," she said. "I wanted to stop by to give you this."

She handed me a pretty paper gift bag with a small daisy image on the front. Peeking inside, I saw an assortment of French bath soaps and lotions. They smelled heavenly.

"It's the real thing," she added. "I promise."

"I believe you," I said. "I heard Anton was quick to spill the names of all his co-conspirators." Captain Bradley had been kind enough to give me an update from Agent Collins. As it happened, state investigators found a plethora of evidence in Anton's apartment—which they immediately turned over to the feds. Consequently, "Philo gang 2.0" was now as defunct as the original.

"I heard that too," she said. "Thank goodness. Also, Spa'Dae hired a third-party chemist to certify all products before they're sold. They had to, in order to save face."

"Oh!" I said, suddenly remembering. "I have something for you too. Would you come into the kitchen for a minute?"

Stashing the gift bag and geode behind the checkout counter, I led Marissa to the back room and set two glasses on the worktable. I added some frozen cherries from the freezer and took Granny's tonic from the refrigerator.

"This is cherry wine, with a twist," I explained. "My granny's special recipe."

"It's really pretty," she said, holding a glass up to the light from the window.

"Granny calls it a 'happy-heart love tonic.' When drinking it, you're supposed to think about what lights up your heart."

"Oh?"

"Yes. No matter what circumstances you find yourself in, never forget that you still have things that bring you joy. They can be other people or—"

I was interrupted by scratching at the door. Laughing,

I let Gus inside. "Or pets," I continued. "Or hobbies or whatever. If you honor what's in your heart, you're sure to find happiness."

"I'll drink to that," said Marissa, raising her glass.

"Cheers." We clinked glasses and sipped the brew. Savoring the sweet-tart flavor, I scratched Gus behind the ears. The truth is, Granny was right. I didn't really need the wine. I had a happy heart already.

Still, a little reminder never hurt.

The End

Acknowledgments

Writing may seem solitary, but creating a book is not. I'm so grateful to all those who have supported me in my publishing journey, from my amazing agent, Rachel Brooks, to my fantastic editor, Nettie Finn. They are my rock stars. I'd also like to thank the entire team at St. Martin's Press, who do such stellar work, with a special shout-out to managing editor John Rounds, copy-editor John Simko, cover designer Danielle Christopher, and cover illustrator Alan Ayers. (Writing a flower-themed series lends itself to such beautiful covers!)

Finally, and always, I have the greatest thanks for my family. Thank you especially to my parents, Tom and Cathy, and my sister Jana, who take the time to read my early drafts and offer their honest critique. And to Scott and Sage, the loves of my life: Thank you for giving me the time and space to write and the encouragement to keep at it. ❤